Amazing a woman like this had gotten involved with such losers

Emily gazed out at the boats again. "The problem with my old life plan was that it required the cooperation of someone else to work. With my new life plan, I don't need anyone else's cooperation."

So that's why she'd gone the artificial insemination route. Her choice made a little more sense to Brad now. But understanding her reasons hadn't changed his opinion of her actions.

Except the timing was lousy. He was in his final year as an E.R. resident and had those Board Certification exams to study for. Finding the hours he'd need to establish a close relationship with Emily was going to be difficult.

But his baby would be a reality in seven months' time—a reality that couldn't be ignored. He was going to be there to see to its emotional, physical and financial needs. That's what a responsible father— and a real man—did.

Her initial life plan had included a father for her child. It was only the bastards she'd picked who had soured her on the idea.

He could make it sweet for her again.

Dear Reader,

Father by Choice is the first book in a new series called CODE RED. This series tells the stories of dedicated medical professionals, police and firefighters as they save lives and fall in love in the fictional community of Courage Bay, located in Southern California.

Courage Bay's residents are proud of their long history of selfless acts of bravery. In this first story we get a glimpse into the community's earliest history after a time capsule is dug up to reveal a hundred-year-old mystery. Solving the case will take the cooperation of two unlikely sleuths: Brad Winslow—an E.R. resident at Courage Bay Hospital and a man on the front lines of the community's emergency teams—and Emily Barrett, the curator of the city's botanical gardens and a member of its esteemed historical society.

As they join forces to find the answers to the mystery unearthed with the time capsule, Brad and Emily soon discover themselves confronted with a few modern-day surprises, as well. And the best of those surprises turns out to be the deep and very unexpected love that they begin to share.

I hope you enjoy Brad and Emily's story. If you would like a personally autographed sticker for your book, send me a SASE at P.O. Box 284, Seabeck, Washington, 98380-0284.

Warmly,

M.J.

Father by Choice
M.J. Rodgers

HARLEQUIN®

TORONTO • NEW YORK • LONDON
AMSTERDAM • PARIS • SYDNEY • HAMBURG
STOCKHOLM • ATHENS • TOKYO • MILAN • MADRID
PRAGUE • WARSAW • BUDAPEST • AUCKLAND

ISBN 0-373-71194-8

FATHER BY CHOICE

Mary Johnson is acknowledged as the author of this work.

Copyright © 2004 by Harlequin Books S.A.

www.eHarlequin.com

Printed in U.S.A.

This book is for Frances Demoor of Kalamazoo, Michigan.
Fran is a real heroine.
Even when faced with the worst of life's heartbreaks,
she always responds with kindness and love.

Books by M.J. Rodgers

HARLEQUIN SUPERROMANCE
1116—BABY BY CHANCE*
1137—FOR THE DEFENSE*

*White Knight Investigations

Don't miss any of our special offers. Write to us at the
following address for information on our newest releases.

Harlequin Reader Service
U.S.: 3010 Walden Ave., P.O. Box 1325, Buffalo, NY 14269
Canadian: P.O. Box 609, Fort Erie, Ont. L2A 5X3

CHAPTER ONE

EMILY BARRETT KNEW WHEN to stop and smell the roses. And those that opened beneath the dazzling April sunshine filling Courage Bay's Botanical Gardens were irresistible.

She buried her nose inside the fragrant petals of "Perfect Moment," a red-orange bloom with a center fold of pure gold and then went on to the "Chicago Peace" behind it, a lush pink that measured no less than five inches across. The bright lemon yellow of "Graceland" farther down the trellised walkway was already producing more flowers than any other bush. And then there was "Unforgettable"—so perfectly named—a robust giant with petals as soft as a baby's cheek.

No gardener could take credit for creating a rose. But when she met their needs, Emily felt as proud as any parent could gazing into their beautiful fresh faces.

"We're going to miss the crane guy," Josh Smithson warned.

She looked up to see her assistant purposely eyeing his wristwatch. Nothing was as impatient as youth.

"Don't you like flowers?" she asked as she straightened, feeling grateful for every one of her thirty-three years.

"They're all right, I guess."

The sweep of Emily's hand encompassed the colorful blooms fluttering in the early afternoon breeze. "All right? What could be more impressive than this?"

"I don't know."

Josh's most frequent answer to any question she asked. Either he knew very little about his own feelings or was hesitant to reveal them.

When Emily was nineteen, she knew exactly how she felt and had no problem sharing it. As her brothers used to complain, getting her to shut up was the real trick. Maybe this was a gender thing. Most of the males she knew refused to acknowledge they even had feelings, much less took the time to examine them.

"You want me to like the flowers, Dr. Barrett?"

If Josh had asked that sarcastically, she would have laughed. But the flat-open sincerity in his words bothered Emily.

"You don't have to like them for me. Or anyone else. Like them for you or not at all."

"You won't be disappointed?"

"Hey, you work hard, and you're dependable. I've never had a better assistant. So if flowers aren't your thing, it's okay."

He greeted her assurance with a bony shoulder shrug.

"What is your thing, Josh?"

"I don't know."

There it was again. And the saddest thing about his words was that Emily believed them. Why did high schools require all kids learn algebra—something which most of them would never use—and yet fail to teach them how important it was to get to know themselves—something they could all use?

"Has taking this year off before going to college helped at all?" she asked.

Another shrug.

"Your folks have any suggestions?" she persisted.

"My dad and granddad want me to study science like they did and join the firm. But I suck at that stuff."

"So outside of being a great assistant, what don't you suck at?"

"I don't know."

Emily gave up. Josh was a good worker, but as a conversationalist he left a lot to be desired. Her thoughts were rudely interrupted by the sudden blast of a leaf blower. Oh, no. Not again. She whirled around, trying to determine where he was. Then the breeze blew a faint whiff of gasoline fumes in her face and she knew

Emily charged up the path through the rose garden, past the swaying beds of fragrant lilacs, and broke into a jog around the lily pond. Turning the corner, she saw Lester inside the greenhouse. He was shuffling to the tune he heard in his headphones, the leaf blower in his hand blasting dirt and debris off the stone path.

She'd asked him repeatedly not to use that polluting piece of crap in the Botanical Gardens, especially not the greenhouse. The toxic fumes were dangerous to the more fragile plant species, not to mention human lungs.

But Lester considered sweeping with a broom to be beneath his manhood. Which was why, every time he thought she wasn't around, he brought out the leaf blower.

Emily waved, trying to get his attention. But he wasn't looking in her direction. She hurried up the cobblestone path toward him, feeling her nostrils burn, trying not to inhale too deeply. She called out to him, but he obviously couldn't hear her above the noise of the leaf blower and whatever he considered music in his ears.

Her temples had begun to throb. She entered the greenhouse, knowing she'd have to grab his arm to get his attention. But before she could, the heat and exhaust hit her full blast.

And she was sinking into a spinning, blinding nothingness.

BRAD WINSLOW OFTEN THOUGHT that working in the E.R. was a lot like going to the theater. It was always high drama with life hanging in the balance. But whether he ultimately found himself part of a mystery, triumph, tragedy or farce sometimes depended less on the skill and

dedication of Courage Bay's team of medical professionals than it did on the assortment of characters coming
through the door.

Today the E.R. was overflowing with crazy fools bent
on tempting fate and the limits of their medical insurance.

Behind curtains one and two were a pair of middle-
aged golfers with head wounds—continuing to exchange
obscenities while they waited for their CT scans. They'd
been so bent on ramming each other's golf carts as they
raced to the next green that they never noticed they'd
taken a wrong turn.

Fortunately, the driver of the industrial-size lawn
mower they'd smashed into had escaped injury. It was the
two idiots who had landed on his windshield that needed
their heads examined.

Then there was the guy behind curtain three who decided to sail his son's skateboard down his daughter's
slide to see how much lift he could get. He lifted over his
neighbor's fence and landed in the swimming pool.

Lucky for him the neighbor had filled it that morning
or he'd have cracked a lot more than a collarbone.

And behind curtain four was the teenage artist determined to have a butterfly tattoo on her boob no matter
how much her parents objected. She'd assembled a sew-
ing needle, candle, some food coloring and had at it—
until her swallowtail turned into an infected swirl of blis-
ters.

Sometimes the most difficult part of being an E.R. physician was maintaining the controlled detachment that was
a necessity in the face of such human folly.

Brad was passing the base radio station when the paramedic line began to ring. The nurse who generally answered the calls was trying to get a naked seventy-year-
old loony balancing a bedpan on his head to return to the
examining room.

Yep, it was definitely the day for crazies. Brad stopped
to pick up the phone.

"Courage Bay E.R. Winslow."

"It's Paramedic Kellison on Rescue Squad Two. How do you copy?"

"Loud and clear, Kellison."

"We're en route to your location with a Code Red."

Code Red meant they were coming in with red lights and siren—the emergency team's protocol whenever they were faced with a possible life-threatening situation.

"We've got a female, around thirty, fell without warning onto a cobblestone path approximately twenty minutes ago," Kellison continued. "Unconsciousness. No observable wounds. Her pressure is ninety-five over sixty, rate about seventy. She's somewhat pale, but nondiaphoretic at this time. ETA to ambulance bay about three minutes."

"We'll be expecting you," Brad said. "CB clear."

"Number Two clear."

Brad signaled to a passing trauma nurse and went to put on a fresh gown and gloves. With a little luck maybe this patient wouldn't turn out to be a loony.

EMILY WAS ENCASED in thick white mosquito nets. She was thankful. The incessant buzzing that was going on outside was getting louder. Last time she'd been bitten by one of those bloodsuckers, she'd endured a painful welt for several days. Had one of the sprinkler systems developed a leak? Was water pooling somewhere? Were they breeding within the Botanical Gardens?

She tried to respect all life. But mosquitoes were a species that stretched the limits of her tolerance. She could hear one of them now—very loud and insistent.

"Wake up, Emily. I know you can hear me."

Not a mosquito. An urgent voice—deep and very male—from someone used to being listened to. Her eyes fluttered open to a blinding light. She grimaced and quickly shut them again.

A hand closed over her forearm—large, warm. "Emily,

you lost consciousness. You're in Courage Bay's Emergency Room.''

She still couldn't make sense out of the blurred words coming through the thick mosquito netting, but the deep resonance of his voice vibrated nicely in her ears.

''Emily, we're taking good care of you. But I need you to tell me if you hurt anywhere. I'm Dr. Brad Winslow.''

Brad Winslow?

''English ancestry. Thirty-one. Six foot three. One hundred ninety pounds. Black hair. Gray eyes. Birthday, March 25. Favorite color, blue. Favorite food, cheesecake. Favorite song—''

''What?''

The sharp demand of his voice sliced through the net surrounding Emily's woolly thoughts and brought her to a full and sudden consciousness. She opened her eyes and blinked into the blurry face of the big-shouldered man hovering over her.

''Tell me who you are,'' he said.

''Emily Barrett,'' she responded to the fuzzy outline. ''Who are you?''

''Dr. Brad Winslow.''

She'd just been dreaming about Brad Winslow. Was she still dreaming? Slowly, her vision cleared and his features came into focus. Thick, dark hair. Straight eyebrows. A face full of strong bones and clean lines. And eyes the color of polished pewter. Wow. No, he couldn't be. Could he?

Pulling herself into a sitting position, she looked around. She was in an E.R. examining room, all right. Fully clothed, thankfully, except for her shoes. A blood-pressure cuff circled her left arm. A nurse was pumping it up.

''What happened?'' Emily asked.

''You lost consciousness,'' Brad said. ''The paramedics brought you in.''

The nurse released the pressure on her arm and took off the cuff. "One ten over seventy."

"How do you feel?" Brad asked.

"Fine." Physically, she was. But mentally and emotionally, she was still reeling from the shock of awakening to find *him*.

"Do you know where you are?" he asked.

"I'm in the Courage Bay E.R."

"And why are you here?"

"You just told me it was because I lost consciousness."

"Lucid and responsive to verbal stimuli," he said to the nurse who nodded and made a note on the sheet attached to the clipboard she held.

"What's the last thing you remember?" Brad asked.

"Walking into the greenhouse," Emily said.

He shone a small flashlight in her eye. She blinked.

"Are you in pain anywhere?"

"No."

"Do you have any medical conditions?"

"No."

He switched the light to her other eye. "Are you on any medication?"

"No."

"Have you had any alcohol today?"

"Of course not."

"Drugs?"

She understood these questions probably had to be asked. But she was beginning to resent them. "Half a cup of coffee this morning," she said. "But I'm trying to get clean."

Not even a twitch to his lip. So much for his purported sense of humor.

"Have you had any operations?" he asked.

"No," she responded.

He turned off the light. "How many fingers do you see?"

"One."

And a strong-looking hand, well formed. At least the physical part of him appeared to be as advertised. When he positioned the listening end of the stethoscope in his ears, she knew what was coming. Even so, she gave a small start when he slipped the circular disk beneath the V-neck of her blouse.

Brad showed no sign that he noticed, but the nurse smiled at her in sympathy. "Cold, isn't it?"

Thankful her response had been misinterpreted, Emily gratefully returned her smile. Before Brad could ask her to take a deep breath and hold it, she had done so.

After listening to what was going on inside her from several different spots, he checked the reflexes in her elbows and knees all the while continuing to ask questions about her medical history.

Emily was proud of her calm and cognizant answers. Especially when she considered how incredible it was meeting him this way. Or meeting him any way for that matter.

Another nurse interrupted the examination when she poked her head into the room. "Two victims of a construction accident en route. Scaffolding collapsed from beneath them when they were two stories up. They're both critical. ETA is four minutes."

"I'll join you when I'm finished here," Brad called over his shoulder before addressing the nurse beside him. "Why don't you go help her prep. I'll handle this."

The nurse nodded and followed the other one out.

Brad's hands circled to the back of Emily's neck and felt their way into her scalp, his probing fingers firm but gentle.

"Do you feel any tenderness here?"

His expression was one of total concentration as he gazed at a blank wall to the right.

She realized she was staring at the slight cleft in his chin and averted her eyes. "Uh...no."

"What about here?"

"No. I'm fine. Really."

He ceased the exploration of her scalp, placed a finger on her pulse. His eyes focused on his wristwatch.

"People who are fine don't suddenly lose consciousness for nearly thirty minutes. Have you had anything to eat or drink today?"

"Breakfast was light. Normally I have a full lunch at noon, but I had to attend to some business about that time. How did I get here?"

Brad glanced at the clipboard that the nurse had left lying on the bed table. "A Josh Smithson called the paramedics. Identified himself as your assistant."

"Poor Josh. I must have scared him to death."

"What is your business?"

"I take care of plants."

"Have you been using any new pesticides or fertilizers in your duties?"

"No."

He released her hand. "Your pulse is a little fast."

With him taking it, she wasn't surprised.

He picked up the chart to make a note. "Any chance you're pregnant?"

Thank God he'd taken her pulse before asking *that* question. "No chance about it. I'm eight weeks pregnant."

His eyes shot to hers. "Why didn't you tell me that when I asked if you had any medical conditions?"

She sat up a bit straighter, annoyed at the insinuated censure of his question. "A medical condition implies something's wrong. Nothing's wrong with being pregnant. That's why I fainted, isn't it?"

"Fainting during early and middle pregnancy is a common experience. The hormone, progesterone, is at an all-time high, relaxing the walls of the blood vessels, making the blood pool in your hands and feet and away from your head. The medical term for it is postural hypotension."

"So, it's perfectly normal."

"Remaining unconscious for nearly thirty minutes is not normal. Fainting is the way the body gets the head down so blood can immediately return to it. You should have come out of the faint in a minute or two. We need to find out why you didn't."

"The leaf blower."

"Excuse me?"

"The exhaust from a leaf blower our maintenance man was using. The smell was bad enough out in the open air, but inside the greenhouse, the concentration was lethal. I've always been sensitive to fumes. When I was a kid, the buildup of carbon monoxide at the back of a school bus could put me out. And often did."

"What's the temperature in the greenhouse?"

"Ten to fifteen degrees warmer than the ambient outside air."

He scribbled something on the chart. "The prolonged unconsciousness could have resulted from the combination of postural hypotension, exhaust fumes and exposure to sudden heat. Your vital signs are normal. I don't see that you've suffered any ill effects. But there's no point in taking chances. I'm going to order some blood work to make sure we're not missing anything."

If he ordered tests on her, there was a good chance that he'd discover her other records at this hospital. Emily couldn't risk that.

"I appreciate the thoroughness, but that won't be necessary. I feel fine."

"Ms. Barrett, it's important you have the tests. For you and your fetus."

"I believe you. And your concern is appreciated. Really. But I have an appointment with my doctor on Monday, and I'd feel more comfortable talking things over with her, woman to woman. I'm sure you understand."

It was the perfect out. No male doctor could argue with a woman about her preference in such a matter.

But Brad Winslow sure looked as if he wanted to.

"Your doctor will want to talk to me. Give me her name so that I can note the chart. When she calls, the nurse will know to put her through."

No way Emily was going to let her doctor call Brad Winslow—or let him know her doctor's real name. He was waiting for an answer. She quickly searched her mind for a substitute and came up with her favorite grade-school teacher. "Landerman."

He wrote down the name. "Is Dr. Landerman new to Courage Bay?"

"Her practice is in L.A.," Emily lied, then realized the other questions that might raise. "She's an old friend of the family, which is why I don't mind driving so far to see her."

"What's her number?"

"I don't have it memorized. Thanks for everything."

Emily could see her shoes on the bottom shelf of the cart next to the bed. She scooted to the side of the examining table, intent on slipping off it and getting to them.

But before she could swing her legs over, Brad stepped forward, rested the hospital chart on the edge of the bed's metal rim and effectively blocked her path.

"Your assistant wasn't able to provide your home address, number and next of kin. Let's take a moment to fill in the blanks, shall we?"

"No reason to take up your time with that," Emily said quickly. "I'll give my insurance information to the clerk in admissions. She'll be able to get whatever she requires from it."

"You sound like you know your way around this hospital."

"I've visited friends here from time to time."

She waited for him to move out of her way. He didn't.

"All right, Ms. Barrett, how do you know about me?"

His authoritative tone had developed an even sharper edge and his eyes were chips of granite.

For a second Emily stared at him. Then it hit her. Dear

heavens. Those things she'd been thinking about him before she came to. She must have said them aloud. Oh, hell.

Don't panic, Emily. You can handle this. Remember, the best defense when cornered is to act innocent.

She squinted at him like someone who'd forgotten her glasses. "I'm sorry. I don't seem to recognize you, Doctor. Do we know each other?"

His skeptical expression told her he wasn't buying the act. The sound of a siren approached. Footsteps rushed past in the hallway. The injured men from the construction site were here. This was her chance to escape.

Second-best defense—run to the nearest exit.

"You have people who need you," she said. "I'd better be on my way. Thank you for taking care of me, Dr...uh... I'm sorry. What was your name again?"

"Where did you find out those very personal things about me?" he demanded, not budging an inch.

She did her best to look confused. "What things?"

"My ethnic background, coloring, height, weight, age, favorite color, favorite—"

"I'm sorry," she interrupted with a regretful shake of her head, "but I don't know what you're talking about."

"You expect me to believe you don't remember what you said?"

"I have no memory of meeting you before today, Doctor. When am I supposed to have said these things?"

"You said them while lying on this bed not five minutes ago. And you know it. You're not leaving here until you tell me exactly where you learned those personal details of my life."

She could see he damn well meant it, too. There was only one choice left.

Third-best defense—scare the hell out of the opponent so he runs to the nearest exit.

Emily plastered a look of excitement on her face. "I told you about personal details in your life? And they were accurate? Well, well. That hasn't happened in quite a while.''

''What hasn't?''

''When I've been in semiconscious states before, I've shown...well, that is, people have told me I display very strong psychic powers.''

For a fraction of a second, something that looked like discomfort flashed across his stoic features.

Emily settled farther back on the bed, no longer making any attempt to leave. As a matter of fact, she was doing her best to convey the impression that she planned to stay awhile.

''Once I collapsed in a store and before I came to, I'd told the owner all about the affair he was having with his bookkeeper,'' she lied blithely. ''Of course, he was a little upset at me since his wife was standing right next to him at the time. But that's one of the drawbacks of being a semiconscious psychic.''

Brad's eyes darted toward the phone on the wall. Debating whether he should call for restraints or a psychiatric consultation?

''This is really exciting, Doctor. You don't know how glad I am you told me. So many people are afraid of acknowledging any sense beyond the mundane five—especially people from the so-called scientific disciplines. Why most doctors wouldn't dream of repeating what you did for fear of being ridiculed.''

His eyebrows inched so tightly together, they were about to meet.

''Please, you must give me the details of everything you said and what I told you,'' she begged. ''When I tell people about this, they're going to want to be sure you didn't give me any hints. Not that I blame them for being skeptical. There are so many fakes out there. Do you mind if I borrow some paper and a pen to take notes?''

To his credit, he didn't so much as flinch. But he was clenching the hospital chart so hard, his knuckles were white. It took an effort of will for Emily to keep a straight face.

A nurse rapped once on the door, then stuck her head into the room. "You want the concussion or the bleeder?"

"The bleeder," he said. "Ms. Barrett is ready to be released."

He shoved the paperwork in the nurse's hands and was out of the room so fast that Emily could feel the gust of air displaced in his wake.

She let out a sigh of relief. Well, she'd managed to dodge that bullet. But only just. On paper, Brad Winslow had been very impressive. In person he was one formidable son of a gun.

"ARE YOU SURE YOU'RE OKAY, EM?" Dorothy Mission asked for the umpteenth time as they worked together to prepare dinner in her kitchen.

Dumping the romaine lettuce she'd chopped into a large salad bowl, Emily sent her friend a look of exasperation. "If you don't stop asking me if I'm okay, I'm going to throw this salad at you."

Dorothy smiled. "Could you wait until you slice in the tomatoes? A green outfit always looks more festive with a nice splash of red."

Emily chuckled as she went back to her task. "Truth is, I nearly had a heart attack when it dawned on me that I'd unconsciously blabbed all that stuff to Brad Winslow."

"Imagine the jolt he must have felt hearing what you said."

"At least he made sure I was okay and everything that was medical had been attended to before he tried to nail me to the wall on it."

"Em, I know you said you never wanted to meet him, but now that you have, are you glad?"

She gave the question some serious thought as she

chopped the carrots. "I admit it did satisfy a certain curiosity."

"Is he everything that you…hoped?"

Emily glanced over at the speculative look on her friend's face. "Forget it, Dot. He's just a man like any other. And, as far as I'm concerned, good for one thing and one thing only."

"Oh, I think they might have one or two other uses," her friend said with a mischievous smile.

"I can open tight jars and take out the trash myself, thank you," Emily said, knowing perfectly well that was not what Dot had been referring to.

"Come on," Dorothy persisted. "You selected Brad Winslow out of the hundreds you could have picked. You must think he's special. What stood out most strongly when you met him today?"

"That he's no one to fool around with. If I hadn't lied my head off and known what button to push, he'd have found me out, and I'd be in serious trouble now."

"Em, I respect your wishes on this, really I do. But you're such a nice person that… I mean even after all you've been through, I guess I still hope you'll…oh, forget it. You're right. I can't pretend to understand what I haven't experienced. And people who say they know how someone else feels are irritating."

"On that we agree wholeheartedly," Emily said.

"You two are agreeing?" Holly Mission said as she entered the room. "Oh, this can't be good."

Dorothy gave her daughter a hug. Holly was both smart and sweet—a seventeen-year-old version of her mom.

"So, is Lester gone?" Dorothy asked Holly.

"Yeah, Josh and I stuck around until he got his stuff together and drove off."

"Did you get his key to the maintenance gate?"

"Oh, hell, Mom. I forgot."

"Key?" Emily repeated.

"Lester quit," Dorothy said. "When I went to bawl

him out about the leaf blower incident sending you to the E.R. this afternoon, I found him loading sacks of organic fertilizer into his pickup."

"He was stealing them?"

Dorothy nodded. "First story he gave me was that he was moving the sacks to the other side of the Gardens so they'd be in place when he fertilized next week. But when I pointed to some of your new rose hybrids in between the sacks of fertilizer in his pickup, he had no convenient lie ready for why they were there."

Emily shook her head. "I've been wondering why so many of our supplies seemed to be missing lately."

"His father has opened a small nursery on the outskirts of town," Dorothy said. "No doubt Lester's been taking the supplies from the Botanical Gardens over to him. I told him he had a choice. Either quit or I'd see to it that you fired him."

"That must have been hard for you, Dot."

"I never should have suggested you hire him in the first place. I love my cousin but her kid is a loser. I swear he got all of his father's genes and not one of hers. When Lester was thirteen, I caught him stealing from her purse so he could buy marijuana from another kid pushing it at school. Supposedly, he got himself clean. But clean or not, ten years later and he's still a thief."

"I'm sorry about forgetting the key, Emily," Holly said. "But I don't think Lester will come back. I watched closely to make sure that he didn't try to put anything that wasn't his into his pickup. Josh was right beside me, scowling at him the whole time he was getting his stuff together. And when he started to drive away, Josh yelled at him not to come back."

"Well, good for our Josh," Dorothy said. "He seems to be working out okay despite his grandfather's claim that the boy's clueless."

"Josh is a very good assistant," Emily said. "He simply needs a little time to find his direction in life."

"Speaking of time," Holly said, "Josh asked me to remind you to meet with the crane guy today."

"I have. The sundial has been prepped and readied for tomorrow."

"Do you need my help on anything?" Dorothy asked.

"Thanks, but I took care of the other last minute details before coming over. Gardens, dignitaries and media are all in line. We are good to go, Mission Control."

Dorothy smiled as she set a plate of sliced roast beef on the kitchen table. Emily put the mixed-salad bowl between the beef and a basket of steaming baked potatoes. The fact that her friend still insisted on eating in the kitchen when Emily joined them always made her feel like one of the Mission family.

"Smartest thing I ever did was to convince my fellow board members to put you in charge of the Founders Day Celebration. It's going to be a smashing success, Em."

"Okay, what are all you smashing women smashing now?" Ted Mission asked with a grin as he came rustling in the back door, keys and briefcase jangling by his side.

Dorothy immediately stopped what she was doing and went to greet her husband.

Ted and Dorothy Mission had been married more than twenty-five years, were past fifty and packed a dozen extra pounds of good living around their middles. But the embrace and kiss they shared were as hot as young lovers'.

"They're at it again," Holly said, shaking her head, but wearing a smile.

Emily watched her friends as she always did—with undisguised envy. Dorothy and Ted had it all—rewarding careers, a long-term love match and a brainy daughter headed for Harvard in the fall.

Once Emily had dreamed of having it all. Now she knew that fulfilling work and a precious baby to love would be enough.

For men might come and go. But a child was forever.

ATTENDING PHYSICIAN Alec Giroux was going over charts when Brad walked by his office on his way out. He waved Brad over.

"You certainly had your share of crazies today," Alec said as he gestured to the stack of charts in front of him. "Nice save on that chest wound."

"We were lucky we didn't lose anyone," Brad said as he folded his arms and rested his leg against the desk.

Alec leaned back in his chair, the expression on his face conveying the fact that he knew luck had nothing to do with it. "You're going to ace those board exams next month."

Brad appreciated the vote of confidence. From the moment he'd begun his residency in emergency medicine at Courage Bay Hospital four years before, Alec had been far more friend and supporter than supervisor.

"You going to take Guy up on his offer of a permanent position here when the exams are over?" Alec asked.

Brad wanted to. In his first month on the job he'd learned more from Alec and his brother, Guy, their chief of emergency medicine, than he'd learned in all his years at medical school. They were the best.

But the money at the community hospital was not. He hadn't paid off all of his eight years of staggering school loans.

"I'm giving it some thought," he said, honestly.

Alec nodded. As a single father, he probably knew how difficult it could be to catch up on bills and make ends meet.

"I was reviewing Emily Barrett's chart," he said. "Surprised to see it among the bunch of wackos we had walking the halls today."

Even hearing her name was enough to get Brad to uncross his arms and plant both feet firmly beneath him. "You know Emily Barrett?"

"My sister, Natalie, says she's a regular in the pediatric and geriatric wards upstairs."

Yeah, Brad figured knowing someone at this hospital was how Emily had really learned that personal stuff about him.

"Emily brings flowers and potted plants to the patients who don't get visitors," Alec continued. "Nice lady."

"Certifiable kook," Brad said beneath his breath.

"I pulled her hospital records," Alec went on, not having heard the comment. "I was hoping they might shed some light on her prolonged unconsciousness today, but no clues there. You were right to suggest more tests. Shame she refused them. All we can do is trust that she'll follow up with her obstetrician."

Brad took a step forward. "She didn't tell me she'd been admitted to this hospital."

"Outpatient in the OB-GYN clinic for her artificial insemination eight weeks ago," Alec explained as he handed over the record. "Dr. Jill Crispin does all of her inseminations and deliveries here."

Brad started, not sure he'd heard right. "Are you telling me Jill Crispin from the Crispin Fertility Clinic is Emily Barrett's doctor?"

"You know Dr. Crispin?"

"I've heard of her," Brad said as he quickly read through the hospital record of Emily Barrett that he held in his hands. This had to be a coincidence. The transactions were absolutely confidential. No way either party could learn about the other.

Except as his eyes fixed on Emily Barrett's maiden name, he suddenly saw that there was one way.

"Brad, is there something wrong? Brad?"

CHAPTER TWO

"WHY DID YOU DO IT?" Brad demanded, working hard to control the anger that seethed beneath his surface calm.

Ed Corbin looked his friend squarely in the eye, took a sip of his beer and swallowed hard. "I didn't have a choice."

"You damn well did have a choice."

Brad's raised voice turned a lot of curious heads in his direction. Ed pulled some bills out of his pocket and slapped them on the bar. "You're pissed. I don't blame you. Give me a chance to explain outside, where we don't have an audience."

Brad didn't argue with the need for discretion. The Courage Bay Bar and Grill was the off-duty hangout for the community's police, fire and medical personnel. Anything overheard here would be on the gossip hotline of every emergency team by morning.

He quietly followed his friend out. A cool night breeze was coming off the ocean, the air filled with one of his favorite scents—the sea. But Brad wasn't in an appreciative mood.

"Is this why you suddenly came up with the suggestion that I donate sperm last year? So she could get it?"

"No," Ed said. "When I told you the Crispin Fertility Clinic was willing to pay top dollar for sperm from doctors, I did it because the director asked me to pass the word, and I knew you could use the money. Those were the only reasons. I swear."

Brad had met Detective Ed Corbin during his first year

at Courage Bay Hospital. A burglar cut himself when he'd tried to escape capture by jumping through a plate-glass window. Ed brought him into the E.R. for treatment.

While a nurse was seeing to his wounds, the guy grabbed a knife and took her hostage. Brad had kept the thief's attention by enticing him with offers of drugs he could sell on the street in exchange for letting the nurse go—giving Ed time to circle behind the man and subdue him.

They'd made a good team that day, and good friends ever since. Brad had never known Ed to lie. He didn't believe he was doing so now.

"What happened?" Brad asked.

"I stopped by Emily's place about three months ago and saw all these sperm-bank questionnaires spread out on her table. When I asked her what was going on, she told me she'd decided to have a kid by artificial insemination."

"You didn't know before that?"

Ed shook his head. "Nearly blew me away. Never occurred to me she'd do something like that. I tried my best to talk her out of it. But Emily's unmovable when she's made up her mind."

"What possessed you to tell her about me?" Brad asked.

"I figured if she was stupid enough to have some stranger's kid, she should at least be sure she was getting good sperm. I mean, what would you have done if she were your sister?"

There was a protective note in Ed's tone Brad had never heard before. They rarely talked about the personal stuff, which was why Brad hadn't even known the name of Ed's sister before today. Emily was clearly very special to him.

Brad found his anger at his friend beginning to fade. "I've never had a sister."

"Count your blessings. They're a damn pain. You love them, and all you want is the best for them. But what happens when you try to help? They tell you to butt out of their business."

"You should have listened to her this time."

"I couldn't. She was going to the wrong place. The Crispin Fertility Clinic is the only one that does a thorough background check on its donors to be sure that they are who they claim. I told Emily about Jill Crispin alerting us when she discovered that a guy using a phony name and profession had applied. He turned out to be an ex-con with two outstanding warrants. That con had gotten away with donating sperm to every other damn clinic around because they never checked up on his lies. Who knows how many more there are like him around?"

"Wasn't steering her to the right fertility clinic enough?" Brad asked. "Did you have to tell her about me?"

"Yeah, I did. You should have seen the flakes she had to pick from even at Crispin. I read the questionnaires these guys filled out. Eighty percent of them were dumb college jocks, barely literate, just looking for some extra cash. The idea that Emily's genes would be mixing with theirs made me want to puke."

"What about the other twenty percent?"

"I suppose some of them were decent, if you could believe what they wrote. The Crispin Clinic is careful that their donors are physically healthy and legally who they say they are. But they have no way of knowing whether these guys are telling the truth when they answer questions about their goals in life and such."

Brad had to admit that was true. He could have lied about those things when he filled out the forms, and no one would have been the wiser.

"But when I tried to impress this fact on Emily, she turned a deaf ear," Ed continued. "Kept telling me she'd decide who was best. Said she didn't need me to make her decisions for her."

"Then why did she take your recommendation on me?"

"I wasn't sure she had. She wanted the best and I wanted the best for her, so naturally I told her all about you so she'd know which one of the anonymous donor questionnaires was yours. But the only thing she said was that *if* she picked your sperm, I was never going to know and neither were you."

"I know," Brad said. "She quoted what I entered on that damn questionnaire verbatim. And when I called her on it, she did the one thing she knew would make me back off."

"What was that?"

"She pretended to be psychic."

"How could she know that would make you back off?"

"Because I put it on the questionnaire. When asked what was the one thing that would make me avoid otherwise nice and pleasant people, I said it would be if they turned out to be superstitious or believed in all that psychic mumbo jumbo."

"Brad, I'm sorry about this. She warned me to say nothing to you. I admit I wanted her to select you for her sake, but I never intended for you to find out."

"I wish to hell I hadn't," Brad said on a long exhale. "What does her husband think about all this?"

"Husband? Emily's not married."

"But she shows Barrett as her married name. I thought—"

"Oh, she was married. Just not anymore. Hell, she doesn't even date now."

Brad stopped walking, grabbed his friend's arm, halting him in his stride. "Are you telling me your sister is planning to raise the baby without a father?"

"She'll be a good mother," Ed said. "I'm not just saying that because she's my sister. Emily's wanted a kid for years, but things...didn't work out for her. She's thrilled to be having this baby."

Brad released his friend's arm and sank to the edge of a nearby concrete street planter, putting his head in his hands. This was getting worse by the minute.

"What's wrong?"

He raised his eyes at the concern in Ed's voice. "My brother and I never had a dad. He took off when we were young, and we never saw or heard from him again. I had a great mother. The best. It's not enough. A kid needs a father. I always swore *my* kid would have one."

"Brad, legally, the child Emily's going to have…it's not your kid."

He didn't need Ed to tell him that. Brad was only too aware that he'd signed away all legal rights to his sperm.

Yes, the money he'd received had helped to pay down his school loans. But the real reason he'd involved himself in the process was because he believed he was doing the right thing helping an infertile couple conceive.

He never imagined that he'd find out who got his sperm. Or that she'd be a single woman.

"What a goddamn mess," he muttered to the night sky.

Ed plopped down beside him. "If you want to shoot me, I'll loan you my gun."

His friend's expression told Brad how badly he felt— despite the fact that he'd been trying to do the right thing for his sister.

"I'm such a lousy shot, I'd probably miss your ugly mug and hit an innocent bystander instead."

Ed nodded. "Then you'd have to patch him up, and I'd have to run you in. See your point. Too damn much paperwork."

They sat for a long moment in silence as cars whizzed by on the street and several pedestrians flashed them curious looks as they passed. Brad was only minimally aware of his surroundings.

He was thinking about how careful he'd been in his relationships with women. Not once had he had unprotected sex. He'd been so sure that something like this was never going to happen to him.

"I have to talk to your sister," he said finally.

"What are you planning to say?"

"Haven't a clue. But I have to do something. Now that I know who's going to have my...the baby and how it's going to be raised, I can't just turn my back and pretend it isn't happening. Could you?"

"No, I guess not," Ed agreed.

"Do you know if she's home?"

"She's out having dinner with friends tonight. Probably won't be back until late. But you could catch her at the Founders Day Celebration tomorrow. I'm going if you want to ride along with me."

The Founders Day Celebration was the biggest event of the year—if not the decade—and had been hogging the local headlines for days. Everyone wanted to attend, and from what Brad had heard, if you didn't have some pretty high-up connections, you couldn't get in.

"You playing bodyguard to some dignitary?" he asked.

"No, strictly there as Emily's brother. She's been putting it together for the past few months so she's my in."

Brad was sure he couldn't have heard right. "Your *sister* is in charge of the Founders Day Celebration?"

"I take it she didn't tell you."

"She told me she was a gardener."

Ed chuckled. "A psychic and a gardener. Boy, did she have fun with you today. Emily's the curator of the city's Botanical Gardens and a member of the Historical Society. She also has a Ph.D. in botany and she's written a couple of books on medicinal plants."

"Jeez," Brad said as his head went back in his hands.

"Yeah, I know. A damn overachiever. Sure put the pressure on me and my brother while we were growing up. Our parents were always so button-popping proud of her. Still are. I planned to push her off a cliff when I got big enough."

"Can't imagine what stopped you."

"It was this annoying habit she had of always making me feel like I was the talented one. No matter what sport I played, she was in the stands cheering for me and threatening the other team's members with the loss of various body parts if they so much as harmed a hair on my head."

The scene materialized so clearly in Brad's mind that it made him wish he'd had such a sister.

"My pass to the ceremonies tomorrow is for two," Ed said. "You can be my date if you promise not to wear anything too low-cut."

"I'll see what I have in my wardrobe," Brad said dryly. "If you were me, how would you approach her on this?"

"Beats me."

"Come on. You've known her all your life. You must have a feel for what would work?"

"It's precisely because I have known her all my life that I can assure you nothing will work. Emily's made up her mind to have this kid alone and raise it by herself. And that's what she'll do."

Brad looked out at the night, hoping for inspiration. But his mind was as hazy and blank as the starless sky.

Ed grabbed hold of his arm and pulled him to his feet. "Come on. We're going back to the bar and tie one on."

"You think getting drunk is going to help?"

"I sure hope so. Tomorrow, I have tickets to the hottest event of the year and look who I'm taking."

THE TEMPERATURE WAS IN the seventies, the air a fragrant kiss across Emily's cheek. In the distance, the Pacific Ocean whispered against white sands. To the north, south and east, the steep mountains circled into a soft blue sky. The gardens all around her were ablaze with sunlight and the beauty of growing things.

"You even arranged for us to have perfect weather," Dorothy said near her ear. "I am impressed."

Emily sent her friend a smile.

The Botanical Gardens were filled with the by-invitation-only spectators. Chief of police Max Zirinsky was among them and so were a lot of his plainclothes officers, unobtrusively milling about and keeping a watchful eye.

On a slightly raised platform sat the city council along with Phoebe Landru and Oliver Smithson, Dorothy's fellow members of the managing board of the Historical Society. The local KSEA TV news crew had set up cameras. Ken Kerr, the society's photographer, was busy taking pictures with his thirty-five millimeter.

"All we need now is the mayor," Dorothy said glancing at her watch.

As though hearing his cue, the newly elected mayor, Patrick O'Shea, turned the corner. The TV crew immediately aimed their cameras at him and started to roll. Emily went over to greet him.

The mayor shook her hand warmly, wearing a genuine smile. In Emily's experience, there were two types of people who went into politics—egoists and idealists. The preponderance of officeholders fit into the first category. Patrick O'Shea, thankfully, fit into the second.

He'd been fire chief before running for mayor, not the kind of job that most candidates for public office held. But maybe the kind that they should. O'Shea knew how to put the welfare of the people of Courage Bay first.

Emily accompanied him to the platform and showed him to his seat. Dorothy had taken her place next to the other members of the Historical Society. The clock in the Botanical Gardens' Heritage Museum was striking the hour. Everything was in place and on time.

As Emily turned to the crowd before her, she felt proud to be a part of this historical moment for Courage Bay. Raising her hands for quiet, she caught sight of her brother at the right of the large crowd and smiled. When she saw who was standing beside him, the smile froze on her lips.

Oh, no. What in the hell was he doing here?

Emily forced herself to turn her eyes and thoughts away. She was going to let nothing and no one interfere with this momentous occasion. "Ladies and gentlemen, it is my great pleasure to welcome you to our Founders Day Celebration. And it is my deep honor to present to you the mayor of Courage Bay, Patrick O'Shea."

Emily took her seat beside Dorothy as Mayor O'Shea approached the podium accompanied by enthusiastic applause. When it had died down, he turned to Emily and publicly thanked her for all her hard work in making the celebration a success.

Dorothy rose and began to clap. The crowd quickly joined her as the mayor, city council and other members of the Historical Society's managing board also got to their feet and applauded. All this focused and very unexpected attention made Emily glad she wasn't a blusher.

Once the audience had sat down again, the mayor faced forward.

"I want to tell you a story my father told me when I was no more than five," he began. "It's a story I've passed down to my children. It's one I hope you will pass down to yours."

The crowd listened with hushed attention.

"In January of 1848, an American ship called *Ranger* was caught in a terrible storm at sea and blown off course to these Southern California shores," O'Shea said. "When the ship was struck by lightning and began to sink, its exhausted crew would certainly have drowned if not for the brave Indians of this land who risked their lives fighting the raging current to bring them safely to shore. In honor of the selfless act of their rescuers, the survivors of *Ranger* named this settlement Courage Bay."

Emily knew this story well. Still, she never tired of hearing it told. These events were a proud heritage that she and all the residents of Courage Bay shared. She found herself caught up in the favorite tale.

"When the Indian chief invited the shipwrecked crew

to stay, they readily agreed," the mayor continued. "Protected by this steep mountain range rising on three sides, our quiet community of Courage Bay remained virtually isolated from the outside world until the late nineteenth century when a road was cut through from the north. Even so, it wasn't until 1904 when the citizens filed their town map with the county recorder's office that Courage Bay was officially founded."

Mayor O'Shea paused as he turned toward the large stone sundial to the right of the platform.

"As a marker of that historic event, the leaders of Courage Bay buried a time capsule beneath this enormous sundial they set in the heart of their community park, a park which has grown over the years to become our beautiful Botanical Gardens."

He faced the crowd. "Today, exactly one hundred years later, we will remove the cover and open that time capsule. I don't know about you, but I can't wait to see what our city's founders have preserved for us."

Emily nodded to the man sitting in the seat of the crane. He turned on the engine and swung the telescoping crane arm over the sundial.

Earlier that morning she'd supervised the operator and his rigger as they'd dug around the eight-foot-diameter stone they would have to lift. After inserting wedges in several spots, they'd slid a metal plate beneath the sundial to protect it from cracking when it was raised. Slipping three sets of straps beneath the plate, they'd tied them together above the stone.

Lifting it now was a simple task. The rigger on the ground grabbed the steel hook at the end of the crane's telescoping arm and fixed it beneath the sturdy straps. He then signaled the crane operator to hoist the stone away.

As Emily watched the progress, she'd found herself wondering what it was the founders of Courage Bay had bequeathed them. The sundial had been chiseled when the time capsule had been buried beneath it, specifying when it was to be opened. On the Roman numerals marking the twenty-four-hour segments were the initials of the men who had been selected to set the stone in place.

But nothing on the sundial gave a hint as to what was to be found in the chamber below. If she were to bury a time capsule today, what would she put inside?

Emily's musings came to a quick close as the stone sundial was lifted and set aside on the cushioned platform prepared for it. The TV camera crew changed position to get a better angle, shining bright lights into the dark chamber below. The big moment had arrived.

Mayor O'Shea and the city council members were the first to reach the sides of the exposed pit and look within. Emily waited in anticipation on the adjacent platform with the other members of the Historical Society.

For a long moment, no one moved or said anything. And then one of the city council members muttered an oath. Another one straightened and stepped back.

Mayor O'Shea calmly turned to face the camera lens. "Ladies and gentlemen, there seems to be a skeleton in our time capsule's closet."

CHIEF OF POLICE MAX ZIRINSKY stood over the pit, instructing the Historical Society's photographer on what angles he wanted him to shoot to get the best pictures of the skeleton that was lying beside the time capsule.

Ed beckoned Brad through the milling crowd—being held back by a line of plainclothes officers—to stand beside them. After introducing Brad to the police chief, Ed got to the reason he'd summoned his friend.

"We need your expertise. If we're at the scene of a murder, no time capsule gets opened today. All of these very important people are going to be asked to leave so a crime team can get in here."

"You want me to take a look at this skeleton and hopefully tell you that death was by natural causes," Brad guessed.

"Can you?"

"I'm not a forensic anthropologist."

"But you studied to be one," Ed persisted.

"Even so, I have to warn you the kind of evaluation you're asking for might not be possible. And even if it is, getting an answer could take a lot of time."

"If we had a lot of time, we'd get a real forensic anthropologist," Max said bluntly.

"How much time do you have?"

"Fifteen minutes, tops," Max answered. "These are not people who are used to being kept waiting."

No, Brad supposed they weren't. Nothing he could do but his best. "I'm going to have to get down in the pit to get a closer look. If this is a crime scene—"

"Don't worry," Ed said, interrupting. "We'll take your clothes and process them along with any dirt or whatever else you may pick up if this turns out to be a murder. Here, take these gloves and put them on. I'll hold your sport coat."

Brad nodded as he slipped out of his jacket and snapped on the thin evidence gloves Ed had handed him. There was only a three-foot drop to the top of the time capsule. Brad carefully slid down on the side opposite both it and the skeleton.

Bright lights followed his progress, as did a TV camera. Since Max was directing the camera, Brad assumed he'd commandeered the crew for the purposes of chronicling the scene and Brad's initial examination of it.

His first glance at the fully articulated skeleton from above had already told him something. Decomposition followed a predictable course. The body had to have been placed here soon after death to leave an anatomically correct and intact skeleton like this.

It was also obvious that the bones had been thoroughly cleaned by insects over time and a couple stained a yellowish brown—most likely by some mineral leached from the soil on which they lay.

Brad went down on a knee and bent his head to get a ventral view of the pelvis, noting the relative narrowness of its opening and that of the sciatic notch on the edge of each hip bone. That gave him a pretty good idea about the skeleton's sex. A cursory look at the leg and arm bones revealed a coarsening, no doubt the result of temperature changes occurring over an extensive period of time.

Then a shift in the overhead light picked up a glint of something near the right pelvic bone. He gently dipped his fingers into the earth, and, to his surprise, pulled out a gold coin.

It proved to be a twenty-dollar Liberty piece bearing the date of 1900. After rooting around in the dirt some more, he came up with something even more unexpected—a mud-encrusted dagger.

Brad's eyes traveled up the skeleton's rib cage and vertebral column. The bright light from above revealed no obvious knife marks on the bones. When he got to the skull, there were none there, either. But there was a round hole over one of the brow ridges. He was leaning forward to study it when he saw a dark lump inside the skull. He reached in and pulled out a spent bullet.

As Brad stood, he found Ed bending toward him, holding out an evidence bag. After slipping the dagger, coin and slug inside it, Brad climbed out of the pit.

"I take it we have a homicide," Ed said as he stared at the dagger, his expression as ill-humored as a man suffering from a toothache.

Brad nodded as he dusted off the knees of his slacks. "Judging by the angle of the entry wound, I doubt that the guy shot himself."

"Shot? He's got a bullet wound?"

"My degree isn't on the forensic side. But I've treated enough live shooting victims to recognize one when I see it."

Brad paused to point at the evidence bag. "Plus which

I found that slug inside his skull. The hole in the bone didn't show any signs of healing, which also leads me to the logical conclusion that the wound was inflicted at the time of death.''

"Bullet must have lodged in his brain," Max Zirinsky said as he came to stand next to them, looking about as thrilled as Ed did at the discoveries. "Didn't have sufficient velocity to exit the skull. I've seen this kind of thing before.''

Brad noticed that the Chief of Police had made sure that even the TV crew was now behind the line of plainclothes police and that his conversation with Brad and Ed was being conducted out of the earshot of everyone else.

"What can you tell us about the victim?" Max asked.

Brad tugged off the evidence gloves. "The cranial sutures are completely closed. It has prominent browridges and robust mastoid processes. The fully erupted teeth are crooked with a fierce overbite. The pelvic opening is narrow.''

"And in English that translates to?" Max prodded.

"Adult male. Twenty-five to fifty age range. Someone will have to look a lot closer at the bones to tell you more.''

"Clothing?''

"Something in the soil near the feet that could be rotted leather boots. Nothing else visible, but I wasn't really looking. Chances are most cloth materials disintegrated over time. Roots are impinging on the sides of the pit. Insect activity has no doubt been steady over the decades. Anything not enclosed within the time capsule was either consumed as their food or broken down by soil minerals.''

"Dr. Winslow, are you telling me that this guy was buried here at the same time as the time capsule?''

Brad nodded as he gestured toward the evidence bag. "I found that 1900 gold coin beneath the body. Can't imagine anyone today carrying it around as if it were change in his pocket. When you add that fact to the absence of orthodontic work and the mineralization of the bones, I'd say it's a safe bet your skeleton is at least a hundred years old.''

Relief washed over Max's face. He grabbed Brad's hand and gave it a hearty pump. ''Thank you, Dr. Winslow.''

''You're welcome,'' Brad said, surprised. ''But I thought that you were hoping it wasn't a homicide.''

''Brad, if this guy was killed a hundred years ago, his murderer's dead, too,'' Ed explained. ''That closes it for us. No crime scene, no need to delay pulling up the time capsule and getting back to the celebration.''

''Let's keep the fact that he was murdered off the news,'' Max said. ''No need to distract from the ceremony. I'll let the mayor know we can proceed.''

As soon as he was gone, Ed held out Brad's sport coat. ''Buddy, you just made me look good in front of the chief. Come on. I want to be the one to break the news to Emily. If you're still bent on talking to her, I suggest you do it after I sing your praises.''

''Sounds good to me,'' Brad said as he put on his coat and started with Ed toward the crowd. ''When she told you about ending up in the E.R. yesterday, she didn't mention meeting me, did she?''

''Not a word.''

''Good. Introduce me to her as though you have no idea that we've met.''

''What do you have planned?'' Ed asked.

''Nothing, yet. I simply want to keep my options open. And don't let on that I know about…you know.''

Brad had refrained from being specific because they had gotten within the hearing range of others.

''Wouldn't dream of it,'' Ed assured. ''If she learns I said anything, she'll kill me.''

When Emily saw Ed and Brad approaching, she broke away from the people she was with and met them halfway. True to his promise, Ed introduced Brad to her as though he had no idea his sister and friend had met before.

"Dr. Winslow and I know each other," Emily said.

Brad nodded as though he had just figured out why she looked familiar. "Yes, of course. You were in the E.R. yesterday. How are you feeling today, Mrs. Barrett?"

"Fine, thank you," she said, but she was studying him intently.

He was studying her, as well. Yesterday, she'd been his patient, and as such he'd carefully restricted his observations to an impersonal list of vital signs.

Today, she was a tall, uncommonly lovely woman with long chestnut hair, large amber eyes and a natural warmth that had effortlessly captivated the mayor as well as the rest of the crowd.

And she was irritating him more by the minute. Why would an intelligent, attractive woman like this—who could no doubt charm most men into doing whatever she wanted—choose to have a child by artificial insemination?

It didn't make sense. Brad needed things to make sense—and this most of all.

"I have some good news, Em," Ed said. "Brad has saved the day. Even though your skeleton appears to have been the victim of foul play, the guy met his maker a hundred years ago. The Founders Day Celebration can go ahead as planned."

"That is good news," Emily agreed, looking relieved. "But you do realize that learning who this skeleton is and how he came to be buried with the time capsule could be as significant as anything else we uncover today?"

Ed shrugged. "That's something for you historians to figure out."

"Aren't you going to investigate?"

"Em, it's not a police matter."

"But if he was murdered—"

"Look, I'd like to help you on this, but I can't. And neither can the department. We have far too many unsolved homicides with living perps running around out there that need to be found. No one has the time to dig into old crimes where the murderers are long dead.''

Watching the disappointment marring Emily's smooth forehead, Brad knew opportunity was knocking and quickly stepped forward to open the door. "I may be able to help you with the skeleton's identity," he said.

She turned toward him, her expression full of that cool, professional calm he thought he had a patent on. "How could you help?"

Before he had an opportunity to answer, a middle-aged woman approached them. Brad recognized her as the one who had sat next to Emily and led the crowd in its applause of her efforts.

Emily introduced her friend as Dr. Dorothy Mission, a member of the managing board of the Courage Bay Historical Society.

"Do you prefer doctor or Dorothy?" Brad asked as he shook the hand offered to him.

"Always depends on who's asking," Dorothy said. "In your case, definitely Dot."

She was flirting with him in that totally non offensive and non serious way that a plump woman over fifty with guts and good humor could pull off. He liked her immediately. "I'm Brad."

"Did I overhear you say something about helping out, Brad?" Dorothy asked.

"Yes, I have some knowledge of forensic anthropology," he said. "There's a lot that can be learned from bones. I'll study the skeleton for you and see what I can turn up."

"That's a generous offer," Emily said, in a tone that was something less than bursting with enthusiasm. "But I wouldn't presume to—"

"I like mysteries," he interrupted. "And you have to admit, this hundred-year-old skeleton presents an interesting one."

"So our skeleton isn't of recent origin," Dorothy said. "No wonder Max Zirinsky was looking so relieved."

"It appears to have been buried with the time capsule, Dot," Emily explained. "And to have been murdered."

"Murdered?" Dorothy repeated.

"Let's keep that fact among ourselves," Ed said quickly. "At least until Brad can examine it and give us the details."

"We'll be delighted to avail ourselves of your expertise," Dorothy said.

Out of the corner of his eye, Brad could see that Emily was not quite so delighted.

He turned to Ed before she could think of any more excuses to brush him off. "Can you arrange to have the skeleton carefully removed and taken to the hospital morgue after the ceremony?"

Ed frowned as he looked over at the chief of police. Brad understood he was going to have to sell his superior on this use of the department's resources for this non-case and clearly wasn't looking forward to the task.

"What the hell," Ed said. "If anybody tries to give me grief, I'll just remind them of all the important noses that would be out of joint if you hadn't been here today. What do you want me to do with this stuff?"

He was holding up the evidence bag with the dagger, coin and spent slug.

"Keep them with the skeleton for now. Could be important to the examination later. That is, if that's all right with you," Brad said as he turned to Emily.

She nodded. That told Brad what he wanted to know. She'd accepted his offer of help, despite her suspicions.

While he was doing this favor for her, he should be able to get close enough to discover what made her tick. Once he did, he could decide how best to convince her that she was wrong to try to bring up a child by herself.

That he would convince her, he had no doubt. Had she really been a superstitious person, no amount of logic could have reached her. But she was clearly intelligent and, even better, a woman of science.

She would respond to reason. He just had to find the right approach.

The mayor advanced toward the podium at that moment and took the microphone in hand.

"Ladies and gentlemen, I'm happy to report that thanks to Dr. Brad Winslow's expert analysis, we know that the skeleton in our time capsule's closet is a fascinating artifact that, no doubt, will become an interesting research project for our Historical Society. Now please take your seats, for we are about to lift the time capsule out of its resting place and take a look inside. Who knows what other surprises lie in wait?"

CHAPTER THREE

"YOU LIED TO ME, EMILY BARRETT," Dorothy whispered in her ear when they had retaken their seats.

"About what?" Emily whispered back.

"Dr. Brad Winslow is anything but just another guy."

"And you're saying that because…?"

"Come on, Em. You know perfectly well that man's the reason we women were given breasts that heave and spines that melt."

Emily contained her smile. Dorothy had insisted Brad join them on the platform in thanks for his help with the skeleton. He sat with the city council, on the receiving end of a lot of appreciative looks from the women in the audience. There was something about the guy, all right. Not that Emily had any intention of admitting that to her friend.

"Does Ted know you lust after other men like this?" she teased.

"I'm not lusting. I'm merely observing and appreciating. But you, my friend, are in a position to lust away. In case you need reminding."

Emily was saved from answering when the grinding gears of the crane caught everyone's attention, and the time capsule was lifted out of the pit.

It was a rectangular, steel-riveted box, about three-by-four feet and at least three feet deep. The rigger on the ground directed the crane's telescoping arm until the capsule was set gently on the large felt-covered pad Emily had waiting beside the podium.

As the workmen went about removing the lid, everyone on the platform circled them in anticipation.

"We'll only be able to get a brief glimpse at what's inside," the mayor cautioned the crowd as he slipped on thin plastic gloves. "The Historical Society must take possession of the contents so that they can be preserved. But once cataloged, our treasure will be shared."

When the lid came up, the mayor lifted out the item on the top—a letter wrapped in string and sealed with wax. He unfolded it very carefully and began to read.

"To the Inheritors of Courage Bay, 2004: Inside this first carton, we send you the images of the white-winged ships that sail into our bay bringing us news and goods from distant shores. There are also photographs of our dwellings made of strong wood and brick, with wisps of smoke lifting out of our chimneys from the fireplaces that keep us warm when winter comes. Rising behind our homes you'll glimpse the steep mountains that for generations have sheltered us from the sorrow and ravages of war. Above them is the sky of pale blue that will bring out scarlet sheets to wrap our sun to sleep tonight. And lastly we send to you our faces—both young and old, fair and less favored, the lines upon all being drawn with life's deft pen.

"What will these pictures mean to you a hundred years hence? This we cannot fathom. Nor can we know what you will find here in your time. But we can tell you what you would have found in ours.

"This is a beloved world, swept with sunshine, the breath of flowers, the song of birds, forests bounding with wildlife and a people with hearts full of gratitude. We, the guardians of Courage Bay, pledge to care for this good land and for one another. When our history is written, may it be recorded with a light and understanding hand."

O'Shea slowly raised his head. "This letter I've just read to you is signed by the mayor and eleven others. They are identified at the bottom as the twelve men chosen to bury the capsule and set the sundial in place. I'm going to close the letter immediately to protect it from deteriorating. Now let's have a quick look at those promised pictures."

The wooden box beneath the letter held at least a hundred pristine photographs, wrapped in cloth. Phoebe Landru, the senior member of the managing board of the Historical Society, had the honor of taking out a few to show them to the crowd.

Emily got a brief glimpse at a picture of the Courage Bay Livery Stable and Feed Store. A blacksmith shop. An apothecary. Then there was a shot of the mountains, heavy with trees that had since been logged. And finally, the photo of a young woman with a lovely heart-shaped face. Phoebe flashed the image briefly to the audience and then carefully put it back in the box with the others.

The mayor pulled the next packet from the time capsule. He identified it as a duplicate of the hand-drawn map of Courage Bay that had been filed at the county courthouse.

After showing it to the crowd and making sure the TV crew got a shot, the mayor stepped aside and invited Dorothy to open the next item in the capsule. It was a box filled with copies of the *Courage Bay Bulletin,* a newspaper that had been defunct for nearly fifty years. One of the copies Dorothy held up for the audience to see had a banner headline announcing that the Wright Bros. Flying Machine had Conquered the Sky. Another proclaimed that the time capsule was to be buried that day.

Beneath the box of newspapers was one with a stack of separate sheets of paper on which townspeople had recorded their predictions for the future. Emily was given the fun of selecting a few and reading them to the crowd.

"This storekeeper says that the marvels of modern ma-

chinery will turn the current drudgery of jobs and house-
work into joyful endeavors, leaving men and women
many hours to take long walks and read well-written
books. Ah, if only he had been right.''

That generated a few smiles from the audience.

''According to the town's newspaper editor, 'Courage
Bay will become a busy city where everyone will move
quickly back and forth in their automobile wagons, horses
having become obsolete. But the wheels of these automobile wagons will be cushioned so the city will be free
from noise.'''

At that moment, a loud screeching of tires and the blast
of a horn echoed from a car on an adjoining street. It was
so perfectly timed, everyone laughed.

The audience was still chuckling when Emily took her
seat.

Oliver Smithson was the one to remove the next box
from the time capsule. A note on the top described the
contents within as letters written by the surviving crew of
the *Ranger,* each giving his individual account of the vessel's sinking on that fateful day, as well as his rescue by
the Indians.

Oliver read off the names of the authors: ''Fitzwalter,
Giroux, Himlot—''

''I'm his descendant,'' Councilman Dean Himlot interrupted. ''That letter from my ancestor belongs to me.''

Emily knew Dean Himlot as she knew most of the no-
tables in this crowd. He could be a bit full of himself,
forgetting sometimes that it was his family's famous name
that had enabled him to get elected.

Still, she'd never known him to be abrasive, especially
in the company of his social peers. Just proof that lots of
money and clout didn't buy class.

''Actually, Dean,'' the mayor said amicably as he took
the mike from Oliver, ''according to the letter that I read
previously, everything in this time capsule was bequeathed to the people of Courage Bay, not any individ-

ual. However, rest assured that you will be given a copy of your ancestor's letter as soon as—"

"Don't open the box," Dean said. "That letter is a family heirloom. You could ruin it by exposing it to the air."

"Get a grip, Dean," Gerald Fitzwalter spoke up from the spectators in a clearly annoyed manner.

Gerald was president of his family's local bank and head of the Chamber of Commerce. He was also a descendant of a *Ranger* crewman. Gerald and Dean had been feuding for twenty years. It all started when they were on opposing football teams in high school competing against each other in a regional championship. A fumble on the field resulted in a fight between them and they both got kicked out of the game. Each blamed the other.

"I wasn't going to open the box of these letters at this time," Oliver said in the tone of a professor addressing dense pupils. "I'm perfectly aware that some of these letters could have been written a hundred and fifty years ago and may, therefore, be doubly sensitive to the elements. Now, if I may proceed?"

The mayor nodded in his direction and Oliver finished naming the surviving crewmen. Emily already knew their names, as she was certain did most of this crowd.

Oliver then put the box aside and opened the next in the capsule. The letters within were written by average citizens depicting community life.

The first one was by a farmer—who, fortunately, didn't have any descendants in the audience—but who, unfortunately, had included more details about raising chickens than Emily ever wanted to know.

The second letter Oliver read started out to be a great deal more interesting. It was from an amateur gardener who claimed to have found a wonderful medicinal plant that had cured her of the blinding headaches she'd had since adolescence. The gardener had included a copper tin that was filled with its seeds, which she described as a soothing intoxicant.

There were two pages to her letter. But to Emily's disappointment, Oliver read what appeared to be only half of the first before he suddenly stopped and closed it.

"We shouldn't expose these documents to the light any longer," he said by way of explanation.

The mayor nodded as he addressed the crowd. "The documents, artifacts and photos will be digitized and placed on the City's Web site. Ladies and gentlemen, the founders of Courage Bay have left us a priceless piece of their history and ours. We'll ensure that it is preserved for all to enjoy."

When the mayor stepped away, Emily retook the podium and invited the audience to reconvene in the reception room of the Heritage Museum behind them, where drinks and hors d'oeuvres were being served.

The mayor and city council quickly joined the spectators headed toward those promised refreshments and the political shoulder-rubbing that was always the highlight of this type of social event.

Emily turned off the microphone just in time to prevent the argument that started behind her from being broadcast throughout the Botanical Gardens.

"How dare you imply that I'm too old and weak to catalog these artifacts correctly?" Phoebe asked in her seventy-three-year-old voice that was about as feeble as a two-by-four.

Oliver's skin was turning a rosy pink beneath his full white beard. "You know damn well that's not what I said, Phoebe. I simply pointed out that when it comes to computers, you are not up to speed."

"Look who's talking," Phoebe said. "Last month, when Dorothy mentioned that we needed to update the Society's hard drive, you were the one who got all hot and bothered because you thought that she was trying to reschedule our spring golf tournament."

Oliver's lips tightened. "I may not be familiar with the terminology, but need I remind you that the pharmaceutical company I ran for forty years is full of computers and competent operators?"

"We are not handing over these valuable items to some computer operator who hasn't the faintest idea how to preserve them," Phoebe said.

"What's going on?" Emily whispered to Dorothy.

"Oliver just got a call from the hospital," Dorothy whispered back. "Wayne won't be able to take custody of the time capsule's contents as planned. He's had a stroke."

"These irreplaceable items must stay in the hands of the Historical Society," Phoebe continued. "Now, my grandniece Fiona is quite competent with computers. Together, she and I can—"

"Only last week you were complaining that Fiona was so tired chasing after her two preschoolers that she didn't even have the energy to come see you," Oliver interrupted.

"I'll hire a sitter for her," Phoebe said, undaunted.

"And how long will that take?" Oliver challenged. "You went through nearly sixty applicants and four months before you finally chose Mrs. Hanna to be the librarian. And what a choice that was."

"Mrs. Hanna's credentials as a historian are impeccable, not to mention the fact that she speaks five languages."

"We didn't need someone with impeccable credentials or who could speak five languages. We needed someone who could work the library's computer! Now we're paying Holly to come in and do it after school!"

"Ken, I need another picture of this imbecile," Phoebe said, pointing to Oliver. "The last one of him I put on my dartboard is already full of holes."

The photographer looked amused but made no effort to comply. Ken—like the rest of them—was used to Phoebe and Oliver's verbal sparring matches. When these two crossed swords, the best thing anyone could do was stay out of the way.

"And that's another thing," Oliver said. "Ken's supposed to be the Society's photographer, but I can't get him to do a damn thing for me. Every time I try he tells me he'll have to clear it with you first."

Oliver was talking about Ken as though he wasn't there. Typical of Oliver. And typical of Ken that he showed no sign of offense.

"He has the editing and printing of the newsletter to see to," Phoebe countered. "He's not one of your lackeys. Speaking of which, where is this illustrious and purportedly proficient historian who was supposed to be on hand today to take custody of the time capsule contents?"

"Damn it, Phoebe, I already told you." Oliver was shouting now. "Wayne had a stroke. Are you going to blame me for that?"

"Please, Oliver, Phoebe," Dorothy interrupted as she stepped between her fellow board members. "I know this is disappointing. I, too, was counting on Wayne's expert assistance. But he's seriously ill. We should set aside concerns about the time capsule for the moment and think of him."

"His doctor told Wayne's wife that the stroke was minor," Oliver said, as though Dorothy was making a big deal over nothing. "He'll be all right."

"That's good to hear," Emily said carefully. "But I believe the point that Dorothy was making is that Wayne needs to know how concerned all of us in the organization are for his welfare."

"Thank you, Emily," Dorothy said with emphasis.

"Oh, very well," Phoebe said. "I'll send him a fruit basket from the Society. And a card."

"And now that that's taken care of," Oliver said, "let's get back to the matter of what we're going to do with the time capsule treasures."

Dorothy and Emily looked at each other and shook their heads.

"None of us on the managing board knows enough to digitize this important information, not to mention putting it on the city's Web site," Dorothy said. "And, as generous as Oliver's offer is to use personnel at the Smithson Pharmaceutical Company, Phoebe's right. These artifacts are too valuable to let out of our hands."

"Josh is employed part-time by the Society," Oliver said. Scanning the now nearly deserted gardens, he called, "Josh? Damn it, where are you, boy?"

"Here," Josh said as he scrambled up the platform steps.

Oliver grabbed his grandson's shoulders. "You took computer courses in high school, didn't you?"

"Yeah."

"So you could do whatever it takes to get images of these items into a computer and put them on the City's Web site, right?"

Josh shrugged. "I don't know."

"Oh, that overwhelms me with confidence," Phoebe said.

Oliver slipped his hands from his grandson's shoulders and let out a huff of disappointment.

When Emily saw the look that flattened Josh's face, she immediately stepped forward. "Josh is doing a superb job for the Botanical Gardens and the Society. He's also been a big help getting things organized for today. I don't know what I would have done without him."

Oliver wasn't listening. He was too busy shaking his head like a windshield wiper on high.

"Damn kids today come out of school dumber than when they went in," he muttered.

Josh slunk off the platform just as Holly came out of the museum. She waved in his direction, but Josh turned away and disappeared into the trees.

Emily was trying to decide whether to try to talk to

Oliver or just kick him when Dorothy raised her hand to get everyone's attention.

"As much as Emily is right about Josh's great work in the Heritage Museum and around the Botanical Gardens, it's not fair to ask him to take on a task of this magnitude. We need someone from the Historical Society who has both experience in document preservation techniques and computer expertise."

Dorothy looked pointedly at Emily.

Emily felt both Phoebe and Oliver's eyes turn toward her as though assessing her right to have the job.

"She has the gardens to see to," Oliver said, "and her own research."

"You're absolutely right," Dorothy agreed. "Which means these important artifacts will not leave this site. That's another plus."

"You said everything would go off today without a hitch," Phoebe complained. "But there was that long delay when the skeleton was unearthed."

"I'm so glad you mentioned the skeleton," Dorothy said, ignoring Phoebe's unfair implication that unearthing a skeleton was somehow Emily's fault. "Isn't it a fascinating find? Emily will be working with Dr. Winslow to identify the remains for us and the items that were found in the grave."

"What items?" Phoebe asked.

"Detective Corbin is sending them and the skeleton to the Courage Bay Hospital morgue so that Dr. Winslow and Emily can study them," Dorothy said. "She'll be able to write the article on everything they discover for the newsletter."

"Since there may be some clue as to the skeleton's identity in the time capsule documents, it makes sense that we look them over as soon as possible," Brad said from behind Emily.

She spun around to find him standing not five feet away, holding two glasses of champagne. He'd left with the mayor in the direction of the reception hall after the ceremony had ended. She hadn't heard him return.

"Dr. Winslow makes an excellent point," Dorothy agreed. "Emily's a whiz with computers. And, since she is a member of our society, we know she will properly preserve these valuable items. I realize this is asking a lot, but will you do it for us, Emily?"

Be the first to see everything that was in the time capsule? Did Dorothy really have any doubt?

"I'll be happy to," Emily said in as calm a tone as she possessed.

"Well, Phoebe, Oliver?" Dorothy asked. "What do you think?"

What both Oliver and Phoebe thought was clear on their faces. Each still wanted access to the contents first. But it was hard arguing with Dorothy's logic and persuasive techniques.

Phoebe nodded. Oliver shrugged. And that, Emily knew, was as close to a "thank you for taking on this incredibly time-consuming assignment" as she was going to get from them. But she didn't care. She was thrilled.

After seeing that all the items had been returned to the time capsule and the lid closed, Phoebe and Oliver set off for the refreshments and the socializing they both reveled in. Ken waved goodbye to Emily and Dorothy and trotted after them.

Brad handed Dorothy one glass of champagne and held out the other to Emily.

She shook her head. "I don't think Sprout would like it."

"Sprout?"

She rested a hand on her stomach. "That's its botanical name."

He nodded as though in tardy understanding. "Of course, the baby. My apologies, Mrs. Barrett. I forgot."

Had he? Or was this a really good act?

As he sipped the champagne he'd offered to her, she

studied him. It could be a coincidence that Ed had brought him today. He certainly gave no indication that he knew she'd had artificial insemination, much less that she'd selected his sperm.

Ed had promised he'd say nothing to Brad. Maybe she'd been worrying for no reason.

"Where do you plan to go over the time capsule contents?" Brad asked.

"My office is on the second floor of the Heritage Museum," Emily answered. "I'll see if I can round up the crane operator and his rigger. Between the two of them, I'm hoping they'll be able to lug it up the back stairs."

"Why don't I give it a try?" Brad offered.

Emily blinked at him in surprise.

"Are you sure, Brad?" Dorothy asked. "It has to weigh at least a hundred pounds."

"Dot's right," Emily said. "You can't possibly carry it over to the museum, much less up all those stairs by yourself."

"Can't I?"

He picked up the capsule and held it as though it weighed no more than an empty orange crate.

"Dr. Winslow, I don't think—" Emily began.

"Light as a feather," Brad interrupted. "Lead the way."

Emily's eyes traveled from the heavy time capsule to the stoic face of the man holding it with such deceptive ease.

"I'll wait here to be sure that no one disturbs our skeleton until Ed can arrange to have it removed," Dorothy offered. "If you need to find me later, I'll be at the reception looking after things."

Still Emily hesitated.

"Go on, Em. It'll be all right."

At her friend's urging, Emily gave in and led the way

to her office. But she did not have a good feeling about this. And she very much doubted everything would be all right.

BRAD'S ARMS WERE IN AGONY and his back was killing him. A hundred pounds. Ha! This damn time capsule weighed a ton. And he still had another eight steps to climb.

What an idiot he'd been, insisting on carrying the blasted thing. He couldn't imagine what had possessed him.

Yes he could. Emily had looked so damn sure when she'd announced that he couldn't possibly do it that the logical part of his brain had ceased to function.

He was determined to prove her wrong—or die trying.

The die-trying possibility was looming ever closer. He set the time capsule down on the next step and collapsed beside it, his heart pounding. Easing out of his sport coat, he let it drop to the stairs.

A bead of sweat rolled across his forehead, zigzagged between his eyebrows and dropped onto his lashes. His arms were so tired that he couldn't even lift a hand to brush the drop away.

"I never should have agreed to let you do this," Emily said. "I knew that container was far too heavy for you."

She stood above him on the second-floor landing. When Brad raised his head, the sweat dropped into his eye, bringing with it the sting of salt. Even with that one eye shut, he could see the "I told you so" look on her face.

"I'm simply taking a breather."

He'd barely had the breath to get the words out. The last thing he wanted to do was lift that damn box again. But with her standing there watching him, he knew he was going to.

Somehow he got himself back on his feet and picked up the capsule. How he managed to carry it up those last steps and into Emily's office he had no idea.

She directed him to set it on the floor beside a walnut

desk. As soon as it was in place, he staggered over to the nearest chair and collapsed. He closed his eyes and sucked in air, wondering if he was ever going to feel his arms again or be able to breathe normally.

Time passed—he had no idea how much and didn't particularly care. He was just thankful that he wasn't carrying that damn thing anymore. When his breath started to come in a more normal rhythm, he felt a hand on his arm and opened his eyes to find her beside him.

"I thought you might like something cold to drink."

She was holding out a tall glass of water. Gratefully, he took it from her, and downed the contents in one long gulp. By the time he'd set the empty glass on the table next to him, she'd taken the chair behind the desk.

The small, exceptionally neat office seemed to be darker than when he'd entered. Glancing around, he noticed that she'd drawn heavy drapes across the windows. A couple of low-wattage lamps were all that now lit the room. They shone off spotless glass shelves and wooden furniture, well carved and built to last.

The room exuded a pleasing calm, not currently reflected in its owner.

"Why did you insist on doing that?" she asked.

He met her eyes. "Weight lifting should be part of everyone's exercise routine. Builds muscle and bone. Makes you strong. Just ask your doctor."

She shook her head. "I realize I should be thanking you for bringing the time capsule up here, but—"

"You're welcome."

"You could have hurt yourself."

The worry in her voice was carefully controlled, but it wasn't superficial.

"Nice of you to be concerned about me."

Her chin lifted. "I was concerned about our liability insurance. Had you sustained an injury carrying these artifacts belonging to the Historical Society, we could have been held responsible."

Her cloak of professional indifference was one he donned often enough to see through. "I wouldn't have sued for much."

Her head shook in frustration. "Dr. Winslow—"

"Call me Brad."

"Are you always this stubborn?"

"Stubborn? I'm not stubborn. I'm totally pigheaded and obstinate."

For a second, a look of overwhelming exasperation claimed her features. Then it vanished and a chuckle— warm and sweet—broke through her lips. The smile that followed was even better.

"There's a bathroom down the hall where you can wash up," she said.

"I look that grungy, huh?"

"Try not to break the mirror."

He got up and headed for the soap and water. As he gazed at the reflection of his dirt-smudged face over the sink, he was grinning. Yeah, it had been really dumb insisting on carrying that damn capsule.

But he'd gotten her to smile. That was worth a few sore muscles.

CHAPTER FOUR

EMILY SWIPED THE CLUMPS of dirt from Brad's sport coat with overly energetic strokes of the clothes brush. When he'd all but collapsed on the stairs, her heart had lodged in her throat.

The man was exactly what he proclaimed himself to be—pigheaded and obstinate.

But it was hard not to admire a guy who boldly admitted his faults, even when he seemed to revel in them.

As he reentered the office, his eyes glanced toward his sport coat, which she'd hung on the coatrack. "Thanks."

She shrugged and gestured toward the chair in front of her desk.

As he settled himself he asked, "How well do you know the guy who had the stroke?"

"Not well. Wayne is one of our senior historians, a longtime friend of Oliver's. He used to be his accountant at Smithson Pharmaceuticals before they both retired."

"Sounded as though Oliver still considers him more of an employee than friend."

"That's Oliver."

"So, what do we do first?"

"You go downstairs to the reception and submit to many accolades while indulging yourself with hors d'oeuvres, which I promise you are delicious if you haven't tasted them."

"What, the accolades or the hors d'oeuvres?"

She refused to smile. "Both will be, I'm sure."

"You're not coming?"

"I've already had lunch. Besides, schmoozing is not my style."

"Not my style, either."

"Dr. Winslow, there are a lot of important people downstairs who are going to want to shake your hand and pump you for information about how you knew the skeleton was a hundred years old. You achieved celebrity status today. Go savor your moment in the limelight."

"I'll pass, thanks. So, what's the best way to go about this document cataloging?"

His eagerness for the task didn't sit quite right with Emily. Her suspicions began to resurface.

"Your offer to help with the skeleton is appreciated," she said carefully, "but being here when I catalog the contents of the capsule isn't necessary."

"And you're saying that because…?"

"Because the chance that something in the documents could lead to the skeleton's identity is pretty slim. If the mayor at the time had known there was a body being buried with the capsule, he would have said something in the letter he wrote."

"How did you know the time capsule was beneath the sundial?"

"That's been common knowledge among local historians since the day it was put in the ground. The date the capsule was to be opened was carved on the sundial as well."

"Who put the capsule in place?"

"Leading citizens of the community were given the honor of lowering it by rope into the pit. That large sundial was then set over the pit. They later carved their initials on the stone face."

"Makes you wonder how they could have missed a body. Is it possible the sundial was later lifted and the body dumped in?"

Emily shook her head. "It took a bunch of strong, able-bodied men to set the sundial into place a hundred years ago. For decades afterward that sundial marked the center of town. No one could have lifted it without an audience.''

"So unless the entire town was in on a conspiracy to keep the death of this guy a secret, we're going to have to look elsewhere for answers,'' Brad said. "The documents might give a clue as to who the guy was, even if they don't reveal how he got there.''

"Your investment won't be worth the slim chance of reward. This is a time-consuming task.''

"Then we'd better get started.''

"You mean now?''

"You had something else planned?''

"No, I'm just surprised you don't.''

"Normally, I do work Saturday and Sunday. But I've pulled a few double shifts this past week, so, at the moment, I'm looking at a whole weekend off. What do we do first?''

This good-looking, single doctor wanted to bury his nose in old records on his rare weekend off when he could be downstairs making important contacts and letting attractive women come on to him?

Emily looked him straight in the eye. "Why are you here?''

He didn't so much as blink. "Do you really want to know?''

Did she? She'd purposely avoided this confrontation yesterday because she believed she could keep the truth from him. But if he had somehow found out she'd gotten his sperm, it would be better to discuss the matter openly than to continue to worry about hidden meanings and motivations in everything he said and did.

"Yes, I want to know,'' she said.

"I got dumped.''

That caught her completely by surprise. "You what?''

"Woman I'd been seeing over the past few weeks canceled our time together. Seems some fortune-teller read her tea leaves and warned her that everyone whose name starts with the letter *B* was going to bring her bad luck over the next few days. She decided to spend the weekend in the far safer pursuits of skin exfoliation and incense burning.''

''Where did the dumping come in?''

''Right after I assured her that she would have felt at home with the ignorant savages who read falling tree leaves a few thousand years ago and got the message to sacrifice the village's virgin to ward off the approaching bad weather.''

Yes, she could imagine him saying that.

''I take it you don't believe in anything beyond the five senses,'' Emily said.

''When someone can't breathe or is bleeding, science provides the tools that enable me to help them. But, I've also seen prayer and nothing but a strong will to live keep someone alive well beyond what should have been medically possible.''

''So you are open to other possibilities.''

''I don't pretend to have all the answers. But I do believe that whatever gives meaning to someone's life shouldn't demean or belittle someone else's. When a person is branded as a threat simply because the first letter of his name starts with a *B,* then the line into superstitious lunacy has been crossed.''

He wore the expression of a warrior who'd gone into conversational battle on this subject more than once. And was weary of it.

''After your brother and I got to talking at the bar last night,'' Brad continued, ''he decided that what I needed was to be dragged to the Founders Day Celebration. Good thing, too, or I'd probably be forced to study for my board certification exams coming up next month.''

''That still doesn't explain why you aren't downstairs shaking hands and drinking the very best in champagne.''

''I've found that I react to people best when I take them

like a potent prescription—one at a time and never mixed with alcohol.''

His explanation filled her with relief. Maybe she hadn't been quite so prepared for that confrontation as she'd convinced herself.

''Too bad your weekend turned into such a disappointment,'' she said.

''Oh, I'd say things are definitely looking up. So, what do we do first?''

He had the kind of smile that made a woman want to smile back. She resisted.

''Go through everything and make a list of what type of things we have and how many,'' she answered. ''Then we can start the process of scanning them into the hard drive.''

She handed him a pad and pen. ''You get the task of record keeping.''

''You can't be serious.''

''You consider it beneath you?''

''I consider it far above me. All those stories you've heard about how doctors can't write legibly? They're absolutely true.''

It was the serious look on his face that had her lips twitching, despite her best efforts. ''How are you at typing?''

He held up all ten fingers. ''My hand-eye coordination has always rated within the top one percent.''

''Of E.R. doctors?''

''Of volleyball players. You can catch our games Sunday afternoons out on the beach near the big barbecue pit.''

The smile was getting harder to contain.

''You'll recognize me,'' Brad said nonchalantly as he shifted in his chair. ''I'm the one who's always falling into the pit.''

She was grinning now, couldn't help it. Brad Winslow

had a very nice personality beneath his staid doctor's countenance.

"So what do you and your husband do for fun?"

Emily's grin subsided. "I'm not married."

"Sorry."

"I'm not."

She faced the computer monitor and opened a word-processing document. After naming it "Time Capsule Artifacts" she came to her feet.

"Okay, Mr. Nimble Fingers, you get the job of entering a list of the contents into the computer file as I read them off to you."

They switched chairs so he could have access to the computer, and she was closer to the time capsule.

Once settled, she raised the lid and slipped on some protective gloves. "First item is the letter Patrick O'Shea read that was signed by the mayor and the eleven other men who were chosen to set the sundial in place."

She heard the confident click of keys as Brad entered the information. Peeking over at the screen, she could see he'd already finished the identifying sentence. Nimble fingers indeed.

"What do you want to list about the letter?" he asked.

"Let's put in the names of those who signed it, starting with the mayor's. This is the first time I heard that there were twelve men chosen to put the sundial in place. There are only eleven initials carved on its surface."

"Whose initials are missing?" Brad asked.

"Something I plan to check on later." One by one she read the signatures at the bottom of the letter to him.

"What's next?"

"The pictures."

Emily picked up the first—a gorgeous shot of a ship in full sail. Even though it was in black-and-white, her mind's eye filled in an azure sky and turquoise sea. Turning it over, she found to her delight that someone had printed the name of the vessel. Every item in the cargo unloaded at the Courage Bay dock was listed.

"I can see why this could become a very time-consuming task," Brad said.

Her head came up at his comment. It was only then that she realized she'd been studying the photo for some time. After describing it briefly for Brad, she set the picture aside.

"Good thing you're here," she admitted. "I could so easily get lost in these."

"Are you one of those people who feels as though she were born a hundred years too late?"

She shook her head. "I admit I'm drawn to the natural beauty of their less crowded time, their deeper connection with one another that came from a slower pace of life. But I'm spoiled. I want my hot showers, Internet access and an epidural when the time comes to deliver Sprout."

He nodded. "When it came to medicine, there was a lot about the good old days that wasn't that good."

"This is the photograph of the young woman that Phoebe Landru showed to the crowd," Emily said as she picked it up. She turned it over and was happy to see a printed identification.

"She's Serena Fitzwalter. I knew I recognized her. Looks as though Gerald Fitzwalter had more than one family member represented in this time capsule."

"He was the one in the crowd who seemed the most irritated when Councilman Himlot balked at having his ancestor's letter read," Brad said as he entered the information about the second photo into the computer. "Is Himlot always so…self-focused?"

"Of all our city's councilmen, Dean's normally the easiest to get along with. I don't know what made him decide to demand that letter from his ancestor. He and his family have generously shared a lot of their historical documents with the Society."

"Maybe he missed out on his bran muffin at breakfast," Brad said.

Emily smiled. "His ancestors as well as many others who settled Courage Bay are represented in family portraits downstairs," she said.

"I'll have to take a look at them sometime. There seem to be a lot of interesting things to study in this building."

There was absolutely no readable expression on his face. Emily decided she'd interpret his comment to mean he was developing an interest in Courage Bay's history.

"Serena Fitzwalter here has a double claim," Emily said gesturing to her picture. "She married into another prominent family, Landru."

"And Phoebe Landru didn't say anything about holding up her ancestor's photo?"

"She wasn't wearing her glasses," Emily said as she set the photo aside. "It was probably just a blur to her."

Most of the next dozen or so photographs were scenes of fishing boats, birds and low tidelands alive with sea creatures and shells. As Emily read off the descriptions, Brad added them to his growing list on the computer.

The next photograph she picked up was of the Smithson Apothecary. She showed it to Brad. "This is where Oliver's pharmaceutical company got its start."

"His was one of the original families?"

Emily explained that the Smithsons weren't descendants of the *Ranger* crew. They'd been Nevada miners. When the silver petered out of their claim, they came to Courage Bay in the latter half of the nineteenth century looking for a new start. Using the Indians' knowledge of native medicinal plants, they opened the apothecary. It grew into a multimillion-dollar business.

"A Smithson ancestor originally owned this building and left it to the Historical Society when she passed," Emily said as she set the apothecary picture aside and came to another set of photographs of people.

She recognized more names. "Look, an O'Shea. Wait

until the mayor finds out he has an ancestor represented. Oh, and here's a Giroux. I have to tell Natalie when I see her. She works at the hospital. You must know her.''

"I work with her brother, Alec, in the E.R.," Brad said. "I don't really know Natalie. Alec rarely mentions her.''

Most brothers rarely mentioned their sisters, a fact for which Emily was growing more thankful by the moment.

"Is Dot a descendant of one of the pioneers?" he asked.

Emily nodded. "Her family arrived from the East toward the end of the nineteenth century. Dot's doctoral thesis chronicled the local history of Courage Bay at the beginning of the last century. She was in time to rescue copies of the old Courage Bay newspaper as well as other memorabilia from neighborhood attics.''

"Are we likely to find a Corbin in here?" Brad asked.

"No. My grandparents relocated here after World War II, like so many other military families who flocked to California.''

"What got you interested in the Historical Society?" he asked.

"Dot recruited me into it last year. There's so much history in the origins of the beautiful plants here at the Botanical Gardens. The origins of the people who planted and cultivated them began to draw me as well. Courage Bay is one of those few Southern California communities where you can still find four-, five-, even six-generation families. I'm still a novice when it comes to the history of the people, of course. But it's nice to live in a place with such sturdy roots. What about the Winslow clan?''

"Don't know much about it," Brad said.

His voice had gone curiously flat. She tried to remember the part of his sperm-bank questionnaire where it asked about his parents, but the only thing that came to mind was that there had been no known illnesses on either side of his family tree.

It was on the tip of her tongue to ask, but too many

questions could make him suspicious. Better to err on the side of prudence and let the matter drop.

As she turned her attention back to the photographs, she found some very interesting group shots of the townspeople, even one of a traveling salesman.

She went through each, reading off the descriptions on the backs so Brad could enter them into the computer. Then she placed each photograph within sheets of acid-free paper and laid it inside a chest in the corner of her office.

"Are the photographs getting special attention for some reason?" Brad asked, as he watched her close the lid of the chest.

"They're in such great shape, I hate to expose them to the elements even for a short time."

"Where will the originals of all these things eventually be placed?"

She retook her chair next to the capsule. "In the basement of this building. Light, heat, humidity and acid are the four enemies of archival treasurers. That dark dehumidified dungeon is climatically controlled to near perfection."

"Oliver Smithson mentioned something about your research. Is it in this kind of preservation?"

"No, my research is the kind that grows in the Botanical Gardens' greenhouse."

"Let me guess. Your favorite TV shows are on The Learning Channel and the Home and Garden Network?"

"Pretty close," she admitted. "I suppose you were hooked on the TV *E.R.* series?"

"Naw, too much blood. What's next?"

Emily caught herself smiling again. Seemed he did have a really good sense of humor, after all.

She began to rethink her earlier comment about this job taking less time because he was here. It might actually take more if she didn't get her mind back on business. She turned back to the time capsule.

A cylinder at the side of some packaged items caught her eye. As she pulled it out, she wondered for a moment what she held.

"Of course," she said finally. "This is an old phonograph record. I doubt there's even a machine around that can play it."

"Probably the newest gadget of its day," Brad said. "If we put the latest CD in a time capsule today, I doubt there'd be an antiquated computer around in the year 2104 that could retrieve the information on it, either."

"By 2104 I imagine most machines will be obsolete. We'll all have a computer chip in our brains to store information."

"Well, at least it's good to know I'll still have a job," he said.

"You sure?"

"Someone's going to have to insert that computer chip."

"Unless they have a robot doing it."

"Oh, great. Just what I needed to hear. Four years of premed, four years of medical school, four years of residency and now I can look forward to being replaced by a robot."

She chuckled.

After a click of keys he announced, "I've entered it as phonograph record of cylinder shape and indeterminate age. What's next?"

"The newspapers." She quickly counted them. "There are sixteen here, randomly selected it appears from the two years before the capsule's burial."

As she started to rearrange them in chronological order, she found one with the same date as the time capsule's interment. The lead story was the fact that it was being buried that day. But what caught Emily's attention was the headline immediately below that one. She grew quiet as she read the story.

"What's wrong?" Brad asked after a moment.

She looked up, only realizing then that she'd been frowning.

"An article in this newspaper reports that a day before the time capsule's burial, five members of a local family died when a houseguest went insane and set fire to their home."

"The article actually uses the word *insane?*" Brad asked.

"Must not have been considered politically incorrect in those days. The family's six-year-old boy awakened to the smell of smoke and saw the drapes in flames. The houseguest was throwing lit candles and crying hysterically about demons. He fled the house to get help, but returned too late. The houseguest as well as the rest of his family had perished."

"That article has upset you."

His voice had grown gentle. When her eyes rose to his, she saw the concern on his face.

"The family's name was Kerr. Ken Kerr is our Society's photographer."

"Are you sure they were his relations?"

"They must be. Dot told me Ken's family has roots in Courage Bay that go back a hundred years."

"Does the article mention who the houseguest was?"

"Agnes Hopper, a widowed neighbor who had befriended them. It says she was staying at the Kerr home because she was caring for their elderly grandmother who was ill. No one knows what caused Agnes Hopper to go insane."

"I take it you had no idea about this happening to his ancestors," Brad said.

Emily shook her head. "He's never mentioned it. No one in the Historical Society has."

"Maybe they don't know," Brad suggested. "It did happen a hundred years ago."

"Except tragedies—especially one of this magnitude— are generally the things people do pass down. Anyway, it's bound to come out now,'' she said, not looking forward to the fact. She finished organizing the newspapers, read off the dates to Brad and then set them aside.

''Now here's the box of letters written by the survivors of the *Ranger* describing the events of that day,'' she said holding it even more gently than she had the other items. She quickly gave him the authors' names and then carefully opened the box.

''Some of these are inscribed on animal skins and their dates are within years of the ship's sinking,'' she said, her voice full of wonder.

''You have a digital camera to take pictures of those things you can't scan into the computer?''

She nodded as she gently sifted through the artifacts, awed at how beautifully they had held up over time.

''Here's the Himlot letter,'' she said gently extracting it from the pile. Her forehead furrowed as she quietly scanned the document. ''This is really hard to make out.''

''Faded from time?''

''No, the penmanship is atrocious.''

''Maybe Himlot was the ship's doctor,'' Brad said.

Emily chuckled.

''What does it say?'' Brad asked.

''Something about setting or putting a thing right side up, I think. This will take someone with more time and patience than I currently possess to decipher.''

She gently put the letter back in the box and tightly closed the lid.

''After I copy the letters into the computer, I'll turn them over to the managing board. They can have the fun of making sense out of them.''

''They'll actually consider that fun?''

''You heard them fighting over the chance to see the contents first. Getting the cover letter and the photographs on the Web site is going to be my number-one priority, especially the photos of the people. A lot of their descendants are going to have a wonderful surprise when they see them.''

''Do you want to put the rest of the cataloging aside for now?'' Brad asked.

''We can't. We have to know everything that's in the capsule. The mayor didn't go much further than we are now for fear of adversely affecting the contents. There could be even more spectacular finds further down.''

She looked over to see him shaking his head. ''What?''

''You're as excited as a kid who's found a treasure chest.''

''We have found a treasure chest,'' she said. ''Don't you think it's thrilling to know you're seeing and hearing about what it was like a hundred years ago? Not some history teacher's version of it, but eyewitness accounts from the people living then?''

He didn't answer, but the way he was looking at her was nice.

Next came the map of Courage Bay. She found it in good condition with the exception of a slight yellowing around the edges. The detail was extraordinary. Streets, shops, houses, farms—all beautifully rendered by hand and including the names of the families who lived in the dwellings.

''The Smithson family certainly held a lot of property then and now,'' Emily commented. ''Hmm, that's curious.''

''What?'' Brad asked.

''This area up here.''

He scooted his chair closer to take a look at where she was pointing. After studying the spot, he nodded. ''That's where the golf course is now. I recognize the big oak tree. Amazing to think how long it's been around. What did you find that was odd?''

''According to this map, the Smithson property line ends outside the oak tree. I thought that area was part of their original land claim. Oliver always talks as though his family has owned that property forever.''

The clock in the tower began to chime. ''Do you realize it's six o'clock?'' Brad asked.

Emily glanced at her wrist. ''Where did the past few hours go?''

''Into fifteen pages on the computer so far.''

Surveying the time capsule's remaining contents, Emily shook her head. She and Brad had not uncovered even half its riches. This was going to take a lot longer than she thought.

''Don't worry,'' Brad said, as though reading her mind. ''We'll grab some dinner and then get back to it. If we work nights and weekends, I figure we should have the stuff cataloged by Christmas.''

She chuckled, hoping his comment was going to end up being a joke.

BRAD LED EMILY TO A FAVORITE spot of his—the rooftop patio of the Courage Bay Bar and Grill. She wouldn't agree to go inside until he agreed to let her pay for her own meal.

The night was clear, the air still. Lights from the ships in the bay twinkled in the distance. The afternoon had gone fast. He hadn't expected to find the time capsule contents so interesting. Or the company.

Long ago he'd come to the conclusion that taste in humor was very much like taste in music. He'd spent time with many attractive women who had quickly lost their allure because they hadn't tuned in to his humor. Emily had both a discerning and appreciative ear.

But she'd been indifferent to his light attempt to flirt with her.

Not the ordinary response he was used to getting from women. But then there wasn't anything about this woman that could be called ordinary.

Despite her obvious ease in the most exalted company,

she had eschewed it for the chance to study artifacts from a past in which she would not have chosen to live. She didn't give a second thought as to whether the work was worthy of her time and talent—much less that it was unpaid. It simply pleased her to find out what was there.

She had a true scientific mind—sharp, curious, questioning.

The very qualities that made her good company were the ones that kept him constantly on his guard with everything he said.

He was certain that she had no idea he knew about her selecting his sperm. If she did, she wouldn't be sitting across from him now.

Which was why he'd lied to her, of course.

Not that the canceled date and getting dumped hadn't been true. Everything he had told her about that had really happened. It just wasn't the reason he'd come to the Founders Day Celebration and offered to stay to help her.

By nature Brad wasn't a liar. But when he remembered how she'd lied to him about who her doctor was and then pulled that psychic routine in the hospital, he decided he could forgive himself for this small lapse of character.

As they sat back and waited for their lobster tails to be delivered, he considered how best to open the subject that would lead him to what he wanted to know.

"Do me a favor?" he asked.

"What?"

"Promise me you'll see your doctor on Monday about the fainting."

Her back stiffened ever so slightly. "I do have an appointment with her. I didn't lie to you."

At least not about that.

"I didn't mean to imply you did," Brad said quickly. "I simply wanted to be sure you mentioned the fainting to her. Doctors sometimes rush their patients through exams and don't give them a chance to talk about what's on their minds. I should know. I've frequently been guilty of it myself.''

Her expression softened. "Your concern is appreciated.''

"Even if the fainting proves to be nothing serious, I urge you to take your partner along to be sure he understands what you'll both be facing as the pregnancy progresses.''

"Partner?''

"The baby's father.''

She turned her eyes from his, looked out at the lights on the water. "He didn't want to be a part of the baby's life.''

Brad picked up a roll. "Having a kid by yourself— that's going to be tough. On both of you.''

He waited for a response, but she said nothing.

After a long moment, he tried again. "What will you tell the child when it asks about its father?''

Her eyes swung to his. "When you were growing up, did you have a life plan?''

The out-of-the blue question threw him. "Excuse me?''

"A plan for how you wanted your life to go. Did you have one?''

"Well, yes.''

"What was it?''

He'd brought up personal matters in her life. She'd become suspicious again if he refused to respond to a question about something in his.

Besides, every time he thought about all the stuff he'd revealed on that sperm-donor questionnaire, he accepted the fact that Emily Barrett was already in possession of more intimate details about him than he'd ever meant for anyone to know.

"My…good friend and I were going to become forensic anthropologists together,'' he said.

"Why didn't you?''

"I decided to go into medicine instead.''

"Why?"

She wasn't going to let it go until he told her. Brad was beginning to wish he'd never started this. He breathed in deeply, exhaled slowly.

"She died."

No matter how he tried to prepare himself, it never helped. The moment he said the words, he was back in the hills once more, kneeling in the dirt, holding Julie in his arms, her face gray and still, the light from it gone forever.

When the restaurant came back into focus, Brad saw Emily staring at his hands. Looking down, he became aware that he'd been squeezing the roll as though it were a heart he was trying to get to beat.

Brad dropped the roll onto his plate and brushed the crumbs from his hand. He grabbed the glass of water, took a long drink.

"How did it happen?" she asked.

He set the empty glass down. "On an anthropological dig. She fell."

"When?"

"Summer break between our freshman and sophomore years."

The absolute attention on Emily's face made her eyes large and still. "And that was the day you changed your college major to medicine because you realized studying the dead wasn't nearly as important as trying to keep someone alive."

This damn woman *was* psychic.

"My original life plan got derailed as well," she said.

"What was it?" he asked, relieved to finally be off his personal affairs and on to hers.

"Nothing very different from that of most people, I suppose. Satisfying work, a happy marriage, kids."

"But something went wrong."

She concentrated on straightening the silverware beside her water glass. "Craig and I married in graduate school.

We agreed to wait until we were settled in secure jobs before beginning our family. Five years later I found out he'd had a vasectomy before we met and never intended to give me children.''

No need to ask why that marriage broke up.

"I don't see you as the type of person to brand all men as bastards because of the actions of one," Brad said.

"I'm not. Two years later I met Vincent. He was an up-and-coming computer entrepreneur who had offices in Utah and Oregon and was opening his third in California. We dated for eight months. He couldn't wait for us to get married and have a couple of kids. I was thinking about it, as well, until I got a visit from the wife and three kids he neglected to mention he already had.''

Amazing a woman like this had gotten involved with such losers.

She gazed out at the boat lights again. "The problem with my old life plan was that it required the cooperation of someone else to work. Now with this new life plan, I don't need anyone else's cooperation.''

So that's why she went the artificial insemination route. Her choice made a little more sense to Brad now. But understanding her reasons hadn't changed his opinion of her actions.

"You don't think a child needs a father?" Brad asked, careful to maintain a tone devoid of both challenge and censure.

"My child will have me. And grandparents who will spoil it silly. And two uncles who will no doubt do the same. It will be surrounded by a whole lot of love. That's what a child needs.''

Their dinners were delivered and they became quiet as they ate. Brad didn't taste much of his food. He was thinking about what Emily had said.

Based on her experiences, he had to admit that her decision to have a child the way she chose made some sense.

But she'd grown up with two parents. She had no idea what it was like for a kid to be without a father.

He'd thought he'd be able to change her mind by appealing to the logical side of her. Now he knew he'd been wrong.

But she was wrong, too. Her child's father did want to be part of his baby's life.

She wasn't interested in having a man around. That had come across clearly. But he could be her friend. Show her that he was someone she could count on—someone who would be there when the going got tough.

When the baby came along, the going was going to get really tough. She had no idea what being a single mother was all about, what it could do to a woman—what it had done to his mother. Emily would be happy for his help then. And he'd show her how happy he was to be of help.

It was a good, solid, workable plan.

Except the timing was lousy. He was in his final year as an E.R. resident and had those board certification exams to study for. Finding the hours he'd need to establish a close friendship with Emily was going to be difficult.

But his baby would be a reality in seven months' time—a reality that couldn't be ignored. He was going to be there to see to its emotional, physical and financial needs. That's what a responsible father—and a real man—did.

Her initial life plan had included a father for her child. It was only the bastards she'd picked who had soured her on the idea.

He could make it sweet for her again.

The fact that she had no idea he knew she was carrying his child was his ace in the hole. She had to have liked him or she never would have picked his sperm.

Winning women over had never been a difficult task. And he could make this one laugh. Hell, that was half the battle right there.

CHAPTER FIVE

EMILY FELT SATED and relaxed as she and Brad exited the Courage Bay Bar and Grill. Dinner had been very good and so had the company. It had been a while since she'd had a conversation with a man that moved past surface pleasantries to real meaning.

A florist's van pulled up to the loading zone in front of the Bar and Grill. The driver left the engine running as he hurried to the side panel and pulled out a huge bouquet of spring flowers with a teddy bear and red-felt heart sitting in the center. Someone inside the restaurant was going to get a nice surprise.

When the deliveryman started toward the entrance, Brad halted him and held out some money. "Any chance you have some red roses in there?" he asked, gesturing toward the van.

The man nodded. "Hold these a sec."

Brad obliged by grasping the edges of the spring bouquet while the deliveryman went back to the truck. He reached into its far recesses and came out with a dozen long-stemmed red roses. When he brought them out, Brad gestured toward Emily.

The deliveryman handed the flowers to her. After taking the money and retrieving the spring bouquet, he disappeared into the Bar and Grill.

"Who are these for?" Emily asked, smelling the roses, but finding little fragrance.

"You."

Emily was immensely disappointed to hear that. They

didn't know each other well enough for him to be buying her flowers as a friend. And men who bought red roses for a woman were generally laying the groundwork to come on to her as a lover.

She needed another lover like she needed anesthetic-free open-heart surgery. Whatever his intentions, there was only one way to handle this. Cut off the pursuit in the proverbial bud.

"Thanks, but no thanks," she said, handing him the roses.

"You don't want them?" he asked, his voice rising in surprise.

"I'm sure you'll find someone who will. It's getting late. No need for you to follow me back to the Botanical Gardens. Thanks for all your help today, Dr. Winslow. Good night."

She swung around and strolled away, satisfied that the brush-off had been properly executed. A woman had to be firm with these things, but not unkind. She'd achieved the right balance. Men had delicate egos—even the best-looking ones. Especially the best-looking ones.

Emily had reached her car at the far end of the parking lot when she heard hurrying steps behind her.

"Wait," Brad's voice called out.

Apparently, she'd underestimated his tenacity.

"Yes?" she asked as she turned to face him.

He was a little out of breath as he stood before her. "I'm sorry about the roses. I thought you'd like them. Most women do."

"I'm not most women."

"Something I should have seen before."

He wore an interesting look on his face, sort of a toss-up between chagrin and curiosity.

"Look, I'd like to return with you to the Botanical Gardens and finish going through the time capsule," he said. "There could be something in there about the skeleton. And even if there isn't, the stuff's fascinating."

She certainly found it so.

"Don't force me to go home and study for those damn board exams."

His desperate sincerity was almost funny.

"What did you do with the roses?" she asked.

"I gave them to the next woman who came out of the restaurant. She thought her husband had put me up to it. Turns out today's some kind of anniversary for them and until I handed her the roses, she assumed he'd forgotten."

"Which he had, of course."

"You can't be too hard on the guy. It's genetically encoded on our Y chromosome to forget these things."

"Is that the same Y chromosome that gives you guys such amazing recall when it comes to sports scores?"

"Ah," he said nodding. "I see you've read the scientific journals on the subject."

His tone and look were totally sober. She fought the need to grin. "You didn't tell her the truth about the roses, did you?"

"While she was hugging him, he slipped me a fifty. I can be bought. If I give you my Boy Scout's word of honor that I will not shower you with any more of those nasty roses, do I get a chance to see what's in the rest of the time capsule?"

As she opened the car door, she glanced at him over her shoulder.

"Were you ever really a Boy Scout?"

"Scout's honor," he said. "Well, until they kicked me out for buying all the little old ladies roses instead of helping them across the street."

It was the completely serious expression on his face that had her chuckling.

"I'll see you back at the Botanical Gardens," she said.

Emily slipped into the driver's seat and drove off. She told herself the decision had been a rational one. She'd made her point. He knew that she wasn't interested in inappropriate overtures from him now. As long as he kept his distance, they could continue to work together.

But none of her logical self-talk eased the disturbing sense that she was steering by a star that refused to stay in place.

Brad Winslow wasn't just some guy she'd met who might have been getting ready to make a play for her. She carried this man's seed inside her.

Meeting him had been by chance. She accepted that. His showing up at the Founders Day Celebration and getting involved with the skeleton had been something over which she also had no control.

But working with him was a conscious decision. And for her to make such a decision wasn't wise.

Even in school she'd always been a sucker for his type. Not the tall, dark handsome ones or the brainy ones or even the ones who could make her laugh— although he certainly qualified in all three of those categories.

No, the guys she fell for were the ones with heart.

From the moment Brad had started to speak about the woman he'd lost, Emily knew she'd been a lot more than just a "good friend." A guy who loved so deeply he still felt the pain of losing that love so many years later was the kind of man a woman wanted to get to know.

Except she couldn't afford to get to know him too well. Her life was on track now because she'd finally put herself in charge of it. The last thing she needed was to invite in a man to screw it up again.

Which meant being with Brad Winslow was going to mean being on her guard every single second.

DURING THE TRIP back to the Botanical Gardens, Brad wrestled with the problem facing him. This was going to be a far more difficult process than he'd envisioned now that obvious overtures were out.

Any of the women he worked with would have been happy with the roses. But they were his colleagues as well as friends. He didn't have such a built-in relationship with Emily.

That should have occurred to him before. He'd been too eager to push ahead, too excited over his "perfect" plan.

She was a beautiful woman. Guys were probably coming on to her all the time. No doubt she'd thought he'd been coming on to her as well.

And it wasn't as though the thought hadn't crossed his mind.

He needed to slow down and rethink his approach.

After Julie died, burying himself in medical school's incessant demands had been all he cared about. Every time he got tired, he felt her lifeless body lying in his arms and found the energy to go on. Between studying and part-time jobs to keep food on the table, he'd had no time to even think about women. The ones who had entered his hectic life since he'd begun his residency had stayed but briefly and left without a trace.

Emily was nothing like his romantic Julie or the willing, but very forgettable, women who had since frequented his bed. She was coolly self-possessed and showed absolutely no personal interest in him.

Why in the hell did she pick his sperm?

Even convincing her that they should continue to work together on the time capsule hadn't been easy. Backing off was the best thing he could do for the present. If he had any hopes of becoming a father to his child, he was going to have to find a way to get Emily to like him.

As he pulled in behind her at the iron entry gates to the Botanical Gardens, he consoled himself with the fact that cataloging the artifacts was going to take some time.

Emily used the remote control in her vehicle to open the gates. He followed her car inside and parked next to her in the Heritage Museum's lot.

When they reached the side door leading to the back stairs, they found it ajar.

"I know I locked this," Emily said, and Brad didn't miss the immediate concern in her voice.

"A straggler from the reception?" he offered by way of explanation.

"The reception was long over by the time we left."

"Cleanup crew?"

"The catering service I used is top-notch. They would have cleaned up and been out of here within half an hour after the reception ended. And Dot would have checked to make sure. No one should have still been in the building when we went to dinner."

Brad leaned down to check for tampering on the lock, but it was impossible to see with only the dim parking-lot lights.

"Maybe you'd better stay here while I take a look inside," he said. "Where's the light?"

"Just to the right on the other side of the door."

He stepped inside, flipped the switch. The hallway leading to the back stairs and the first-floor rooms was empty. He made his way through the adjacent library, a large reception hall and several side rooms and gave the rest rooms a quick once-over, as well.

No one was there and nothing seemed to be disturbed. He checked the front door. It was locked.

By the time he'd returned to the hallway, Emily had stepped inside. He answered the question on her face with a head shake.

"I need to check the second floor," she said.

"Let me go first."

She didn't argue but followed behind as he led the way up the stairs. As soon as Brad reached the second-floor landing, he saw the door to her office was open. He'd watched her close and lock it, just as he'd watched her lock the back door behind them.

"Stay here," he said.

He kept his eyes on the open door as he quickly checked the other doors off the second-floor landing. Each was closed and locked. He stepped through the doorway into Emily's office.

Switching on the light, he felt the tension that had built in his shoulders ease as the shadows retreated to the empty corners of the room.

The drapes had been opened and the larger of the sash windows was up, a light breeze flipping the paper calendar on the desktop.

He made his way to the window and found the screen gone and the wooden sill sporting a fresh gouge. Below was the parking lot, deserted except for their two cars. But something or someone had gone through this window within the past two hours.

When he turned around, he saw that Emily had followed him in. She stood over the open time capsule, her expression one of shaken disbelief.

"What's wrong?" he asked as he hurried over to her.

"The contents are gone."

His eyes followed hers to the bottom of the empty steel-riveted box.

"The pictures," she said and scurried to the chest in the corner. When she opened it, he could hear her exhale of relief. "At least they didn't get the pictures."

DOROTHY WAS THE FIRST of the managing board to arrive. She entered the library, where Emily and Brad waited after giving their statements to the detectives. The moment she saw Emily, she crossed the room to give her a hug.

"You're all right," Dorothy said. "That's the important thing."

Emily pulled back from her friend's arms. "Thanks, Dot, but no one was after me. I've checked through every room of the museum. The contents of the time capsule were the only things stolen."

"The time capsule contents have been stolen?" Phoebe said from the doorway, her voice a horrified screech.

Emily looked over to see that Ken was beside Phoebe and Oliver stood behind her.

"How did it happen?" Oliver demanded, the anger lines etched deep around his mouth.

"The back door was ajar when Dr. Winslow and I returned from dinner and—"

"You left the documents unguarded?" Phoebe said, her tone clearly accusing.

Emily was still reeling from her own severe disappointment. She was not in the mood to become Phoebe's punching bag. But she'd learned long ago that striking back in anger only made things worse. Taking a deep breath, she started to count to ten.

"How could you let this happen?" Oliver said. "Those artifacts are priceless! Irreplaceable! I knew they should have gone to the vault at the pharmaceutical company where security guards would have seen to their safekeeping."

Emily started her count to ten again.

"If I had taken them home as *I* wanted to," Phoebe said, "we'd still have them. I've never let myself get distracted by a man."

"Phoebe, don't—" Ken began.

"Don't what, Ken? Don't get angry? Too late. I'm already angry."

"This is a terrible blow for all of us," Dorothy said carefully, her normally diplomatic tone a little raw around the edges. "But please keep in mind that it is the thieves who deserve our anger. Emily could not have foreseen—"

"She should have taken the proper precautions," Oliver interrupted. "You convinced us the artifacts would be safe in her care and now, within a few short hours, she's let them get stolen. It's inexcusable!"

"When word of this devastating loss gets out to the rest of the members," Phoebe piped up, "they're going to expect us to take firm measures. Emily, maybe you'd best think about turning in your resignation."

Emily wanted to. Her patience in light of these unfair accusations was quickly deserting her. But if she quit the Society, that would be tantamount to admitting she'd done something wrong.

"Emily is not resigning," Dorothy said in no uncertain terms. "She is a valued member of our Society. This was not her fault. I will not allow you to—"

"Dorothy, you may be our media liaison," Phoebe interrupted, "but don't forget *I'm* this Society's membership chairperson."

"And *I'm* it's archives director," Oliver said. "Phoebe's right. This is a matter for the members at large to decide. We'll see what they have to say."

"Yes, I'd be interested in hearing their reaction, as well," Brad said.

Emily recognized the deep note of authority in his voice. It was the one she had awakened to in the E.R. Everyone in the room turned toward him.

"What do you mean?" Oliver demanded.

"Just what I said. I'm curious how they'll react when I tell them that I personally watched Dr. Barrett lock both her office and the back door when we left the museum at six. And that there were only a handful of people who knew the time capsule would be here—the same handful of people who are currently in this room."

For a long moment, Phoebe and Oliver stared at Brad, the unsavory implications settling on their faces.

"But it's ludicrous to think that we—" Oliver began to protest.

"Is it?" Brad interrupted again. "A common thief wouldn't be interested in the artifacts. Everyone knows that. Their value can only be appreciated by historians like yourselves."

"You're implying that one of us—" Phoebe began.

"I'm implying nothing. I'm simply stating the facts. I heard you and Mr. Smithson fighting over the right to get possession of them. Now they're missing. I wonder what the society members will make of that...coincidence?''

Phoebe's eyes no longer seemed able to blink. Oliver's skin color drained to match the whiteness of his beard.

"I didn't think to mention your argument to the police when they questioned me, but it's an oversight that can be quickly remedied,'' Brad said. "They are still upstairs, processing the crime scene. I'm sure they'll be glad to hear that you've arrived.''

Phoebe and Oliver stared at Brad, slack-jawed.

"No doubt they'll want to take you down to the station for questioning,'' Brad continued. "If I were you, I'd consider calling a lawyer. I can vouch for Dr. Barrett's whereabouts at the time of the theft. Can anyone vouch for yours?''

Emily decided right then and there that she could really get to like Brad Winslow.

"Come on, Dr. Barrett,'' he said. "We have to amend our statements to the police. When they asked us if we knew of anyone who might want to steal the historical treasure, we were obviously in too much shock to think of the obvious.''

"But, but, but,'' Oliver sputtered like an old auto engine on a cold morning.

"I didn't do it,'' Phoebe protested in what for her was a faint squeak.

"Even so, if word gets out that you're suspects, your reputations in the Society will be irrevocably compromised,'' Dorothy said. "Much in the same way that Emily's reputation would be compromised should an implication be made that this theft was in any way her fault.''

Both Phoebe and Oliver averted their eyes in sudden, uneasy shame. Nothing like being on the other end of a swinging stick to feel the sting.

Ken turned to Phoebe. "Is there something you want to say to Emily?'' he coaxed.

"I didn't mean to imply you were at fault, Emily,''

Phoebe said after a moment of troubled quiet. "It was the shock of learning the artifacts were stolen. I...wasn't thinking clearly."

"Phoebe's right," Oliver said. "We were upset. Spoke out of turn. You understand."

What Emily understood was that Brad had done a perfect job of coming to her defense by putting them on the defense.

"Are you ready to talk to the police now, Dr. Barrett?" Brad asked in that solid, authoritative tone that was growing on her more by the minute.

Phoebe and Oliver stared at her in stricken silence as they waited for her response.

"I think they'll be able to find the thief or thieves without any additional help from us, Dr. Winslow."

The relief on the two board members' faces was immediate.

"Then I'll see you to your car," Brad said formally.

"Go on, Em," Dorothy said, with a small smile. "I'll lock up after the police leave. As I'm sure Dr. Winslow will attest, all the stress and strain of tonight can't be good for your baby."

"Baby?" Phoebe echoed. "You're pregnant? Oh my heavens. I didn't know! And even with that wonderful distraction you still did such a great job on the Founders Day Celebration. We haven't thanked you enough, Emily, dear."

"A woman in a family way should not be working such late hours, Emily," Oliver scolded like some doting father.

"Oliver is right," Phoebe said. "You must go home now and get off your feet."

Emily accepted Phoebe and Oliver's sudden concern for her welfare with as much grace as she was currently capable of showing.

On her way toward the door, Emily stopped to give Dorothy a warm hug and a whispered thank-you.

While she walked with Brad toward their cars in the lot, she was still searching for the right words to say to him.

"I don't know how you kept your cool back there with those two," he said suddenly. "If they'd pulled that crap on me, I would have punched their lights out. I don't care how old they are."

The angry edge to his voice was as surprising as his words.

She stopped at the door to her car and turned to face him, feeling off balance by both the force of his reaction and hers.

"You should resign," he said. "Don't tell them about the pictures you saved. Or about what you had me enter into the computer. Leave them high and dry. Serve them right."

The nicest thing about Brad's words was their ring of honesty. That told Emily something very important. He hadn't come to her defense to try to impress her.

She laid her hand on his forearm and looked him in the eyes. "Thank you, Brad."

Withdrawing her hand, she got into her vehicle and headed for home.

BRAD STOOD IN THE PARKING LOT, staring at her disappearing taillights, flat-footed with surprise.

He'd been so carried away with his anger at Phoebe and Oliver's unfair attack on Emily that he never considered how she would respond to his taking them on.

He'd simply been doing what he knew to be the right thing. But the sincerity of her thank-you told him that it hadn't been that simple for her.

When his cell phone began to ring in his pocket, he realized his fingers were running over his arm where she'd held it.

He pulled the phone out of his pocket and answered with his name.

"We've got a problem here at the hospital, Dr. Winslow."

Brad didn't recognize the voice. And this wasn't the way he was used to being summoned when there was an emergency. "Who is this?"

"Albert down in the morgue. Someone tried to break in here tonight."

This was obviously a wrong number.

"Albert, are you aware I'm an E.R. physician?"

"Yes, Doctor. I'm calling you because the only remains in the morgue tonight have your name on them. I thought if someone were after those remains, you'd want to know."

Remains with his name on them? The light finally came on in Brad's brain. Of course. Albert meant the skeleton.

"Someone tried to steal the skeleton?" he asked, suddenly on full alert. "Did they get it?"

"Yes, Doctor. I mean, no, Doctor. I mean they tried, but I came back from my lunch break early and scared him away."

"You got a look at who it was?"

"Well, no. I was coming out of the break room when I saw someone in a cloak at the other end of the hallway in front of the doors, banging on the lock. I think it was a man, but I was a distance away. I yelled and whoever it was ran off."

"You're sure he didn't get into the morgue?"

"The lock on the door had been damaged, but I still needed to use my key to get it open."

"Did you touch anything?"

"No, I just went inside to see if anyone was there. And to check the bodies. There's only one in the trays. Except when I opened the tray, I found a skeleton instead of a body."

"Have you called the police?"

"Right away. But that was at least ninety minutes ago and no one has showed."

Brad rather doubted that the police considered a break-in at a morgue to be high priority on their response list.

"I'm sorry to bother you about this," Albert said, "but I—"

"No, I'm glad you called. You did the right thing. That skeleton in the morgue you're guarding is very important. Sit tight. I'll be there in thirty minutes."

Brad flipped his cell phone closed and headed for his car. The artifacts had been stolen from the Heritage Museum, and an attempt had been made to get at the skeleton.

Someone seemed to be going to a lot of effort to possess everything that had been unearthed with the time capsule.

WHEN EMILY WAS COMFORTABLE in bed, she drew the journal out of the bottom drawer of the nightstand. She traced her hand over the cover, a collage of tiny shoots and buds bursting with new life.

She flipped it open to where her bookmark lay from the last entry and turned to a fresh page. After picking up the pen from the nightstand, she began to write.

Dear Sprout,

I spent time with your biological father today, and I must say you have some very nice genes. His sperm-donor questionnaire asked that he describe his personality. He listed such traits as goal oriented, a critical thinker, serious but with a good sense of humor. They're all there. He also possesses a sense of fairness and will not hesitate to speak out in the face of injustice.

Tonight he spoke out in defense of me. Your mom's no shrinking violet, Sprout. I'm not only up to fighting my own battles, I prefer it. But what he did was…well, pretty special. Remind me to tell you all about it someday.

I hope you enjoyed dinner, but don't get used to the lobster. I've already started your college fund.

Goodnight and sleep well. I love you. Mom.

Emily was putting the journal away when the phone rang. She picked up the receiver and said hello.

"Em, the local news is running the story of the time capsule," Dorothy's voice said excitedly in her ear. "Quick. Turn it on."

Emily reached for the TV remote control and hit the button. The time capsule was indeed the lead story. She'd missed the first few minutes. The film rolling on the screen was of the sundial being removed by the crane. And then Brad inside the pit bending over the skeleton.

"There's your guy," Dorothy said in her ear.

"He's not my guy, Dot."

"He sure came through for you tonight."

"No argument there."

They grew quiet so they could listen to the TV broadcast.

The reporter was talking about the surprise of the skeleton's discovery and how it had been buried with the time capsule. Nothing was said about the skeleton having met its end through suspicious means.

Mayor O'Shea reading the letter from the capsule came next. Then the film cut to his promise at the end of the ceremony that the artifacts would be preserved by the Historical Society for all to enjoy.

"As our reporter mentioned at the beginning of tonight's story," the news anchor said, "the contents of the time capsule were stolen this evening from the Heritage Museum, where they were being cataloged. No suspects have been identified."

"Well, I guess there was no hope of keeping the theft quiet," Emily said into the phone.

"Have you talked to Ed?"

"I called him when I got home. They're still processing the scene. He promised to get in touch tomorrow and fill me in on anything important."

"Do you think the photographs will be safe in the museum's basement?"

"They should be. The place is like a vault. Besides, just a handful of people know they're there. The police aren't going to tell the press that they weren't stolen."

Emily was about to switch off the TV when the news anchor put up his finger as though urging her to hold on while he listened to something in his earphone.

"We've just received an update to the story," he said. "The police are now reporting an attempted break-in earlier this evening at the Courage Bay Hospital morgue, where the skeleton unearthed with the time capsule is being housed. The thief was interrupted and the skeleton was not taken. The hospital is increasing security. We'll keep you informed as we learn more."

"Dot, did you hear that?" Emily asked.

"Yes," Dorothy said through the phone. "First the artifacts and now the skeleton? I don't understand this. What in the hell is happening, Em?"

CHAPTER SIX

BRAD FOUND EMILY in the Botanical Gardens' greenhouse early Sunday afternoon. She was busily humming to a tray of tiny plants that she was repotting and didn't notice him when he entered.

She wore a light lemon shirt tucked into faded jeans. Her long hair was pinned to the top of her head with a large gold barrette. She dipped her fingers into various potting-soil mixes, taking out a smidgen of this and a smidgen of that like a master cook creating a special dish from one of the myriad of recipes in her head.

When he'd seen her yesterday in her formal dress suit, he would have sworn she was in her element among Courage Bay's elite. But today she looked like what she'd initially told him she was—someone who simply took care of plants. And from the happy little tune she was humming, he had the unmistakable conviction that this was where she felt most at home.

He never knew what to expect from her.

Last night when she'd thanked him, she'd meant it sincerely. That was the reason he'd taken this chance to visit her unannounced. But although she'd warmed to him somewhat, how she'd greet him today he couldn't guess.

When she turned and saw him, he braced himself. For an instant, surprise stilled her features. Then her lips curved into a welcome.

He stepped forward, an emotion far stronger than simple relief behind his returning smile. It was getting so that he didn't know what to expect from himself when he was around her.

"I saw Dot up at the museum getting the locks replaced," he said. "She told me you'd be here. I would have called first, but she warned me that you don't carry a cell phone when you work in the greenhouse."

"The ringing disturbs the plants," she said as she continued to repot the new shoots.

"And the planter?"

"Modern gadgets are great. But everyone needs a quiet place where they can avoid them once in a while. Do you have such a place?"

"Not since I entered medical school. You generally work on Sundays?"

"No, but the gardens were closed yesterday because of Founders Day. And getting ready for that event has put me behind on a few things."

"So what are you growing?"

"Some hybrids of a number of traditional medicinal plants. This one is from *Cardus marianus,* what is commonly called milk thistle."

Brad had heard of the plant. "A folk remedy for liver health. I get it. You're planning on opening up an herb shop across the street from the hospital, where you will dispense healing plants that will cure the sick and put us bumbling doctors out of business."

She smiled. "Tempting, but I'm much too busy here identifying, naming and classifying these hybrids. I'm also propagating a few new lilacs for the Botanical Gardens and attempting to bring some of the rarer roses we have here into cultivation for home gardeners."

"Was taxonomy your area of specialization in botany?"

"I vacillated between that and genetics. At one time I seriously considered devoting all my time to the study of plant heredity and variation."

Brad's eyes took in the rows and rows of new green

leaves poking out of the containers all around them. "Any of these plants experiments in genetics?"

She shook her head. "When I got out of graduate school, Craig and I both went to work as geneticists in a large biotech lab, inserting desirable genes into plants to produce bigger and better yields of useful products. I thought it would be such important, worthwhile work."

"But it wasn't," he surmised when she paused.

"I guess botanists are not very different from the plants we study. Even though we all carry the same title, we require different environments to make us thrive. Every gardener knows that what works for beardeds will kill the moisture-loving Louisiana and Siberian irises."

"What was killing you?"

"I was this replaceable cog in a corporate wheel, forced into competition with my co-workers, pushed to work longer and longer hours, shut up in an enclosed lab away from natural light and air. A bit too dramatic to say that those things were killing me, of course, but they were killing my joy for botany."

Brad could understand that. As much as he loved medicine, there were aspects of it he would never want to specialize in.

"When I tried to explain how I felt to Craig," Emily continued, "he had no idea what I was talking about. Told me I was foolish to even be thinking of quitting my well-paying position, especially since I'd recently been promoted."

"Money-grubbing lout," Brad said, keeping his tone light.

A tiny grin flashed across her face. "Anyway, I tried to hush the inner voice that kept telling me the fast track I was on headed nowhere I wanted to be. When that voice finally wouldn't keep quiet any longer, I got out."

"Was that when your marriage broke up?"

"It was a month later when I learned about...when we split."

Because the bastard had lied to her about wanting a family. Didn't sound to Brad like her ex had given a damn about anybody but himself.

She stepped over to the sink and gave her hands a quick wash. "The moment I accepted the job as curator of the Botanical Gardens and built the greenhouse for my research, I knew that this was where I belonged. There's something about being out among all these beautiful growing things that keeps me nourished. It's hard to explain."

"You feel connected to life's pulse here."

Her look was one of pleased surprise. "That's it, exactly. How did you know?"

"It's the same kind of feeling that keeps me in the E.R., even on the days when I'm certain that nothing I'm doing is making a difference."

"Do you really feel that way some days?" she asked as she dried her hands.

"Oh, yeah."

"But when you save a life it must be so satisfying to know that your knowledge and expertise helped to make a difference."

Brad thought of the call he'd gotten early that morning to help out with a sudden overload of emergencies in the E.R. And how much of a "help" he'd been.

"Sometimes even when you do everything right, it still doesn't make a difference," he said.

She rested her hip against a row of sturdy wooden trays and studied him. "Who was this patient you weren't able to help?"

"It's not important."

"I'd like to understand."

Yes, he believed she would.

And maybe that was why he suddenly found himself telling her about the man who had had a heart attack behind the wheel of his car and ended up hitting a mother and her child who were walking to church.

He was DOA. So was the mother.

Brad saw it all again in his mind's eye. The paramedics rolling in the five-year-old girl on the gurney, one holding the saline drip above her while he negotiated the corners into the trauma room, the other frantically performing CPR.

"No BP, no pulse," the paramedic holding the bag of saline reported. "We figure she was down ten, twelve minutes before we got to her."

The paramedic was Ramirez, big and congenial, always known for his absolute cool in any crisis. He was sweating.

And then the little girl was in their hands and the respiratory therapist was grabbing the Ambu bag while Brad was groping for a pulse. And not finding one.

He barked the staccato orders that were the E.R.'s trade lingo. After four years in emergency medicine, they came easily. But working on a child never did.

Her face was bloodless, her lips blue when she was hooked up to the heart monitor. A nurse climbed onto a stool and started chest compressions where the paramedic left off.

Brad grabbed the size-five ET tube out of the tray. So damn tiny.

He looked up and saw a rhythm on the monitor at the same time that the nurse said, "Heart rate of fifty."

His eyes went to the other nurse who was groping at the child's neck.

She shook her head. Still no pulse.

"Put in another line," Brad said as he rushed to the head of the table. "Epi, atropine."

He was behind her now ready to intubate. The child's jaw was slack. As he peered inside her mouth, he could see the vocal cords. Gently, he slipped the beveled edge of the ET tube through. He straightened, pulled out the stylet. Textbook perfect.

"We're in."

The respiratory therapist bagged the child.

Brad pulled the ends of the stethoscope to his ears. He could see the little girl's lungs beginning to expand. A good sign. He listened at her chest wall. Breath sounds. An even better sign.

He looked up at the heart monitor. 58...62...64. Still too low.

"Pulse?"

At some point, Alec Giroux had come into the room. He stood now with his fingers on the little girl's carotid. He shook his head in response to Brad's question.

Brad put his hand on the child's right groin, searching for a femoral pulse. A century passed before slowly, faintly, it appeared. His eyes shot to the monitor again. 77...79...80.

"We have a blood-pressure reading," a nurse said. "Sixty over forty."

She had a blood pressure. She had a pulse. Her heart rate was climbing. And her skin? Yes! Her skin was pinking.

"We had her fully stabilized before she went up to the OR," Brad said to Emily as he finished the story. "The X rays revealed broken ribs, a ruptured spleen. The surgeons operated successfully."

"You saved her."

"Her brain was deprived of oxygen too long, Emily. She's in a coma. She may never come out of it."

In the silent moment that followed, Brad's eyes sought out the growing things around them, all resolutely reaching for the sunlight.

"Give me a minute to lock up," Emily said.

Following her out of the greenhouse, Brad realized that it had given him a kind of release to tell her about the little girl.

He never talked about this stuff—not even to other physicians—especially not to other physicians. Medical pro-

fessionals were trained that they were most effective when
they maintained a strict emotional distance.

Objectivity enabled them to think clearly in chaos and
respond in a way that was most beneficial for the patient.
A doctor who could not check his emotions at the door
was worthless in an E.R.

But the way Emily had listened so attentively to his
story and accepted it without jumping in to offer insipid
and meaningless platitudes afterward made him feel better. He didn't know why.

The Botanical Gardens were open to the public today
and visitors were meandering down the lanes. Brad had
been to the gardens a few times before, but he'd never
really taken the time to notice them. As he did so now,
he could see the plants and vistas were beautifully arranged like individual outdoor galleries, with varied colors
and themes.

Emily took a side path along the lily ponds, away from
the public area, through an arbor in the process of being
constructed next to a cool waterfall that whispered over
gray California river stones.

She obviously didn't only see to the plants; she also
created these outdoor exhibits with a true artist's eye.

The Heritage Museum was closed to visitors today.
When they reached the back door, the new lock was in
place and Dorothy was gone. Emily drew a slip of paper
out of her pocket. Referring to it, she punched in the combination.

Up in her office, she opened the closet door where she
kept a small refrigerator, fetching a bottle of springwater
for herself and one for him. After they'd both sampled
their cool drinks, she asked him why he'd come.

"You heard that someone tried to steal the skeleton last
night?"

"I saw the TV news report," she said. "Do the police
have any leads?"

"Nothing yet. Hospital security is on full alert. To even

get down to the morgue now requires going through the equivalent of an airport-security check. I doubt whoever it was will try again. But, just in case, I thought I'd better get to the analysis right away. The pathologist isn't in today so the autopsy room will be free."

"I thought Sunday afternoons were reserved for volleyball?"

"I can fall into the barbecue pit another day. Want to be there with me when I look over the skeleton?"

"You came out here to see if I wanted to go to the morgue?"

"Sorry," he said, not sorry at all. "I forgot that most women are squeamish about such things."

Brad very much doubted that was the case with Emily. But he implied what he did as a nudge for her to prove him wrong by agreeing to be in on the examination. He wanted, needed her there. His excuse to be with her had vanished with the contents of the time capsule.

She thought about it a moment before getting to her feet. "I'll follow you."

He was careful not to show his relief. She could not know how important this was to him—or why it was so important.

THE AUTOPSY ROOM WAS quite cold and smelled strongly of antiseptic. Emily was beginning to regret that she'd let herself get caught in the need to prove she wasn't some stereotypic sissy female.

She wrapped her arms around herself and tried not to shiver.

"Here," Brad said, slipping out of his sport coat and holding it out to her.

"You're going to need that in this freezer," she said. "Don't be gallant."

"Gallant isn't part of my job description. But being naturally warm-blooded is part of my genes. Go on. Take it."

When she still hesitated, he shook his head in frustration and swung it around her shoulders. "And I thought I was stubborn."

The warmth of his jacket did feel good. His scent was on the fabric of the coat. She pulled the edges closer around her.

"I thought you were pigheaded and obstinate," she said too sweetly.

He sent her an amused look as he circled the center table where the skeleton lay, the evidence bag near the bones of the feet.

"I'm going to turn on the tape machine and make a record of what we find to eliminate the need to take notes," he said. "Remind me to remove the tape when we leave."

She nodded as he flipped a switch and adjusted the microphone suspended over the examining table.

"What we have is a fully articulated skeleton found in the dirt beside the time capsule buried in April 1904," Brad began.

"Was this how it looked in the pit?" Emily asked.

He nodded. "The police evidence gatherers did a good job of placing the bones on this gurney in the precise position in which they lay in the time-capsule grave."

Brad circled the skeleton one more time. "The bones are thick, chalky-white for the most part, slightly discolored in certain sections, no doubt from something leached out of the soil during their extended period in the ground."

Old bones were not Emily's thing. Still, as long as she was here, she decided she might as well try to get into the spirit of things.

"You mentioned at the site that it was a he," she said. "How did you determine that?"

"At first glance you can see that these bones are pretty massive. That's your first indication that they belong to a male. Then there's the pelvic opening. See it there?"

She followed his pointing finger and nodded.

"Overall it's quite narrow and this subpubic angle here is relatively acute, plus which the sciatic notch—"

"Hold on a minute," Emily interrupted as she moved closer. "Remember you're talking to a layperson here. What's a sciatic notch?"

"Sorry. That's this small V-shaped indentation on the edge of each hip bone. It's about the width of a thumb. And on this skeleton, quite narrow."

She bent forward to take a closer look. "Narrow as compared to what?"

"As compared to a female's," Brad said. "Being able to interpret information like this comes from having seen a lot of bones and noticing patterns."

"You learned this when you were studying to be a forensic anthropologist?"

"Most of it. Of course, medical school also emphasizes skeletal anatomy. But it doesn't take too many anthropological digs before you can tell fairly quickly whether you're dealing with a male or female skeleton."

He paused to point. "The pelvis is always the best indicator—a female's being proportionately wider to allow for the passage of a baby. But the skull can also give you clues."

He had a contagious appreciation for his subject. Emily found herself being drawn in.

"Show me what you mean," she said.

"Well, this skull has large browridges—a male trait. And these pyramid-shaped bones that project down behind each ear are called mastoid processes. Their strength and thickness also confirm maleness."

She noted the areas he was pointing to and then something else. "Is that round hole above the right browridge what I think it is?"

He nodded. "I found a spent slug in the skull case. It's in the bag at his feet. And you can see that there is no bone healing around the wound so it had to have occurred at the time of death.''

Actually, Emily could see nothing of the sort, but she took Brad's word for it.

"What else can you tell about him?"

"You see these lines here on the skull? They're the cranial sutures. When a baby is born, they aren't yet fused so that they can overlap and allow the head to pass through the birth canal. As an individual ages, they permanently join and close. Happens somewhere in the mid-twenties. Our skeleton was at least that old when he died. After I take a closer look, I should be able to give you a definite age range.''

"Height?" Emily asked, becoming more intrigued by the moment.

"By studying the bones of people whose height is already known, scientists have been able to estimate the stature of someone based on the long limb bones like the forearm or thighbone. There's a chart that will help to give us his height when I take a measurement of his femur. Will you hand me that tape measure over there?''

Emily followed his pointing finger and retrieved the item. She then watched as Brad extended the tape over the thighbone. Once he had the reading, he went over to the shelf and took down a reference book. He flipped through the pages until he found what he was looking for.

"How are you at doing equations in your head?" he asked.

"Balancing my checkbook is the extent of my higher math skills.''

He looked around until he spied a calculator on a table behind him. Referring to the book's open page, he punched in several numbers on the calculator. Then a few more.

So, he couldn't do the math in his head, either. For no reason at all, that made her feel good.

"This guy was about six feet.''

"Since the average man is around five-nine, our skeleton would have stood out in a crowd. What about weight?"

"That's going to be a lot more difficult. Muscles show up on bones, but not fat. If this guy had a spare tire around his waist, we'll never know by looking at his skeleton. Want to help me find evidence of his muscle?"

"Show me what I have to do."

"You can start here," he said, pointing to a bone edge. She moved closer.

"Every time we use our muscles," Brad said, "a bone's surface becomes rougher in order to anchor the attached tendons. See how rough it is here on this guy's shoulder bone?"

"That means he had a lot of muscle there," she surmised.

"Exactly."

She reached out a finger to touch the edges of both shoulder bones. "It's rougher on the right. Does that mean he was right-handed?"

"You would have made a good forensic anthropologist. Another place to look is the hand bones. Examine them and tell me what you find."

"Do I get tested on this later?"

"Forty percent of your grade will be based on willingness, another forty percent on accuracy and you get an additional forty percent if you don't step on my feet."

"You do realize that's over one hundred percent?"

"Yeah, well, I use a calculator to balance my checkbook."

She turned to her task, amused and having a surprisingly good time. After careful scrutiny, she decided the edges on the wrist bones of the right hand seemed rougher than those on the left. But as she traced her finger lightly across more of the bones, she noticed something else.

"I vote for right-handedness, but what's this mark?" she asked.

Brad bent to take a closer look. "Seems to be a nick in the bone. Could be caused by the teeth of mice."

Their shoulders brushed ever so slightly. It had been a long time since the touch of a man could give Emily so much as a tingle. This was more than a tingle.

She straightened, took a cautious step back.

"Would you get me the magnifying glass on the table over there?" he asked, pointing without looking.

He was hunched over the hand bones, hardly aware she was there.

She headed for the table, glad his attention was consumed by the examination, irritated at herself for reacting to him.

This wasn't a case of simple lust. Lust had never been simple for her. When a guy turned her on, it was because he possessed qualities that went far beyond basic physical attraction.

Brad hardly gave her a glance when he took the magnifying glass out of her hand. "Thanks."

For the next several minutes he said nothing, totally engrossed in the task before him. Finally, he straightened and faced her.

"He was stabbed in the hand."

"You don't think it's a mouse bite?"

"Rodents have U-shaped incisors. This is a V-cut, like a knife."

Brad moved to the bottom of the skeleton's feet where the bag with the dagger, coin and slug lay. He extracted the dagger from the bag, took it over to the right wrist bone he'd been studying. Carefully he inserted the blade into the cut in the bone.

"It fits. Definitely a knife wound. Maybe even from this knife."

"Had the bone healed on this wound?" Emily asked.

"Good question," Brad said, removing the dagger from the bone. "And the answer is no. So, it, too, had to have happened at the time of death."

"Two assailants?" Emily wondered aloud. "One with a gun and one with a knife?"

"Possibly," Brad said. "This guy could have put his hand up and received a defensive wound."

Brad picked up the magnifying glass once again and took a closer look at the right hand, picking up the bones one at a time until he'd examined them from all sides. "No, scratch that. Not a defensive wound."

"How can you be so sure?"

"Come here and I'll demonstrate," he said.

When she stepped forward, he picked up the dagger. "Now, pretend I'm about to strike you with this knife and you don't have time to run away." He raised the dagger to a menacing position. "What do you do?"

Emily put her hand up to shield her face.

"That's right," Brad confirmed. "An automatic defensive maneuver. Now hold that position. If I continue my forward dagger thrust, like so, I would strike you there."

He lightly touched the side of her wrist with the dagger's edge.

"You'd slice into the bone on the side or inside of the wrist," Emily said understanding. "Not on the top."

"That's right. And yet there are no slice marks on the side or inside of this skeleton's wrist. There's only the one slice mark on the top. So what does that tell you?"

She gave it a moment's thought. "That the skeleton's right hand was down at his side when he was struck?"

Brad shook his head. "I'll show you why that's unlikely. Put your right hand by your side."

She did so.

"Remember, I'm intending to do you bodily harm. Why would I strike your right hand when it was resting by your side?"

"I see what you mean. You'd be more likely to stab me in a way that would incapacitate me."

"Exactly. Now assume the assailant was right-handed as most people are. In order to inflict a knife wound to your hand down at your side, I would have to approach you from behind like this.''

He moved into position. ''If I were intent on doing you bodily harm, why would I waste a stroke on your wrist when I could stab you in the back or grab you and aim for your exposed throat like this?''

Brad demonstrated by wrapping his left arm around her, pulling her securely against him and bringing the knife in his right hand in front of her throat.

Emily knew he'd just asked her a question. But for the life of her, she couldn't remember what it was. The feel of his hard body pressed against her back, his strong arm beneath her breasts pulsating with warmth, snatched every coherent thought from her head.

Then she became aware that the pounding through her chest had a deep, vibrating echo, and his breath near her ear was fast.

BRAD WITHDREW HIS ARM from around Emily and stepped back.

He'd gotten so caught up in demonstrating the manner in which the skeleton had met its end that he'd forgotten who he was with. By the time he remembered, it was too late. God, she'd felt good.

He still wasn't sure how he'd managed to let her go.

For the next minute, he concentrated on breathing in and out and trying to think of what to say to save himself. She'd walked away from him when all he'd done was present her with roses.

Having held her so intimately for several exciting seconds longer than any demonstration required was one giant step over the line. He'd felt her heart pound. He'd probably scared the hell out of her.

''I'm sorry,'' he said when he could do so with a semblance of normalcy. ''I shouldn't have... I should have warned you what I was going to do. I didn't...think.''

Understatement of the year.

He waited a moment, but she didn't respond.

"I was only trying to…" he began again, then stopped. Nothing he said now was going to matter and he knew it.

"It's okay," she said, her words barely audible.

"Is it?" he heard himself ask stupidly.

She turned, faced him. "I know you were only trying to demonstrate what could have happened."

Her voice was full of reason, her expression calm. But her hand resting on the edge of the table was quivering.

Brad couldn't believe how dense he'd been.

Her pounding heart when he'd held her, the fact that she'd made no attempt to pull away from him and now her acceptance of his apology. They told him what he should have known from the first.

She *did* like him. That's why she was so uncomfortable when he gave her the roses. They were too close to a romantic overture. The possibility that she'd lose control over her carefully mapped-out life plan by letting a man— any man—get close to her again was something she was fighting against.

"What I was trying to point out is that it was unlikely an attacker would have simply slashed this victim's wrist," Brad said, feeling more confident and at ease than he had since meeting her.

She had herself in hand now. Hadn't taken her long to recuperate. No matter what she felt, she could control it.

The challenge she presented made his pulse quicken with an excitement that he hadn't felt in a long time.

"So, how do you think this guy got the knife wound?" she asked.

"I think his hand was at waist height," Brad said, "and the slashing wound was a downward stroke administered by someone standing to his right."

He demonstrated on himself this time, mimicking a slash across the top of his right wrist using his left hand. She copied the position of his hand by holding up her own, waist high, thumb up, palm parallel to her side.

"Was he attempting to shake hands with someone when his assailant struck him?" she ventured.

He put a note of challenge in his voice to make her reassess the possibilities. "You think that's what happened?"

"Okay, why would someone hold their hand in this position if they weren't in a hand-shaking mood?" She was thinking out loud, not really asking a question.

He remained silent.

"If his hand was extended like this he might have been holding something," she amended. "A weapon?"

He nodded, pleased at the quickness of her mind. "It would explain why the assailant with the knife struck him."

"Are there any other knife marks on the rest of his bones?"

"None on his right or left hands. It will take a lot of close, slow scrutiny for me to check on the rest."

"So what we've deduced so far is that our skeleton was holding something, and an assailant on his right side wounded him with a knife, getting him to drop whatever it was he was holding, at which point the first assailant, or another one, shot him in the head."

Brad nodded. "Probably a second assailant. If the first one had a gun, it would have made more sense for him to use it instead of the knife."

"Reading these bones paints a picture of considerable violence. This was certainly the Wild West back in 1904."

"It's not a whole lot tamer now," Brad said. "If you have any doubts, spend a Friday or Saturday night with me in the E.R."

"What happens then?"

He gave it a moment's thought. "I take back my invitation. Never come down to the E.R. on those nights—or any other nights."

"You think I'm too much of a wimp to handle it?" she asked, her tone only half-serious.

He studied the gentle lines of her face. "I think you're too wholesome and nice to be exposed to the violence and self-destructive behavior that rushes through the doors at those times. Someone once told me that whatever we fill our minds with is what we become. I believe that. Focus on your beautiful plants. They'll keep the right curve on your lips."

She was silent for a moment with that deep quality of attention that drew him in.

"What about you?" she asked. "How do you see what you do and deal with the grief?"

"I've been trained to deal with a patient's grief and their family's."

"I meant the grief you feel when you lose a patient."

"Grief in an E.R. doctor is a self-indulgent waste of time. Emotions don't help us save lives. They interfere with our ability to do so."

After studying him for several seconds she smiled. "You don't consider being pigheaded and obstinate emotions?"

"Absolutely not," he said straight-faced. "They are highly valued marks of professional persistence."

She chuckled.

"And what about your sense of humor?" she asked.

"So you think I have a sense of humor."

"You always make me want to smile."

The way she was looking at him made him want to do other things.

The cell phone in his pocket rang. He pulled it out and answered with his name. A few seconds later he said, "Okay, I'll be there in five."

He flipped the phone closed. "I have to report to the E.R. Another physician was called away on a family emergency and they're shorthanded."

"You went in this morning, as well. I thought this was your weekend off."

"I was due to report back in tonight anyway. I'll stop by the morgue on the way and let them know to put the skeleton back. What's your schedule like next week?"

"Obviously a lot better than yours. How long are your shifts?"

"Sixteen hours. Five times a week. Plus call-ins like now."

"You work an eighty-hour week plus overtime?"

"Used to be a hundred and twenty hours. The Accreditation Council for Graduate Medical Education passed new rules last year that got the workweek reduced to eighty for residents."

She was shaking her head. "*Reduced* to eighty. I never should have accepted your help on this stuff."

"I never would have offered if I couldn't handle it. I'll give you a call when I have a break, and we can get back to analyzing the skeleton."

She hesitated.

"I'm young, healthy, strong and clearly not too smart," he said. "Take advantage of me before I wise up."

She was trying not to smile. "Let me give you my numbers."

He pulled out his phone and entered her office and cell-phone numbers into his address book as she recited them.

"Do I keep the tape?" she asked.

"The tape," he repeated, having forgotten. He reached over to turn off the recorder, slipped out the tape and handed it to her. Then he busied himself with putting a fresh one into the machine.

"Thanks for the reminder," he said. "Pathologist wouldn't have been pleased if he'd found our discussion on one of his autopsy reports."

"I figured it was going to be part of my final grade," she said. "So, what was my final grade?"

"Out of a hundred and twenty points, you got a hundred and nineteen."

"What happened to the other point?"

"You couldn't do the math equation in your head, remember?"

She laughed.

He really liked making her laugh. And holding her in his arms.

He planned to do both again—very soon.

Becoming Emily's lover was a far more appealing goal than his initial one of simply being her friend.

CHAPTER SEVEN

Dear Sprout,

I was with your biological father again today, and he was teaching me some very interesting things about forensic anthropology. I know I told you he was a doctor, but he used to study the other before he switched his major to medicine. He lost someone he loved, and it changed his life direction.

On his questionnaire, he listed his favorite song as "Forever Love." I can't help wondering if he loved her like that—forever.

There were a lot of things on his questionnaire that stood out from all the other candidates whose genes I could have selected for you. I'll tell you more about them as we go along. But right now I can barely keep my eyes open.

Probably the pregnancy hormones. Or the caffeine withdrawal.

Which reminds me. As of tomorrow morning, we will be officially and totally off coffee. Yep, not even a quarter of a cup. So, if you feel a little sleepy or grumpy, you can blame it all on me for being such an addict that it's taken me three weeks to wean myself off the stuff.

Sleep well, my little Sprout.
Love, Mom.

EMILY PUT HER JOURNAL away and turned off the light. As she lay back in the bed and closed her eyes, Brad's face remained clear in her mind.

When he'd held her that afternoon, he hadn't done it with the intention of coming on to her. She knew that, which was why she'd accepted his apology. But he'd been affected by the contact just as she had.

She should have left immediately and put an end to any plans to see him again. That would have been the sensible thing. But she hadn't been sensible. She'd given him her phone numbers and agreed to be there when he studied the skeleton next.

Why? Because he'd told her she was wholesome and nice? Because he wanted to shield her from the sad things he had to see in the E.R.?

Men who implied she couldn't face the rawer realities of life generally annoyed her. But she'd liked what he'd said, and the way he'd made her feel when he said it.

She liked entirely too much about him. When he called, she would do the smart thing and end this.

EMILY ARRIVED AT THE HOSPITAL Tuesday morning to find Oliver standing at Wayne's bedside, his back to her. She stopped at the entrance to the room, not wanting to intrude.

"I'm sorry about the money, Oliver," Wayne said.

"I'll find it somewhere. When we get these damn artifacts back, I want you to take possession of them. How soon do you get out of here?"

"I can probably go home today. But the doctor said I have to rest up. Oh, hi, Emily. Are those roses for me?"

Oliver spun around to see her standing in the doorway. He gave her an awkward nod of welcome.

"Actually, they're for another patient," Emily said in response to Wayne's question. "How are you feeling to-day?"

"Good," Wayne said. "By the way, the lilacs you brought by are still holding up beautifully." He paused to point to the vase sitting on his nightstand. "My wife says we should use you as our florist."

Emily smiled. She didn't know Wayne well, but he had always struck her as a nice man, although she felt he let Oliver browbeat him too much.

"Oliver tells me the Founders Day Celebration went off well because of all your hard work."

"Thanks," Emily said, sending Oliver a big smile.

He wore an embarrassed look, no doubt remembering how he'd treated her. She hadn't appreciated being on the receiving end of his anger over the stolen time capsule contents. But she understood how hard such a loss was for a true historian like him and was prepared to put it behind them.

"So Oliver tells me that you were given the job of going through the artifacts," Wayne said. "Did you find anything interesting before they got stolen?"

Wayne was another true historian. Emily could understand his disappointment at not seeing the time capsule treasures first. Sitting at his bedside, she filled him in on what had been unearthed, letting all of her own excitement come through.

"Thanks, Emily," he said afterward, his voice warm with appreciation.

"Did you see the TV coverage?" she asked.

"No. I was still pretty out of it."

"I'll drop a copy of the TV video by your place in a few days," she promised him as she got up to leave.

"I'm glad you were given the artifacts," Wayne said. "And when we get them back, I know they'll be safe in your hands. Try to overlook Oliver's...possessiveness."

Emily was a bit surprised to hear Wayne open up that way until she glanced around to see that Oliver was no longer in the room.

"I overheard a part of your conversation with Oliver a few moments ago," Emily said. "Is he in financial difficulty?"

"No, he simply wanted to borrow some cash. All his money is tied up in long-term investments. I did his personal taxes as well as the corporation's for years. Kept telling him that he needed to have liquid assets to cover emergencies. But he's never been willing to sacrifice the few percentage points in interest to provide for the contingency."

Wayne shook his head. In his accountant's view that was clearly a serious flaw.

"You said something about not being able to give him the money?"

"The most cash my wife would have been able to pull out of our accounts by tomorrow was twenty thousand."

"How much did he need?"

"A hundred thousand. Emily, don't worry about Oliver. He's not a drinker or a gambler. Whatever came up so suddenly that had him coming to me to borrow money was probably a family thing. I heard a granddaughter is getting married. It was probably that. He's an ornery old goat, but when it comes to family, he'll always go the extra mile."

After wishing Wayne well, Emily left to make her second stop.

She'd learned that the little girl she was looking for was named Samantha and she was still in a coma. They were trying to trace her father. According to the minister at the church she and her mother attended, Samantha's parents had recently divorced, and her dad had traveled out of state to take a new job. Unfortunately, that was the only information the minister had.

Normally no one but staff and a patient's family were allowed in the ICU. But the very nice nurses and doctors who worked there always bent the rules when Emily visited. She had no fear of being stopped.

As she entered Samantha's room, however, she stepped sideways and concealed herself behind a curtain.

Brad was standing beside the little girl's bed, studying the chart in his hands.

Emily knew that stabilizing a patient for transfer to surgery or other appropriate medical discipline was supposed to be the extent of an E.R. doctor's responsibility. But here he was, checking up on the little girl he'd saved two days before.

After storing the chart away, he stood beside the girl's bed and gazed at her still face as he stroked her hair. Then he bent down and gently kissed her forehead. The next second he had straightened, turned and walked out of the room.

Emily smiled, warmed from within. For all Brad's protestations against emotional attachment to his patients, deep inside him beat a heart that cared.

She emerged from her hiding place to set the vase full of roses on the bedside table. Then she took the girl's hand in hers.

"These lovely flowers are for you, Samantha. I've watched them grow from the tiniest seed into these beautiful, strong buds. They'll be pushing open their petals soon to smile at you. That's not something you're going to want to miss. It's a beautiful world out here, little one. Wake up and smell the roses."

"EVERYTHING GO OKAY at the doctor's yesterday?" Dorothy asked when she entered Emily's office at the Heritage Museum.

"Fine," Emily said. "She's confident the fainting is nothing serious after hearing about the circumstances that brought it on. She ran a few tests to be sure and called me this morning to say that everything came back normal."

Dorothy plopped onto the chair across from Emily's desk, flushed and fanning herself.

"You okay?" Emily asked.

"It's those two flights of stairs I have to climb when I come to see you," she complained.

"Flight and a half actually," Emily corrected. "Register any and all complaints with Oliver's ancestors. They built this monstrosity."

"Without which we'd have no Heritage Museum," Dorothy said, trying to be fair, as always.

"Thirsty?" Emily asked.

"Very. The Santa Ana winds are in full force today. Must be at least ninety outside."

Dorothy took the bottle of cold springwater Emily got her and drank it down immediately. "Thanks. I called you about thirty minutes ago. Got no answer."

"I sneaked down to the basement so I could put the time capsule photographs back under lock and key. The museum is filled to the brim today with visitors. Must be all the publicity about the stolen artifacts."

"Whether publicity is good or bad doesn't seem to matter," Dorothy agreed. "I had to wade my way through the bodies to get to the stairs. One curious couple tried to follow me when I slipped behind the roped-off area. Thankfully, the security guard intervened. How's the scanning coming?"

"It's done," Emily said proudly. "All the time capsule pictures are in the computer, a backup CD is filed in the basement and I've printed out copies of what Dr. Winslow and I cataloged for you, the other board members, and Ken."

Emily handed Dorothy several copies of the list of cataloged items.

"This is great, Em. Thanks."

"Ed also got me a copy of the TV tape of the ceremony so we have some film on the artifacts that were taken out on Saturday."

"At least if we don't get the originals back, we'll have something."

"We're going to get the originals back," Emily said, a

little worried about her friend's disheartened demeanor. "Do you know what's holding up the pictures from Founders Day?"

"Phoebe says that no one is going to see Ken's pictures until the Historical Society's newsletter comes out in a week or so."

Emily shook her head. "Sounds like Phoebe. When is she expecting me to have the article ready on the skeleton?"

"She hasn't called to bug you about it?" Dorothy asked.

"Not a word."

"Well, that's out of character. Maybe she's still ashamed about the way she treated you after the robbery. Which reminds me. The reason I was trying to get a hold of you is that the police came by this morning. Phoebe, Oliver and I have agreed to taps being put on our phones."

"Good."

"I don't know about that. They didn't say it outright, but I got the impression that they think one of us might have received a ransom call from the thieves and not reported it. Has Ed mentioned anything about this to you?"

She nodded. "The police think that all the publicity surrounding the 'priceless' time capsule being opened on Founders Day got some thief's attention. They did expect you'd get a call by now."

"So they've ruled out an inside job. Well, that's a relief at least."

"Did you really think that Phoebe or Oliver had some part in the theft?"

"No, of course not," Dorothy said. "But being suspected of something like this...well it's damn uncomfortable for anyone. What made the police decide it was an outside job?"

"Well, for one, they verified that the lock on my office and the one on the back door were picked."

"And since you and I and Phoebe and Oliver all had keys to the back door, they assumed we would have used them."

"Also the scratches on the sill over there told them that the contents of the time capsule were put in sacks and lowered by rope out the window to the parking lot. They didn't think a historian would have done that."

Dorothy's eyes followed Emily's pointing finger. "Those irreplaceable items were put in sacks and dropped out a window?"

"I know. The thought turns my stomach, as well."

"How many of them were in on it, do you think?"

"The police figure just one thief. That's why he or she didn't take the capsule. It was too heavy for one person to lift."

"But Brad carried the capsule up the stairs by himself."

"That he did," Emily said, her head shaking in wonder. "The police are still processing it for fingerprints and fibers. They estimate that, filled to the brim, it probably weighed two hundred pounds."

"Your man has some serious muscles," Dorothy said.

"*The* man is lucky he doesn't have some serious back problems."

"Em, when the police put the tap on my phone, I told them about Lester. I want you to, as well."

Emily knew how difficult it must be for Dorothy to say this. She didn't have the heart to tell her friend that she'd already mentioned Lester to Ed, and that the police had been unable to find him.

"Does your cousin know?" Emily asked.

Dorothy nodded. "She called me yesterday, asked if I'd seen him. He hasn't been in contact with her for more than a week. I filled her in on what happened. She called his home number. The phone just rang. She went over to his apartment. No one answered her knock."

Emily knew from her conversation with Ed that the police had done that, as well.

"She even called her ex," Dorothy continued. "He claims not to have seen Lester for days, but the louse could be lying to her. He and my cousin's divorce wasn't what you'd call amicable. I hope the police are right and this is a ransom matter. If the thief has any sense at all, he'll try not to damage what he's got."

"If he had any sense at all," Emily said, "he wouldn't have stolen the stuff in the first place. I can't believe whoever did this is dumb enough to think we'd reward the thievery by submitting to a ransom demand."

Dorothy shifted in her seat. "Dean Himlot came by the house on Sunday. He told me he's willing to put up the money to get the contents back. Dean said that he was going to go on TV and offer a reward for the safe return of everything. No questions asked."

"That's the same as paying a ransom."

"That's what I told him. But I understand his frustration. He really wants that letter from his ancestor. Those things mean so much to his family."

Emily wondered if it would still mean as much if he knew the shape it was in.

"Anyway, Dean apparently thought it over," Dorothy continued. "He called me this morning and told me I was right. Offering a reward wasn't the way to handle the theft. Have the police asked to put a tap on your phone, as well?"

She shook her head. "It's your name the press have as media liaison. They think this thief is an amateur who will contact you, or possibly Phoebe or Oliver. Your numbers are the only ones listed in the Historical Society's directory."

"Why an amateur? Because of how the artifacts were treated?"

"That and how clumsily the lock was picked on my door and downstairs. There were a lot of scratches. The police figure it took maybe ten minutes to break in. Experienced thieves can open antiquated locks like the ones we had in seconds.''

''I wanted to put new locks on the museum last year, but Oliver kept insisting that they would deface the historical architecture of the building,'' Dorothy lamented.

''Well, thanks to your quick work this weekend, we have good, reliable locks on all the doors now.''

''Yeah, I've closed the barn door good and tight now that there's nothing in the barn.''

Emily didn't like the uncharacteristic defeat in her friend's voice.

''Dot, you did not steal the stuff and you did not delay putting the right locks on the door. For heaven's sake, don't become one of those fools who blames herself for the actions of others.''

Dorothy sent her a tired look. ''You're right. Don't know what got into me. Guess this thing has been draining me more than I realized.''

''Maybe you should think about canceling your classes this week.''

''Can't,'' Dorothy said. ''My students are counting on me. And look who's talking. You're the one who's pregnant and shouldn't be stressed with this mess.''

''Don't worry about me. I've never felt better. Outside of a little queasiness now and then and the fact that I'm suddenly sleeping nine hours straight every night, so far this pregnancy has been a breeze.''

''You're lucky. From the moment I was pregnant with Holly, I felt so rotten, nothing I nor anyone else did was right. Ted took to calling me the witch of the West.''

''I don't believe that for a second, Dot.''

''Okay, maybe he didn't say the name out loud. But I'm sure he was thinking it.''

A knock came at the door. Emily called for whoever it was to come in. Josh pushed open the door. When he saw

Dorothy was there, his face went blank, as though he'd forgotten what he'd come to say.

"Yes, Josh?" Emily prompted.

"I...uh...swept the paths. Anything else?"

"Thanks, Josh, but that's all that needed doing."

He nodded, shut the door.

"I can't imagine what Holly finds to talk to him about," Dorothy said, shaking her head. "Is he doing Lester's old job now?"

"He's pitching in for a few days. There'll be a new, full-time maintenance person starting on Thursday."

"Just as well. You'll be losing Josh soon, I'm afraid. Since he's shown no interest in going to college, Oliver's created a job for him at the Smithson Pharmaceutical Company. Josh is dragging his heels about taking it, but I have no doubt Oliver will convince him it's his family duty to join the firm in the end."

"Josh told you this?" Emily asked.

"Josh?" Dorothy shook her head. "Please, Em, that boy can barely put two words together when he's around me. Oliver was the one who laid out his grandson's future. He came to me because he's worried about Josh and Holly spending so much time together. I've tried to tell him that Holly sees Josh only as a friend, but, as usual, Oliver isn't listening."

"Why does the thought that Holly and Josh might like each other bother Oliver?"

"Oliver considers himself above us. With the exception of Phoebe, most of the active members of the Society do not have pure enough blood for him. He pushed his son into marrying the daughter of a wealthy business associate from back east who, I understand, can trace her lineage to the *Mayflower*. He plans to do the same with Josh."

"Has he forgotten we're living in the twenty-first century?"

"We may be, Em. But Oliver's still back in the nineteenth. And sometimes the sixteenth."

"I never realized he was that much of a snob."

Dorothy got to her feet. "I'm all for family pride, but when it leaves someone with the impression that they're better than someone else, it's just another word for prejudice. How's the study of the skeleton coming?"

Emily held up the autopsy-room tape. "Findings so far are recorded on this. We got interrupted when Dr. Winslow was called to the E.R."

"Anything on its identity?"

"Nothing but general stuff like height and age at this point. I'll put the info into the computer as we go along so it becomes part of the time capsule's records. You haven't said anything to anyone about the guy being murdered?"

Dorothy shook her head. "The last thing we need is more negative publicity. The press would have a field day with that. See you later."

When her friend had left, Emily slipped the tape into a machine, rewound it and hit the play button. But instead of entering the information into the computer, she rested her elbows on her desk, put her chin in her hands and listened.

As the deep resonance of his voice filled the room, she remembered how fun and informative Brad had made the examination for her. How it felt being held so securely in the circle of his strong arm.

She was so deep in reminiscence that she gave a start when her telephone rang. Hitting the recorder's stop button, she picked up the receiver and answered with her name.

"The autopsy room is free for the next few hours," Brad said on the other end of the line. "Want to come down and resume our study of the skeleton?"

This was her opportunity to end their collaboration on a polite, friendly note. All she had to say was that her schedule was too busy and ask him to call her back with what he found.

But Emily couldn't get the image of Brad bending down to kiss the little girl in the ICU out of her mind.

"Are you still there?" he asked.

She clutched the receiver. "Yes."

"So you're coming?"

"Yes."

She stared at the phone a long time after she'd hung up.

Your decision was a perfectly reasonable one, Emily. You're the Historical Society's representative. It's important that you be present when the artifact is being examined.

She held out her hands. Steady as a rock. But she could feel the warning tremor in her epicenter.

EMILY WAS WEARING a sweater when she entered the autopsy room this time, wise woman that she was. Brad was disappointed that he wasn't going to be able to offer her the thick cardigan he'd purposely brought along.

That she had shown up at all was something of a relief considering her obvious hesitation over the phone. He understood she was worried about liking him.

"What will you look for today?" she asked as he turned on the tape.

"First, I think we'll try to estimate the skeleton's age a little more closely," he said as he picked up the magnifying glass. "For that, we need to check the spine."

He bent down and gave it a careful once-over. "If you'll look here, you'll see that the vertebrae are clean."

"Clean of what?" she asked, inching closer.

"There's no sign of the lipping and ridging that begin to show by the midthirties."

She was straining her neck to see but couldn't because she wouldn't let herself come close enough.

Brad straightened, laid the magnifying glass on the table and retreated a foot. "Go ahead and take a look."

Moving into position, she picked up the magnifying

glass. He pretended interest in another part of the skeleton while she studied the vertebrae.

Giving her lots of space was important now. The less romantic interest he projected, the more comfortable she'd feel around him. He intended to make her feel very comfortable.

"So what we have is a male between the ages of twenty-four and thirty-five," she said when she straightened.

"Right. Let me show you something else."

He held out his hand for the magnifying glass, allowing her to come to him. She stepped forward and placed it on his open palm. When she stepped back, she leaned on the table for balance.

With a loud crack, the skeleton's femur broke beneath her hand.

She let out an exasperated breath. "Please tell me that part of your examination of this skeleton requires one of the bones be broken."

"The bone shouldn't have broken that easily."

"You don't have to be nice. I was careless."

"I wasn't being nice, Emily. When I said that the bone shouldn't have broken that easily, I meant it. Something else is going on here."

Brad moved down the table to the cracked femur and bent over it with the magnifying glass. After closely examining the sharp, brittle edges along the break, he next passed the magnifying glass over the skeleton's mandible.

"What are you looking for?" Emily asked.

Before answering, Brad went back to the bones of the arms and legs, running the magnifying glass over them.

"There was a guy who came into the E.R. with a fractured forearm last year," he said. "Alec treated him. The guy had been playing football with his kid and fell. He kept insisting that his arm couldn't be broken because it had hardly touched the ground. Tests revealed he had massive but fragile bones."

"Are you saying that's what this skeleton has?"

He nodded. "The base of the skull and the cortex both show greater than average density and thickness. There's also evidence of several healed fractures in the long bones."

"What causes massive but fragile bones?" Emily asked.

"I'm not sure. I'll need to check it out in my reference books at home. Come on."

He was at the door before he realized she hadn't followed him. His enthusiasm for the medical hunt had caused him to forget that his apartment was definitely dangerous ground for a woman who wasn't comfortable around a man. This was going to take some finesse.

"You don't look very eager to find out," he said. "Have you tired of the chase?"

She was clearly conflicted. He knew she wanted to go with him. What she needed was to feel nonpressured, safe.

"If you think it would be a waste of time to watch me sift through medical texts," he said, "I can call you later with what I find."

He waited. She was still thinking.

"You might as well take the items found with the skeleton," he said as he picked up the evidence bag and handed it to her. "I doubt we'll be needing them anymore."

He started toward the door.

"You forgot the tape," she said.

"Oh, right."

He retraced his steps to the machine and ejected it.

"Where do you live?" she asked while he was unwrapping a new one to insert in its place.

"Five minutes away. Doesn't pay to live too far from the E.R."

He pretended to have trouble getting the new tape in the machine to give her more time.

"I'd like to come along," she said.

"Okay by me," he said as casually as he could, slipping in the tape and then hurrying to the door before she changed her mind.

EMILY HAD LEARNED the hard way that men were good at hiding things. But the place a guy called home was a clear road map to his personal habits as well as the inner workings of his mind.

Brad's apartment was strewn with body parts.

Greeting her at the front door was a life-size model of a skeleton, dangling from a metal hook. Plastic human torsos, legs, arms—all thick with muscle but stripped of skin—were mounted on stands and scattered about the small living room.

A dismembered hand—far too lifelike—reached menacingly over the top of the sofa. A human eye, at least five times life-size, stared at her unblinkingly from its position on a windowsill. And covering every inch of the walls were anatomical charts in raised relief, depicting bones, muscles and organs in every part of the human body.

Any serial killer worth his salt would have fallen in love with the place on sight.

Brad stepped over a model displaying the muscles and blood vessels of a dismembered foot on his way to the coffee table, nearly hidden beneath books. "Make yourself at home."

He had to be kidding.

Rummaging through the medical books, he eventually pulled one out and plopped down on a chair beside the table. He flipped through the pages, becoming immediately engrossed in the contents, seemingly unaware that she was still standing just inside the door.

Emily looked around to see where she might sit, should she choose to. Aside from the chair Brad occupied, the living room contained only a couch—littered with yet more medical books.

Off to one side was a cubbyhole of a kitchen. Off to
the other side, a short hallway leading to what was probably a bedroom and bath.

His head came up suddenly.

"Don't stand on ceremony, have a seat," he said, gesturing toward the uncomfortable-looking couch. "There
may be something to drink in the fridge if you're thirsty."

It was as good an excuse as any to get a closer look at
his kitchen.

"Want anything?" she asked as she carefully stepped
over the carnage on the carpet.

"Whatever's there," he answered distractedly.

Emily had met two kinds of men: those rare finds who
washed their dishes after use, and those who left them
scattered on tables and counters inviting swarms of bac-
teria to feast.

Brad fit into a whole new category. He had no dishes.
The cupboards in his tiny kitchen were completely bare.
His silverware drawer contained one knife. The only thing
that adorned the countertop was a roll of paper towels.

Inside the refrigerator she found six soft drinks, a gallon
jug of drinking water, and not one scrap of food.

Pulling out a soft drink for him, she decided she'd pass
on the selection.

His head was still buried in the book when she returned
to the living room. As her shadow crossed the page, he
looked up.

"Thanks," was all he said as she put the soft drink in
his hand. He took a quick swig and resumed his study.

She circled the coffee table, pushed some of the books
aside, then settled on the lumpy couch. Spying a volume
on pregnancy under the rubble beside her, she pulled it
out.

She was lost in a wonderful collection of photographs
that charted the development of a fetus inside its mother's
womb when she heard his book close.

"He had osteopetrosis."

"Isn't that common among the elderly?"

"You're thinking of osteoporosis. But you're on the right track. Osteopetrosis is also a bone disease."

She closed her book and put it aside.

"There are three forms," Brad went on. "The two varieties that appear in infancy and childhood are very serious, often fatal. The third is called tarda and appears in adulthood. That's what our skeleton had."

"So the tarda type isn't fatal?"

"Someone with osteopetrosis tarda can have a normal life span but will be plagued by brittle bones."

"That can fracture easily," she said, nodding. "Too bad we don't have the doctor's records for Courage Bay a hundred years ago."

"We may still be able to trace him through his disease. Osteopetrosis is both hereditary and very rare. Remember Alec's patient in the E.R. last year?"

"Are you thinking that man might be related to the skeleton?"

Brad came to his feet in a single, effortless move. "Wouldn't hurt to check it out. As you said, this is one of the few communities in Southern California where the founding families are still well represented. Come on. I need to go back to the E.R. and look through those records."

BRAD LED EMILY to the medical supply room where he knew an unoccupied computer terminal waited. He offered her the lone chair, but she insisted he take it since he was the one who was going to use the computer.

Opening the search area under patient records, he entered osteopetrosis and hit enter. Only one record came up. It was dated the year before.

As he read the information, he recognized the specifics of the case Alec had told him about.

"Legally, I can't show you someone else's medial record,'' Brad said. ''But if you were to just happen to glance at the name on the monitor…''

Emily was standing behind him. As she bent forward to read the information on the screen, she rested her hand on his shoulder.

The fact that she was touching him so unthinkingly told Brad that all his efforts to make her feel at ease were working. At the same moment he was congratulating himself, however, he was having to make a concerted effort to ignore how warm the room was getting.

''Leonard Landru was the patient,'' Emily said excitedly, her breath caressing his ear. ''He's Phoebe's grandnephew. Could it be that the skeleton is a Landru ancestor?''

Brad kept his face toward the screen.

''A very good possibility,'' he said. ''Didn't you say that the genealogy records of the founding families were kept at the Heritage Museum?''

As she straightened, her hand slipped from his shoulder. He couldn't decide if he was relieved or disappointed.

''Yes, we should check them next,'' she said. ''They could tell us if a Landru went missing right after the time capsule was buried.''

He glanced at his watch.

''When are you due back in the E.R.?'' she asked.

''Right after dinner.''

As he stood, she was shaking her head. ''You obviously don't have time for this. I keep forgetting how impossible your schedule is. I'll check out the genealogy records and let you know. Do you have an answering machine at home?''

She'd pulled out a pen and pad from her purse. He couldn't let her work on this without him. Every second he spent with her was important.

''What, after all my hard work, you're not going to let me be in on the finish?'' he asked.

"Are you suggesting I wait until you're off duty again?"

"Our skeleton has been unidentified for a hundred years. What's a couple more days?"

Those lovely arched eyebrows of hers were drawn into a frown. "You should be using the little free time you have to study for your board exams. I don't feel right about this."

No, she didn't. She was genuinely concerned for him.

"Don't worry about the exams, Emily. I'm not."

Her expression said she was anything but convinced.

There was only one thing left to do. Maybe it was risky, but he couldn't take the chance that she'd cut him off now.

"Let's grab something to eat while you think about it," he said.

Her head started to shake. "Maybe I should—"

"There's a place a few miles away," he interrupted. "Tonight they're serving a great roast chicken with olive-raisin sauce. For dessert, we can have brownies topped with whipped cream and berries. And if the chef takes a liking to you, everything's free of charge."

"I don't believe it."

"Good for you. A true scientist should never accept a testimonial as empirical evidence. Come along and test this out for yourself."

CHAPTER EIGHT

EMILY WAS CONFUSED when Brad pulled in front of a ranch-style home in an established residential neighborhood. She was surprised when they were greeted at the door by a gray-haired couple somewhere in their seventies who Brad proceeded to introduce as his good friends, Harry and Irene.

"Emily, it's nice to meet you," Irene said with a big smile. "I was so pleased when Brad called to say you were joining us for dinner."

"Yeah, we were beginning to wonder if Brad still liked women," Harry said, winking at Emily.

"I believe I mentioned that Emily and I are working together on the time capsule," Brad said.

Irene grinned, clearly amused he'd gone so quickly on the defensive. "He made us promise to be on our best behavior with you, Emily. We're not supposed to say or do anything to embarrass him. And here I was all ready to show you the skull-and-crossbones tattoo on my butt."

"And I was going to share this amusing anecdote with you about the time Brad got the chicken pox and I convinced him it was because he ate too much chicken so he wrote a letter to the AMA saying he'd solved the chicken-pox problem. All they had to do was stop feeding kids—"

"She gets it, Harry," Brad interrupted, shaking his head.

"Wish you could have seen him before he started to shave," Irene said. "That dark mop of hair and those pretty gray eyes were so cute when all he had was peach fuzz on his face.''

Out of the corner of her eye, Emily could see Brad looking at the ceiling. She chuckled. These were fun people.

"Everything's ready," Irene said. "Brad never has much time when he comes for dinner so we know the drill—sit down, shove the food in our mouths and hope to get a little conversation in between swallows. Harry will show you the way while I go grab the grub.''

She scooted off in the direction of the kitchen.

Harry slipped an arm through Emily's and led her into the dining room. "So you're the curator of the Botanical Gardens. I always wondered who the magician was who could get all those plants to grow. What's your secret?''

"You promise you won't tell?" Emily asked very seriously.

Harry held up his palm, ready to give his oath. "You have my solemn word.''

"I hum to them when they're tiny, and threaten to break out into song if they don't hurry up and grow. Works like a charm.''

Harry's eyes twinkled. "Well, no wonder nothing in my damn garden grows. All I've been doing is dumping horse manure on their heads.''

Emily laughed because it was impossible not to.

When they reached the dining room table, Harry held out a chair for her. "We watched the unveiling of the time capsule on TV. Irene has some friends with ancestors who lived in Courage Bay then. She was wondering if one of those unopened letters might have been from one of them. Damn shame about the theft. Do they have any leads?''

"Not so far.''

"Any ideas on why someone would take them?" Harry asked as he slipped onto the chair next to her.

"The police are convinced it's an opportunist thief who will ask for a ransom."

"Who's your number-one pick?"

"We had a maintenance man who was given the choice of quitting or being fired for petty theft. He still has his key to get into the gardens. I wouldn't put it past him to have used it."

Harry nodded in understanding. "What's up with the skeleton?" he asked as Brad sat across from him.

"The guy was shot in the head, Harry. Looks like someone tried to hide his murder by burying him with the time capsule."

"They didn't mention anything about his being murdered on TV," Harry said.

"It would have dampened everyone's enthusiasm for the celebration. Outside of Emily, me and now you, only the police and a member of the managing board of the Historical Society know. We'd like to keep it that way."

"Must have been exciting to be there in person when the cover of that sundial came off," Harry said. "When I saw you on your knees next to those old bones, it sure brought back memories for me."

"How do you mean?" Emily asked.

"Harry is the one who got me interested in forensic anthropology," Brad explained. "About a million years ago."

"He was this skinny little kid, Emily—no more than six—dressed as a skeleton, banging on our door one Halloween, trick-or-treating. Irene invited him in and put an apple in his hand while I showed him an old skull from one of my excavations. It had a mouth full of teeth that had been rotted away by cavities. I warned him that would happen to him if he ate all the candy he'd collected in his sack."

Emily chuckled. "You must have been *really* popular with the kids in the neighborhood."

"They called him crazy old Harry," Brad said.

"They still call him crazy old Harry," Irene chipped in as she came out of the kitchen. She had a large tray with four plates full of the promised roast chicken with olive-raisin sauce. The smell was mouthwatering.

"Soon as he got home from school every day," Harry continued, "he was knocking on our door, pestering the hell out of me and Irene. Only way we could get rid of him was if she filled him up with milk and fruit, and I fed him stories of my anthropological digs."

"By the time I was eight, he'd taught me the names of every bone in the body," Brad said. "He'd even taken me along on one of his expeditions."

"I had to," Harry confided. "The little bugger wouldn't stop hounding me until I did."

The rough affection on Harry's face couldn't have been greater if he'd been speaking of a favorite grandson.

Emily sliced off a piece of chicken and took a bite. "This is wonderful," she said with feeling.

Irene beamed at her. "You're getting extra whipped cream on your dessert brownie."

"Sounds like Harry and Irene unofficially adopted you," Emily commented later as Brad walked her to her car.

"I guess they did."

"Your parents didn't mind?"

"There was only my mother, and she was working long hours to support my older brother and me. Made her old and tired before her time."

"Where is she?"

"When I was sixteen, she fell asleep behind the wheel while driving home from her second job. Ran into a power pole. Never knew what hit her."

Brad's tone and expression had remained perfectly even, but Emily didn't doubt the sadness that dwelled behind those words.

"What happened to your dad?"

"He was one of those fathers who didn't want to stick around."

The emotion that lay beneath those cryptic words had a far different feel to it.

They'd reached her car, and she turned to face him. "Who cared for you after your mother died?"

"My older brother. He was nineteen at the time." Brad paused, a small smile lifting his lips. "Going on fifty."

"Harry and Irene never had any children of their own?"

He shook his head. "When I got old enough to understand, Harry explained that he'd had a bad case of the mumps when he was a kid that left him sterile."

So, that's why Brad had donated sperm. He wanted to give a great couple like Harry and Irene the chance to have children.

"I enjoyed meeting them."

"I'm glad you decided to come. I'll call you as soon as I can, and we'll pick up the investigation with the Landru genealogy."

She could have called him back as he started toward his car and told him no, but she didn't.

BEFORE BRAD SIGNED IN for his shift in the E.R., he made a stop up in the ICU. The moment he entered Samantha's room he saw the beautiful roses in the vase near her bedside.

"We finally found the little girl's father, Dr. Winslow."

Brad turned to the ward nurse. "Is he here?"

"On his way from Seattle. He doesn't know that she's in a coma yet. Only that she was badly injured."

Brad was glad he wasn't the one who was going to have to tell a father such news.

"Where did the flowers come from?" he asked.

"There's no card with them. But these roses have beautiful color and a fresh fragrance—not like the kind you get from florists. I'd say they were a gift from the curator of the Botanical Gardens.''

Alec's words replayed in Brad's mind. *"Emily brings flowers and potted plants to the patients who don't get visitors. Nice lady."*

Very nice.

EMILY WAS CAREFULLY brushing off the last of the dirt embedded on the dagger that was found near the skeleton when she realized there was a faint carving on the worn wooden handle. Holding it under the light, she thought it looked like a shield, but she couldn't be sure.

After taking several close-up shots with the digital camera, she carefully placed the dagger in a fresh protective bag. When she got back to her office, she'd scan the images she shot into the computer to see if she could enhance the detail.

She was affixing the label to the outside of the dagger's protective wrapping when she heard a voice behind her.

"I'm glad I finally found you."

Emily glanced over her shoulder to see Phoebe standing just inside the entrance to her workroom. "I didn't hear you come in."

"It's these new shoes of mine," Phoebe said, advancing toward her. "Cushioned soles. I'm startling everyone these days."

Yes, Emily could see that. Phoebe—a statuesque woman who generally walked around in the most conservative of pumps—was wearing thick-soled running shoes with iridescent pink stripes on the sides. They were a bit incongruous when combined with her crisply tailored navy-blue suit and perfect coiffure.

"I know they look ridiculous," Phoebe said. "But Fiona gave them to me and they're comfortable. So I'm wearing them."

"Good for you," Emily said, meaning it.

Phoebe's eyes went to the workbench. "Is that the dagger that was found with the skeleton?"

"I didn't realize you knew about the dagger."

"Ken told me he shot pictures of it in the pit."

"When are those pictures going to be available?" Emily asked.

"What he decides to use will be in the next newsletter. Let me see."

Emily held out the dagger. "I just finished cleaning it."

Phoebe's glasses were hanging from a chain around her neck. She set them on her nose as she took the see-through package from Emily's hand.

"It's just a plain dagger," she said after several minutes of close scrutiny under the light.

"I beg your pardon," Emily said with feigned indignation. "That is a hundred-year-old artifact."

Phoebe smirked as she handed it back.

"Would you like to see the coin?" Emily asked.

"Coin?"

"Ken didn't tell you about the gold coin?"

"Oh, the *gold* coin. Yes, let me see."

Phoebe took her time giving it a good look before handing the coin back. "Dorothy gave me my copy of the list of things you and Dr. Winslow cataloged from the time capsule. Thank you, Emily."

"You're welcome."

Phoebe distractedly fingered several items on the workbench. "What I said the other day… I really didn't mean it."

"Losing the contents from the time capsule was a hard blow for us all," Emily said simply.

"You have a forgiving heart. That's a nice quality. I had nice qualities myself once. I wasn't born a cold-hearted old spinster."

"No one sees you like that. I can't tell you how much I enjoyed reading your 'Dear Miss Phoebe' column, especially when I was a teenager. It was always full of good humor and gutsy advice.''

She waved away Emily's praise as though it annoyed her. ''I wanted to get married and have children. But, by the time I came of age, my brothers were already producing progeny, my mother was dead and my father decided I'd be of more use taking care of him and his household.''

''Hard for me to imagine a woman of your considerable strength of will going along with that.''

''He needed me. My father was a big, hearty-looking man who ran an important business. Everyone looked up to him. When he hurt himself, he'd hide away in the house in shame. I can't tell you the number of times he was laid up and I had to run and fetch for him because an arm or leg or both were broken and on the mend.''

''He had a lot of broken bones?'' Emily asked.

She nodded. ''Every time he banged his arm or leg, he seemed to break something.''

Sounded to Emily as if Phoebe's father had osteopetrosis.

''The older he became, the worse it got,'' Phoebe continued. ''I kept telling him to take it easy. But he was determined to project the image of health and vitality. Ended up causing us both a lot of pain. By the time he passed, I was pushing forty. My chance was gone.''

''You sure about that, Phoebe? I seldom see you without Ken these days.''

Phoebe laughed. ''Ken? Please. He's not only a decade younger, he's like the brother I never had to boss around.''

''I understand you've worked together a lot of years.''

''Work is the right description. There's nothing personal between us—nor could there ever be. It isn't only because I don't feel that way toward him. Some woman broke Ken's heart once upon a time and he's never gotten over it.''

''Really? Who?''

"Never found out. It happened before I met him."

"I never would have guessed."

"No, Ken isn't someone who most people picture harboring a grand passion. Probably because he comes across as too Milquetoast with that slender frame and good manners. Now a big, gruff man like Oliver is more the type to..."

"To?" Emily prodded when Phoebe's voice trailed off.

"Forget it," Phoebe said. "Not important."

Emily thought she might be getting the picture. "Oliver's only what—a year or two younger than you?"

"Don't be silly," Phoebe protested too fast. "All we do is fight. Besides, it's only been a couple of years since his wife died. And, anyway, I could never respect a man who..."

"Who what, Phoebe?"

"I think it might have been Oliver who took the time capsule artifacts."

Emily gave a start.

"I didn't want to say anything before," Phoebe continued. "I kept telling myself that I had to be wrong. Maybe I am. But if I'm not and by keeping quiet I'm helping him to..."

"Phoebe?"

"It was when we were at the reception that afternoon. I had just come out of the ladies' room when I overheard Oliver talking to someone on his cell phone. He had his back to me, but I distinctly heard him say that the only way they could be sure that the truth didn't get out was to take it."

"Take it," Emily repeated. "You think he was referring to something in the time capsule?"

"When the items were stolen, my first thought was the same as everyone else's. It had to be an outside thief. But later when no ransom demand was made and the particulars of that conversation came back to mind, I started to wonder...well...if he..."

"Have you talked to Oliver about this?"

"Of course not. If he did steal what was in the time capsule, he's certainly not going to admit it to me. And if he didn't, well, he'd never forgive me for believing he would."

So, Phoebe did care what Oliver thought of her.

"You could tell the police," Emily suggested.

"Last year I called the police when I saw a suspicious man looking into my neighbor's windows. The patronizing patrolmen who answered my call treated me like a pathetic old spinster who was so lonely for company she'd fabricate a suspect. When my neighbors were burglarized a week later, those same fools were back on my doorstep asking me to repeat my description. They hadn't even listened to what I'd told them."

"My brother would listen to you," Emily said.

"No, your brother will listen to *you*. Tell him what Oliver said. Just keep me out of it. Anyone at the reception might have overheard his cell-phone conversation. Ken was taking pictures. Dorothy was close by talking to Dean and Gerald. Holly and Josh were head-to-head in the corner. No one need know that I was the one who told you."

"If I approach my brother about information concerning a crime, he has to make an official report. That means he's going to need to know my source."

"You can't give him my name. If you do, I'll deny I told you anything."

Emily had a feeling she would, too.

"Have you thought about making an anonymous call?" she asked.

"I watch *CSI*. With all the gadgets they have today, they could not only trace the call but also do a voice recognition that would identify me. You're a smart woman, Emily. I know you'll think of something."

Emily couldn't imagine what that might be. She was just about to say as much, but when she looked around, Phoebe was gone.

"I'M GLAD YOU CALLED," Emily said when Brad identified himself. "I've been wanting to talk to you, but I didn't have your number."

That was the best news he'd had all day.

"Then let's rectify that right now," he said as he gave her his cell- and home-phone numbers. After giving her time to write them down, he asked, "You've learned something?"

Emily told Brad about Oliver's cell-phone conversation that Phoebe had overheard at the reception.

"I assume you've let Ed know?"

"Yes. He's going to try to keep Phoebe's name out of it and treat it as an anonymous tip. But what she said got me thinking. Remember when we looked at the map in the time capsule and the oak tree was shown outside the Smithson property line?"

"You checked with the county to see what was on the map filed in April of 1904 when the Town of Courage Bay was founded," Brad guessed.

"You sure you don't have some psychic in you?" she asked.

"Maybe you're rubbing off on me," he said, glad she couldn't see him smile. "So, do the maps match?"

"The original map is gone, along with a lot of others," Emily said. "There was an earthquake that destroyed the courthouse in the 1920s. However, a new map was redrawn soon afterward that shows the oak tree within the Smithson property lines."

"So the map redrawn in the 1920s doesn't match."

"There could be any number of reasons for that. But I found it interesting to learn that it was Edgar Smithson, Oliver's grandfather, who drew the replacement map of Courage Bay that was filed in the new county courthouse built soon afterward."

"Which means that Edgar Smithson could have re-drawn boundaries in favor of his family's holdings."

"And if Oliver knew, then he probably realized that the map from the time capsule would have exposed what his grandfather did. It's only a little over an acre of land, and in 1920 that part of Courage Bay wasn't commercially viable, so it wouldn't have been worth much."

"What's the value of that piece of land today?"

"Probably a couple million because of its location," Emily said.

"Sounds like a good motive to me."

"Still, this is all speculation. And it doesn't really fit with the person I know Oliver to be."

"How so?"

"Oliver is a gruff, hard man. But he's also a die-hard historian. I'm having a difficult time believing he'd handle the artifacts the way the thief did."

"He may have had to make a choice. Protect history or protect his family name."

"Good point," she conceded. "For a proud man like Oliver, there would be no doubt what his choice would have to be. Ed's going to do an official check on the land-transfer deeds from the time to see what they say."

"In the meantime, I can be there in thirty minutes to go over the Landru genealogy. Shall I bring a couple of Irene's leftover brownies?"

"Best calling card I can think of. I'll give your name to the security guard downstairs so he'll know to let you through."

EMILY HAD THE LANDRU genealogy records sitting on her desk when Brad arrived. In addition to a brownie, he handed her a carton of milk.

They sat across from each other, munching their brown-ies and sipping milk as they reviewed the several binders containing the very-well-documented family tree.

Each individual's birth, marriage, offspring and date

and cause of death were chronicled. Additionally, all born with the Landru surname had a few paragraphs written about them—sometimes lasting several pages—delineating their accomplishments.

There were quite a few Landrus in Courage Bay at the turn of the twentieth century. However, by April of 1904—when the time capsule was buried and the skeleton was buried with it—many family members had succumbed to tuberculosis.

"The only Landrus left at the time the capsule was buried were Frances, age sixty, Eugena, sixty-two, Norman, twenty-four, his father Randolph, fifty-six, and Randolph's wife, Eloise, fifty-three," Brad said. "And none of them is shown missing afterward."

"Hmm."

He looked over at her to see she was engrossed in something she was reading.

"What is it?" he asked.

"Norman and Serena Landru had a baby boy on November 1, 1904."

"Something about that obviously interests you."

"Remember when we went through the pictures from the time capsule and I came across Serena's?"

"Yes. You recognized her."

"On the back of the photograph it identified her as Serena Fitzwalter. In November she is shown as being married to Norman Landru and giving birth to their baby. It's only seven months later."

"I see," Brad said. "Does it show when their marriage took place?"

Emily flipped back a few pages to check the Landru marriages. "A week after the burial of the time capsule."

"Either their baby was premature or they made their decision to get married because it was on the way. How does Phoebe fit into the line?"

"Serena and Norman were Phoebe's grandparents. William, the baby born to them in November of 1904, was her father. According to their genealogy, all of the Landrus in Courage Bay today are descended from him. She told me she took care of him as an adult because he was always laid up with broken bones."

"Sounds like William had the osteopetrosis that got passed down to Leonard," Brad said. "And yet there is no Landru missing in April of 1904 according to these genealogy records."

"Serena was a Fitzwalter. Maybe she was the one who passed the osteopetrosis to her son."

"Do the Fitzwalters have their lineage as well documented?"

"All the founding families do. Their records are down in the basement archives where I got these. Won't take long to bring them up."

Emily stood and began to replace the Landru records in their storage container.

"I'll go with you," Brad said, rising to help her.

"Okay. But let's make a stop on the ground floor first. I want to show you something."

When they had descended the stairs to the first floor, Emily and Brad threaded their way through the museum's visitors to a large painting hanging on the far wall. The names listed below the portrait identified the solemn-faced people as Serena Fitzwalter Landru, her husband Norman Landru and their son, William, age nine. The family portrait was signed by the artist and dated 1914.

"Those are the faces that match the names on the genealogy records," Emily said. "I know serious decorum was the fashion of the time, but it's a shame their expressions are so emotionless. Makes it difficult to get a sense of who they were. I remember a painter, Alice Neel, saying that the subjects of her portraits assumed a pose that demonstrated what the world had done to them and their retaliation."

"If she had painted this portrait, I'd have to say that

her subjects had retaliated by assuming the poses of patients under anesthesia.''

Emily smiled. ''I wonder what it's like for Phoebe to walk into a museum and look up at a portrait of her ancestors.''

''I would imagine it beats walking into the post office and seeing them up on the wall,'' Brad said.

Emily was chuckling when a voice said from behind them, ''I'll second that.''

She turned to see Ken Kerr. ''I didn't realize you were here.''

''I just arrived,'' he said. ''Thanks for the list you made of the contents of the time capsule. It's going to be helpful when I put the newsletter together.'' He turned to Brad. ''How's the skeleton's identification coming?''

''We're making progress,'' he said.

''Whatever you can get me by press time will be appreciated,'' Ken said. ''Needless to say, I thought I'd have a lot more material for this issue than is currently available. Speaking of which, while you were cataloging the papers, Emily, did you get a chance to read any articles in the *Bulletin* that was dated the same day as the time capsule's burial?''

Ken's unexpected question caught Emily off guard. ''I did glance at a couple of things,'' she admitted, not able to meet his eyes.

''The fire at the Kerr family residence being one of them?'' Ken asked, surprising her by his bluntness.

''Yes.''

He smiled, surprising her even more. ''Don't let it bother you, Emily. It doesn't bother me. Looks like Gerald Fitzwalter is on his way over, and I doubt it's me he wants to see. Keep me informed on how the article is going.''

She nodded as Ken swiftly took his leave.

As Gerald approached, she smiled in greeting. ''Do you know Dr. Winslow?''

Gerald nodded to Brad. "We met at the Founders Day reception. Emily, I'd like to talk to you."

"Dr. Winslow and I are involved in something at present. Why don't you give me a call later?"

Gerald's eyes went to the storage container Brad held with the Landru genealogy prominently displayed on its identifying label. He frowned.

"Does it have something to do with the time capsule?"

"Gerald, what's on your mind?" she asked, careful to maintain a noncommittal tone.

"Winslow, you want to give us a minute here?" Gerald asked.

Brad looked to Emily. She nodded.

"I'll be admiring more of Courage Bay's founding families over here," Brad said as he gestured toward the portraits on the opposite side of the room.

When he'd stepped out of earshot, Gerald faced Emily. "Is Winslow the reason you're always turning me down?"

"Gerald, this conversation is finished."

When she started to turn away, he grasped her arm. "No, wait. Emily, I'm sorry. You're right. That was out of line."

She stared at his hand. He withdrew it from her arm.

"That's not what I wanted to say at all. Look, I need your help. There's a rumor going around that you were the one who was given the time capsule contents to catalog when Wayne had his stroke. Is it true?"

Emily nodded. "What is it you're after?"

"Did you read the letters from the crew members of the *Ranger?*"

Emily thought about her answer. "No, I didn't read the letters."

Her conscience was clear. Technically, that was true. She had tried to read one letter and had not been successful.

Emily couldn't tell whether Gerald was relieved or disappointed at her answer.

"You heard Dean Himlot was ready to offer a reward for the artifacts?" he said.

"I know he talked to Dorothy about it. I also know he's withdrawn his offer."

"He thinks there's something in them that's important."

"What does he think is in them?"

"Dorothy won't listen to me," Gerald said, ignoring Emily's question. "But she'll listen to you. Tell her that if she doesn't call the local TV news station and offer a reward for the safe return of the stuff on behalf of the Society, I'm going to offer it on behalf of the bank."

"What do you mean on behalf of the bank?"

"If I get the artifacts back, I'm digitizing them into the bank's computer, posting them on the bank's Web site and keeping them in the bank's vault."

"The artifacts belong to the Society, Gerald, not to your bank."

"The letter the mayor read said the contents of the time capsule belong to the citizens of Courage Bay. My family's bank was a part of this community decades before anyone even thought about organizing a historical society."

"Your bank is privately owned. These are public documents."

"What public, Emily? Far more residents of Courage Bay have accounts with my family's bank than are members of the Society."

"It's not a question of numbers, Gerald."

"Look, I'm not trying to be difficult about this. I'll go through the Society. But I'm not waiting forever. You can tell Dorothy that she has the weekend to act or I will."

He stalked out of the museum.

"Think he'll do it?" Brad asked from behind Emily. She turned to him. "You heard?"

"I've been two feet behind you from the moment he put his hand on your arm."

A jolt of pleasure shot through her.

"Sounds to me as though Gerald is worried that Councilman Himlot is going to learn something or destroy something," Brad said.

"I wonder which it is."

"Will Gerald offer the reward if Dorothy doesn't?"

"He isn't one to make idle threats. Remind me to call Dorothy when we get back upstairs. I doubt the police are going to be too thrilled with these proposed reward offers. Let's get those records."

THE BASEMENT OF the Heritage Museum was an enormous cavern with long rows of well-labeled storage files. It was also dim and chilly.

Knowing how Emily liked sunshine and fresh air, Brad had no doubt that she spent as little time down here as possible.

She led the way to the genealogy records and pointed to the area where the ones for the Landru family should go. As he stored them away, she started searching the labels for the Fitzwalters.

"What do you know about the history of the Himlot and Fitzwalter crewmen aboard the *Ranger?*" Brad asked.

"According to the story handed down, Gerald's ancestor was one of the sailors who kept an injured crewman afloat in the storm-tossed sea until the Indian boats arrived to take them safely to shore."

"And the Himlot crewman?"

"When the *Ranger* was struck by lightning, it was Dean's ancestor who wrenched a sail free and wrapped it around the burning clothes of a fellow crewman to put out the fire and save his life."

"And these stories were passed down through the generations?"

Emily nodded.

"Maybe Dean Himlot and Gerald Fitzwalter are afraid their ancestors' firsthand accounts aren't as heroic as the tales that have been a part of their family histories."

"I'd say that's the obvious explanation."

"Would they really be so concerned about a change in a story that happened more than a hundred and fifty years ago?"

Emily nodded. "A heritage of heroism is a big part of their image. Councilman Himlot comes from a long line of politicians who were elected on mottoes of selfless public service. And it's a trademark of the bank that Gerald inherited. During the Depression, when banks all over the country closed to protect themselves, the Fitzwalter Bank remained open and honored its depositors' requests to withdraw funds. They nearly went bankrupt doing it. Both men come from proud lines."

"How did Gerald's pride take it when you turned him down?"

"Why do you assume that happened?"

"It was pretty obvious from the way he looked at you, Emily."

Her attention went back to the rows of metal files. "I think he was mostly surprised. Women generally come on to him. Here are his family's genealogy records."

She picked up the large metal container.

"Let me carry that," Brad said. As he grasped the box, his hands slid over hers.

He held her eyes for a long moment, the container between them, before she slowly withdrew her hands from beneath his and turned toward the door.

Brad mentally patted himself on the back for his continuing restraint, all the while wondering how much longer he could count on it.

He took a couple of deep breaths before he followed her up the stairs.

CHAPTER NINE

ONCE BACK IN HER OFFICE, Emily left a message on Dorothy's answering machine about her conversation with Gerald. Then she and Brad got to work.

There were ten men with the Fitzwalter surname living in Courage Bay in 1904. Emily and Brad located four more males who were descended from the female line of previous generations and carried different surnames. All fourteen were still alive and accounted for in Courage Bay's genealogy records in 1905.

Emily closed the books and set them aside. "So, the skeleton was neither a Landru nor a Fitzwalter. This is disappointing."

"And surprising," Brad said.

"You really expected it to be an ancestor of Leonard Landru?"

"Especially after you told me about Phoebe's father exhibiting the same symptoms. You remember Occam's razor from your science courses?"

She nodded. "The principle that states when you have two competing theories, the simpler of the two is the better."

"And the simpler in this case is that the skeleton is William Landru's ancestor. It's beyond reasonable mathematical probability for two unrelated people to be carriers of the same rare hereditary disease and to be living in the same small community of Courage Bay a hundred years ago."

"I just thought of something," Emily said. "There may

be another way to identify who the skeleton is. Remember my telling you that Dot saved a lot of the early newspapers printed here in Courage Bay?''

"While she was writing her graduate thesis."

"You're a good listener."

"Depends on who's talking."

Emily looked away from the smile on his face. "Dot put them on microfilm and donated them to the Historical Society. The rolls are filed in an office down the hall. There could be some copies of the *Courage Bay Bulletin* from around the time the capsule was buried."

"What's in those newspapers that can help?"

"The weekly *Bulletin* listed births, deaths, marriages, people moving in and out. All the day-to-day events of a small community. Everyone knew everyone back then. If someone from the community went missing after the capsule was buried, there might be a story about it."

He was already on his feet. "Let's go see."

The room down the hall from Emily's office was small and crammed with old storage files. She located the right time period, pulled out a roll of microfilm and loaded it into the viewer.

"This appears to be what Dot was able to salvage of the newspaper for the six months before the time capsule was buried and the eight months after. A lot of issues are missing, but we still might find something useful," she said. "You may have the honor."

He slid two chairs in front of the viewer and waited until she took one before sitting next to her. "I haven't used one of these antiquated things since I was a kid."

"You'll want to be careful," Emily said. "The knob is a little loose."

"Yes, I'd already noticed."

The first copy of the *Courage Bay Bulletin* from October 1903 came into view on the microfilm reader. The newspaper was four pages long and six columns wide with an eclectic mix of ads and stories, both national and local. Brad slowly advanced the film.

"This story is about the upcoming burial of the time capsule," he said, pointing to the bottom right of the screen.

Emily eased closer to read the reference. It said that the citizens were being encouraged to submit what they would like to have included. All items except the mayor's letter and the final newspaper would be boxed the week before.

> To coincide with the filing of the Charter, the newly elected mayor and eleven other men will be given the task of digging the pit to accommodate the capsule a week before its burial. Those wishing to apply for the honor should do so in writing and will be selected by a means to be determined.

Emily was so caught up in the history unfolding within the words that she was startled by the sudden jerk of the screen, followed by a soft curse beside her.

"What's wrong?" she asked.

Brad said nothing, simply stared at the knob that had broken off in his hand.

That was when she realized she'd leaned over so far to read the screen that she was nearly in his lap.

Emily quickly withdrew and got to her feet. "It'll be easier and faster to go through these if I print out the issues. That way you can read through half while I take the other half."

He nodded.

"While I print, you might want to clear off that table near the window so we have a place to lay them out," she suggested.

He got up and went to tackle the task.

BRAD WAS TAKING DEEP BREATHS as he stacked the papers and pamphlets on the surface of the table. He was only too aware that Emily had rubbed against him without intent. But his body still hadn't gotten that message.

Forcing himself to concentrate on the pamphlets in front of him, he saw they described historical items. From what he could tell, they were handouts given to visitors so they would understand the history behind each of the paintings and artifacts on display in the main rooms of the Heritage Museum.

One in particular caught Brad's eye. It featured a dramatic painting of the *Ranger,* on fire in the harbor, along with a vivid description of the sailors' heroism and the rescue by the Indians. According to the brochure, the painting and description had been created in the 1930s.

"Caught the history bug?" Emily's voice asked from behind him.

He faced her, only then becoming aware that the noise of the printer had stopped. She was holding the finished pages in her hands.

"Is there an antidote?" he asked.

"None I'm aware of."

"Who wrote this history about the rescue of the *Ranger*'s crew?" he asked, pointing to the circular.

"Some early historians, from the accounts given to them by descendants. The drawing of the ship was an artist's vision gleaned from those same accounts."

"These were done twenty-six years after the burial of the time capsule, more than eighty years after the sinking of the ship."

"Yes. The letters in the time capsule would have gone a long way toward verifying the accounts of that day. I still get a thrill every time I remember that I held the actual letters written by those survivors. Probably seems strange to you."

"Not at all. In that moment you felt in touch with them."

She looked at him with warmth. "In the meantime,

these newspapers should be interesting to read. Dot salvaged twenty out of the possible thirty-four copies from the eight months following the burial of the capsule. Let's each take ten and concentrate on headlines that mention missing residents.''

''You've never seen these before, I take it?''

She shook her head as she handed him the copies. ''To be honest with you, I forgot they were even here. Feel free to mark up what you think might be important.''

As he was reaching for a highlighter, he couldn't miss the look of disbelief spreading across her face as she glanced at her first copy of the *Courage Bay Bulletin.*

''What is it?'' Brad asked.

''This news item on the first page. Says here that a navy lieutenant was dismissed from service by a court of inquiry for conduct unbecoming an officer when it was discovered he reneged on his promise to marry a woman. Looks like in those days a man had to stand by his word or suffer the consequences.''

''Was he someone from Courage Bay?'' Brad asked.

''Good question. Let me see if it says.''

As she read further, he found himself staring at the sunlight from the window swimming through her hair.

''No, this took place back east,'' she said. ''It's a national news item. Now I'm not going to let anything else sidetrack me. On to missing persons.''

Time he turned his attention to the newspapers in front of him, as well. Brad was on the back page of the first when he came across an article that caught his attention.

''Emily, listen to this.

'''Local man still missing, feared drowned. L. P. Norland has not been seen by friends or neighbors for two weeks. His sister went to his home last Sunday where she found the door unlocked and no one inside. Although Mr. Norland's personal belongings appeared to be undisturbed, Mr. Norland himself was nowhere to be found. He was last seen walking along the beach in a state of considerable inebriation and is feared to have been drowned.'''

"What's the date on the newspaper?" Emily asked.

"Two weeks after the burial of the capsule. It's the right time frame. There was nothing about any missing people in the previous newspaper—the one issued the week after the burial."

"The ten copies you have are the ones Dot salvaged that immediately follow the time capsule's burial. I have the next ten that follow them. Do any of your other copies mention if they found Norland?"

Brad did a quick check of the headlines for the rest of the issues he held. "This *Bulletin* is dated five weeks after the burial. There's no mention of Norland, but there is an article on the front page you might like to see."

She scooted her chair closer but, he noted, she was careful not to touch him this time. They silently read the article together.

Cox's Elixir Wagon Found in Mountain Ditch

A group of local loggers reported yesterday that they were gathering firewood in a mountain ditch when they found the smashed remains of the familiar Cox's Elixir Wagon that spent several months in this vicinity last winter. R. C. Cox, the inventor and purveyor of Cox's Miracle Elixir, left town five weeks ago to return to his home in San Francisco. It is suspected that as he traveled through the mountain pass, he was caught in a windstorm that forced his wagon off the road. Since neither Mr. Cox nor his team was found, he is presumed to have continued the rest of his journey on horseback.

"Technically, that makes two men unaccounted for," Emily said. "Might be a good idea to read through the rest of these to see if we have any more."

Emily went back to her copies, and they scanned the remaining issues of the *Courage Bay Bulletin* that followed the burial of the time capsule. They found no further references to Norland or Cox, nor any other reports of missing men.

"If they did find their bodies, it could have been in the death notices of the issues of the papers we're missing," Brad said.

"Frustrating not to have the whole picture," Emily agreed.

"Speaking of pictures, is there any chance we have some photos of these men from the time capsule? I seem to remember that Norland name. Might have been one I entered into the computer when we went through the photographs."

"Would it help if we did have pictures?"

Brad nodded. "There's a computer program that can superimpose the picture of someone's face over the skull of a skeleton and make an identification."

Her voice rose excitedly. "You have this program?"

"No, but Harry does. He's a top-notch forensic anthropologist. Even the Smithsonian has called him in on cases. I've watched him work the program a number of times. Amazing what it can reveal."

Emily was already out of her chair. "I'll be right back."

When she returned a couple of minutes later, her arms were full of photographs he recognized from the time capsule.

"Those aren't the originals," Brad guessed from the fact that they were neither wrapped nor boxed.

She shook her head. "The originals are stored in the basement under lock and key. When I scanned the pictures into the computer, I put numbers in the upper right corner to match your entries in the computer. This is a set of the printed copies and the legend for them."

Placing the pictures on the table, she picked up the list

and quickly looked through it. "We do have an L. P. Norland. He's in picture number sixty-one."

Brad located the photograph and pulled it out of the pile. "This is a group shot in front of a church. Which one is Norland?"

"Top row, third one from the left," Emily said as she referred to the legend.

Brad noted that Norland was taller than the men he was standing with. That fit with the skeleton's above-average height. He sported a full mustache, as did all the men in the picture, clearly a fashion of the time. Guessing his age wasn't easy.

"Could it be him?" Emily asked.

"Hard to tell. Harry's computer program can enlarge his image and get rid of the facial hair. That will help us see if there's a match to the skeleton. Is Cox listed?"

She ran her finger down the names. "I don't see him, but I remember a picture of a traveling salesman. Try number eighty-seven. It's labeled Elixir Wagon."

Brad located the photograph with eighty-seven in the upper right-hand corner. "This is it, all right. Cox's Miracle Elixir is printed on the wagon."

She moved to his side to look at the photo. Standing in front of the team of two sturdy horses was a brawny man. He appeared to be somewhere between twenty and thirty but it was hard to tell how tall he was since there were no other people in the picture.

"He could be our skeleton, as well," Brad confirmed. "Maybe there's something in the earlier issues of the newspaper that will give us more information about these men."

She nodded and quickly divvied them up.

On the second issue he read, Brad found an ad in the upper left column that he knew could be important.

"Look at that," Brad said as he slipped the newspaper over to her and pointed at the column.

She read the ad.

Cox's Patented Miracle Elixir. The perfect tonic for women. Mrs. D. F. Jones, of San Francisco, suffered for six months with frightful episodes; but writes that a half bottle of Cox's Miracle Elixir wholly cured her in two hours.

"I wonder what was so frightful about her episodes," Emily said. "And what was in the elixir."

"Probably fifty percent alcohol. Most of these so-called elixirs were full of it. After half a bottle, Mrs. Jones was probably so soused she wouldn't have even remembered she'd had a frightful episode."

"Be interesting to check what was in the stuff," Emily said. "I wonder if there's a way to access the old patents through the Internet."

"Even if there is, the so-called 'patent medicines' peddled by salesmen of that time rarely had patents on them. The term was loosely used as a way to suggest that the product was sanctioned in some way or possessed a potent secret formula."

"So these guys were your basic snake-oil salesmen?"

"Snake oil would have been a lot healthier than the junk they put in their cure-alls. Their testimonials were always made-up. You'll notice that this one is from a woman in San Francisco with a common name like Jones. Very unlikely anyone in Courage Bay would be able to check the facts."

"What's the date on the newspaper where that ad appears?" Emily asked.

"January." Brad did a quick check of the other issues of the *Bulletin* in front of him. "That's the earliest one. I have another in February."

Emily glanced through her batch. "I have one of his ads appearing in a March issue and another in April, right before the time capsule burial, so he was still in town then. Looks to me like this traveling salesman stayed in the southern part of the state for the winter peddling his wares before heading north in the spring."

"Guy wasn't dumb. Better weather down here."

"Seems odd he stayed in Courage Bay for three months, considering how small the community was. I would think that a traveling salesman would want to be in town only long enough to sell his stuff and then move on."

"He might have run his ads in the local newspaper of several Southern California communities and then traveled among them during the winter."

"That would make more sense," Emily agreed.

They went back to reading.

"I've found Norland," Emily said after a few minutes. "Or, rather, his wife. Mrs. Lawrence P. Norland succumbed in December of 1903 to a fever, according to the death notices."

"If he was despondent over her death that would explain why Lawrence was seen drinking on the day he disappeared."

"In which case he may have walked into the sea and drowned. But what could have happened that would have caused him to be shot and dumped in the pit with the time capsule?"

"Only crime I've read about in these newspapers is a resident being jailed for being drunk and disorderly," Brad said.

"I know I joked about the Wild West when we saw the skeleton's injuries. But the truth is, I don't remember reading anything in the Historical Society's records about Courage Bay having a problem with violent crime. It was still a peaceful little town during the early part of the twentieth century."

"That's definitely how the mayor's letter made it sound," Brad said. "How did he put it? 'A beloved world, swept with sunshine.'"

"And people protecting the good land and one another," Emily added.

Down the hall, the telephone in Emily's office rang. She left to answer it. When she came back a moment later, her face had lost its color.

Brad stood. "What is it?"

"They've found Lester, the missing maintenance man."

"Is he talking?"

"He's dead," Emily said.

ED WAS WAITING FOR THEM in front of an apartment building when Emily and Brad arrived.

"This is his girlfriend's place," Ed explained. "Her story is that she was out of town for the past week, didn't even know Lester was here. When she came home about an hour ago, she found him lying on the kitchen floor."

"How did he die?" Brad asked.

"The kitchen's a mess with broken dishes and other debris all over the floor. There's blood on the back of his head. Looks like a fight. He's been dead a few days. Coroner's going to have to do an autopsy."

At that moment, the bagged body was carried out the front door on a stretcher.

Emily looked away. Brad's warm hand circled hers and held it securely.

"I have to tell Dot," she said after a moment.

"A detective is already with her," Ed explained.

A crowd of curious onlookers was beginning to form on the lawn in front of the apartment building. Gesturing to Brad and Emily to follow him, Ed made his way to his unmarked car at the curb. He opened the back door and pulled out an evidence bag.

"Em, you recognize this?"

While Ed held up the evidence bag, Emily's eyes scanned the single piece of paper within. "I can't be sure but it sounds like one of the letters that Oliver read at the

Founders Day Ceremony—the one written by the gardener. She's drawn a sketch and is describing the native plant she found that helped relieve her headaches.''

''Yeah, that's what I figured. We discovered a long rope and several burlap bags in the pickup in the garage. Looks like you were right, Em. Lester was the thief.''

''Where are the rest of the contents of the time capsule?'' she asked.

''This last page of the gardener's letter is all we found. It was on the floor underneath his body. If he's hidden the rest, doesn't look like he stashed it here. We'll know more when we have a chance to process the scene, determine how he died and check the girlfriend's story.''

''How long will that take?''

''Hopefully, no more than a day or two. I'll need to retain this letter as evidence. Keep Lester's involvement in the theft and other particulars to yourselves until we release the information.''

''When will the news be picking this up?'' Emily asked.

''Right about now.'' Ed pointed behind them. A local KSEA TV news van was pulling up to the curb. ''So unless you want to get grilled, I suggest you two make yourselves scarce.''

Emily understood now why Ed had told them to park around the block. She and Brad unobtrusively made their way toward their cars.

''I'm still wondering what the tie-in is to the skeleton,'' Brad said.

''You definitely think there is one?''

''All I know is that someone went after it, as well. In order to use Harry's computer program to try to identify who the skeleton was, I'm going to need to borrow your digital camera to take pictures of the skull. If there's a lull in the E.R. tonight, I'd like to slip down to the morgue and take the pictures.''

''When do you report in?''

He checked his watch. "Little over an hour."

"You have to eat before then?"

"Skipping a meal won't hurt me. I'd rather use the time to pick up the camera."

"The digital camera is at my place. It's a ten-minute drive. I can fix you something to eat before you head in for your shift."

EMILY LIVED IN A WELL-KEPT 1930s style bungalow about a block from the beach. The inside was full of sunlit windows, built-in cabinets, spotless hardwood floors and soft upholstered furniture. It exuded welcome and warmth.

She said she'd be back in a minute and disappeared down the hall.

Brad walked over to the large picture window that overlooked the backyard. She'd turned the small area into a private, secluded garden shaded with white trellises covered by blooming climbers. Paths of clover intersected colorful flowers, weaving their way to the corners where palm trees swayed in the ocean breeze.

When she returned to the living room, she carried the digital camera.

He stepped forward to take it from her. "Nice," he said gesturing about him. "I'm beginning to wonder why you didn't run screaming when you saw my place."

"Yes, I've been wondering about that, as well," she said with a faint smile.

"I don't live there like you live here, Emily."

"Where do you live?"

"Good question. I suppose you could say the E.R. has been my home for a long time now."

"Well, if you're going to make it *home* in time for your next shift," she said glancing at her watch, "I'd better get started on dinner."

He followed her into a kitchen of cream countertops and light maple cabinets. The view out its window revealed another peaceful alcove of plants.

In fifteen minutes flat she had produced a fresh green salad, broiled salmon seasoned with lemon juice and dill, steamed mixed vegetables, cherry tomatoes, and a cup of mandarin orange and banana slices sprinkled with fresh walnuts for dessert.

They ate side by side at the kitchen counter in a companionable slience. When he was finished, Brad rested back on the bar stool, downing the last drop of the rich coffee that she'd brewed for him but hadn't touched herself.

He exhaled in satisfaction as he set the cup on its saucer. "A woman who can cook. One of my favorite kinds."

She opened her mouth to say something, then closed it, having clearly reconsidered.

"What?" he asked.

"It was on the tip of my tongue to ask what were your other favorite kinds when I suddenly realized that was a setup line, specifically designed to get me to inquire further."

He smiled at her. "You're a very intelligent woman, Emily Barrett. Another one of my favorite kinds."

She got to her feet and began to collect the dishes, sending him an amused glance. "You're a very sneaky man, Brad Winslow. One of my least favorite kinds."

As she headed toward the dishwasher, he gathered the rest of the dishes and followed her.

"What's your favorite kind of man?" he asked as he placed the dishes on the counter while she stacked the dishwasher racks. "Let me guess. A botanist who's a history buff on the side?"

She turned to face him. "The kind who has a heart. Thank you for what you did today."

"Emily, I didn't do anything."

"When they brought Lester's body out."

He nodded in tardy understanding as he stepped forward and took her hand for the second time. "You're welcome."

Her eyes darted nervously to the clock on the wall. "Shouldn't you be on your way?"

He looked at her with no attempt to hide what was on his mind. "Should I?"

She took a very deep breath. "The invitation tonight was for dinner only."

He leaned forward until he was close enough to smell the sweet scent of her hair.

"I know. But there's something you need to know. Emily, I've been wanting to do this for so very long," he said as he pressed his lips into the hollow of her cheek. "And this."

He kissed her longer and harder than he had intended or was wise. But after days and nights of thinking about it, he couldn't help himself. Especially since she was cooperating fully. The second he could snatch at a semblance of sanity, he forced himself to pull back.

She drew in a shaky breath. "Brad, I didn't want this to happen."

He rested his forehead against hers. "I know. But I'm not going to lie to you. I'm happy as hell it has."

Her face was flushed and beautiful and the last thing he wanted was to leave her. But he was due at work, and if he stayed any longer, he was going to do something rash.

"I'll call you tomorrow," he said.

He scooped up the digital camera on his way out.

Dear Sprout,

I promised to tell you some more about your biological father and I guess this is as good a time as any since I can't think about anything but him tonight anyway.

He was asked on his sperm-donor questionnaire what he thought the most important quality a human being could have. He said empathy for others.

Someone died today, and, although I would never have called that person a friend, I felt bad. He instinctually knew and took my hand. And suddenly I didn't feel bad anymore.

On his questionnaire, he agreed to meet with you after you turn eighteen and answer your questions if you wish. He wrote that he is a firm believer that a loving home is what truly shapes a child, but, as a doctor, he's also aware that knowing your genetic information could be crucial to your health.

I hope you will take him up on this offer and meet with him when the times comes. You will not be disappointed.

Goodnight, my little love.
Mom.

EMILY SET HER BOOKMARK in place, put the journal away and turned off the light, knowing sleep was very far away.

She could still feel his lips on hers.

BRAD WANDERED OVER to the newborn unit to look at the babies.

He and Julie had talked a lot about having children. Since her death, he hadn't given them another thought. His commitment to medicine had become his total focus. He'd been content to immerse himself in its demands.

But during this past week as he thought about his baby on the way, he found himself becoming curiously, surprisingly elated.

Look at all those little squirming bundles of new life.

"You're smiling, Brad. Sure you're feeling all right?"

He turned to see Alec beside him. "Funny."

"The nurse told me I'd find you up here. I didn't believe her."

Brad turned, started down the hallway. "What, a guy can't take a walk to get the kinks out when we get a lull?"

"I understand your visiting the little girl in the coma, Brad. But they tell me this detour to the newborn section has become a regular stop with you, as well. The hospital staff's beginning to talk."

"Yeah? And what are they saying?"

"That your biological clock must be ticking."

Brad looked over to see a grin spreading wide on his friend's face. He should have known. Courage Bay Hospital's staff took almost as much pleasure in passing gossip as they did in saving lives.

"You didn't just come up here to deliver that dumb line. What can I do for you?"

"There's a Josh Smithson in the E.R. to see you."

It took a moment before the name registered with Brad. "Lanky? Late teens? Mostly shaved dark hair?"

"That describes him and most of them. He won't tell me what's wrong. Says it's a personal matter."

Brad nodded as they headed back to the E.R. The morning had quieted down after a hectic night. With any luck, he could tend to Josh's problem quickly and get back to completing the stack of patient records that waited for him. Seemed that half of his time was spent filling in charts.

Out in the reception area, Josh was standing at the nurse's desk, looking ill at ease. Brad beckoned him into an unoccupied examining room and closed the door.

"Have a seat, Josh. Tell me what's wrong."

Josh shook his head as Brad gestured toward a chair, resting his backside against the examining table instead. "I'm not sick."

"Okay. Why did you come?"

"I saw you helping Dr. Barrett with the time capsule and I thought... I mean when I tried to talk to her...well, I couldn't because Dr. Mission was there, and Holly says she's really stressed. And my grandfather likes her so telling him is out.''

Brad mentally waded through the quagmire of Josh's sentence, finding himself confused. ''Why don't you tell me what's bothering you,'' he suggested.

''I was driving by the hospital last Saturday night. That's when I saw her.''

''Saw who, Josh?''

''Phoebe Landru. She was turning into the parking lot near the ambulance entrance.''

''She was here at the hospital?''

''Yeah. I thought maybe she was visiting a friend or something except the visitor parking is on the other side. And then I heard the next day that someone had tried to steal the skeleton. I was going to tell Dr. Barrett, but Dr. Mission was with her, and…''

''And you thought the news would stress her,'' Brad finished for him. ''You think that Phoebe Landru might have tried to steal the skeleton?''

He shrugged. ''I don't know.''

''Why would she do that, Josh?''

''I don't know.''

''You sure it was her you saw that night?''

''Yeah. She drives this totally ancient 1932 two-tone DeSoto. Nothing else like it around.''

Brad remembered seeing the distinctive car in the parking lot at the Heritage Museum.

''So, you'll like check to see if she was visiting someone or something?''

''Yes, Josh. I will. Thanks for telling me.''

He shrugged and started toward the door.

''Josh?''

He stopped, turned.

''About what time was it when you saw Phoebe turn into the hospital parking lot?''

''Close to seven-thirty.''

The time fit. It was right around seven-thirty when Albert surprised the person trying to break into the morgue.

Even so, Brad couldn't imagine the woman he'd met sneaking into a hospital morgue trying to steal a skeleton.

Still, it might not hurt to check it out.

CHAPTER TEN

EMILY WORKED DILIGENTLY on the computer trying to clarify and amplify the image on the handle of the dagger. It was a slow process—eliminating some pixels here, emphasizing others there, and then adding contrast.

Finally, she was able to produce a faint outline of a black lion on a white shield with an elongated helmet above.

She recognized it immediately as a family's coat of arms. But she had no idea whose. Saving the image to the computer file, she printed out a copy of the family crest and went in search of the heraldry book in the library downstairs.

Holly had a part-time job filling in for the Society's librarian three days a week after school. She handled all of the computer work that Mrs. Hanna staunchly refused to become involved with.

Emily found Holly sitting in front of the computer at the checkout desk when she arrived.

"I'm sorry about Lester," Emily said after greeting her.

"Don't sweat it," Holly said. "I hardly knew him, and, quite honestly, what I did know I didn't like. Now the police tell us he stole the time capsule stuff. The loser went looking for trouble and found it. I just feel bad for his mom and mine."

"I've been trying to reach your mom."

"She's going to call you today," Holly said. "She's been looking after Lester's mom and swamped with phone calls ever since reporters showed up. Is it true what they're saying about his being murdered?''

"I don't believe the police know what happened.''

Josh entered the library then and came over to the desk. He nodded a greeting at Emily. "I swung by your school earlier, Hol, but they said you'd cut your afternoon classes.''

Emily stared at Holly in surprise. This straight-A student cut school?

"They were grilling me about Lester,'' Holly answered in response to her look.

"What do you mean, 'grilling'?''

"The guy was my second cousin and they were treating me like we were joined at the hip. They kept asking me questions like, did he show me the time capsule stuff he stole? Did I know who his accomplice was that killed him? I never realized before what being related to a criminal does to a family.''

"The police only mentioned Lester had been sought for questioning in the case of the stolen time capsule contents,'' Emily said.

"Everybody knows that's police code for he did it and skipped,'' Holly said.

"Still, the police said nothing about his being murdered.''

"Didn't you see the TV news this morning?'' Holly asked.

Emily shook her head.

"A neighbor of Lester's girlfriend was interviewed,'' Holly said. "He claimed to have gotten a look through her kitchen window before the police came. According to him it was obvious Lester had been in a fight with someone who killed him.''

No doubt Ed was delighted with that turn of events.

"You want me to reshelve books or something?'' Josh asked.

"Yeah, if Emily doesn't need you,'' Holly said.

"He's all yours," Emily said.

"Not really," Oliver's gruff voice said from the doorway.

Emily started. From the startled looks on both Holly and Josh's faces, she knew she wasn't the only one who hadn't realized Oliver was listening to their conversation.

"Josh, I need to see you outside," Oliver said.

"I'm supposed to be working now," Josh said.

"That's one of the things I want to see you about," Oliver said. "Outside please."

Oliver wasn't really making a request. Josh shuffled toward the door and left with him.

"I hear Oliver is worried Josh is sweet on you," Emily said.

Holly snickered. "He's clueless. Josh and I are just friends. Although Oliver is right about Josh wasting his time with these part-time jobs around here. He should be in college. He can write."

"I had no idea," Emily said, surprised.

"He doesn't talk about it because his father and grandfather give him so much grief every time he does. But he gives me his stuff to read. The stories remind me of Isaac Asimov's sci-fi thrillers. They're good, full of heart. If I had relatives like Josh's, I'd disown them."

"You lucked out."

"Except for Lester. I know you didn't come down here to talk about him or Josh. Can I help you find something?"

"The heraldry book."

"Two rows down, top right shelf."

"I'm impressed. Do you have the placement of all of the volumes memorized?"

Holly smiled. "Only the heavy ones I curse every time I have to lift them."

Chuckling, Emily went in search of the book. She didn't find it two rows down on the top right shelf. Or anywhere else in that section of the library. She returned to the desk.

"Any chance the book is checked out?" she asked.

Holly checked the library's database. "The heraldry book should be on the shelves," she said. "Let's go see if it's misfiled."

Together they searched all the shelves in the small library. The book wasn't there.

"Mrs. Hanna probably took it home to do research," Holly said. "She's done this kind of thing before. I wish she'd tell me so I could update the database. Anyway, I can help you with a heraldry search. We don't need the book. They have all that family crest stuff on the Internet. What name are you looking for?"

"I don't have a name," Emily said, as she followed Holly back to her desk, "only a partial image of a crest."

"Oh," Holly said. "Now that's going to be a lot harder."

"Maybe not. This would be a Courage Bay family crest. Do you have a listing of all the family surnames of residents from the early twentieth century?"

"That kind of information is what this library is all about," Holly said as she took her seat in front of the computer and pulled up a file. She printed it out with a click of a key.

"They're alphabetical. Is that how you want me to pull up the family crests?"

"As good a way as any," Emily said as she unfolded the paper she'd brought with her containing the faint image of the shield, lion and helmet and laid it next to the keyboard. "This is the one I'm trying to find."

Holly took a quick glance at the image before she started through the list. The first family crest she pulled up on her screen had a shield and a lion, but varied significantly from the image on the dagger.

Emily's cell phone rang. It was Ed, but she was having

trouble hearing him so she told him to hold on and stepped outside the museum.

Out of sight on the other side of a thick hedge she could hear Oliver's voice.

"I don't want you hanging around her, Josh. Her cousin's a thief! I would think that you'd have more pride in your name and heritage than to descend so low as to associate with such a family."

"Holly's not her cousin," Josh protested, his voice barely audible.

"Damn it, boy, you're not listening to me. Josh, where are you going? Josh, come back here!"

The hedge rustled and Emily quickly retreated behind it in time to see Josh hurrying past her toward the Botanical Gardens. He was clearly too upset to notice her. A couple of seconds later she heard Oliver's footsteps stomping toward the parking lot.

She came out from behind the hedge cover and descended the front steps of the museum in time to see Oliver get into his car, slam the door and drive off.

"I'm sorry, Ed," she said as she put the cell phone to her ear. "An unavoidable delay there. What was it you were saying?"

"The Smithson family acquired that acre around the old oak tree at a public auction in June of 1904," Ed said over the phone. "Transfer of land was legit. When a Smithson redrew the map for the county that was supposed to duplicate the one filed at the time the community was officially formed, he either made an honest mistake or didn't think it mattered because the timing was so close."

"Out of curiosity, who was the previous owner?"

"Kerr."

The Smithsons must have acquired the land right after the fire. Legitimate transaction or not, to Emily's mind the acquisition lacked a certain sensitivity.

"Did you get a chance to talk to Oliver about the conversation that Phoebe overheard?" Emily asked.

"He claims he was talking to his son about a business matter," Ed said. "We checked the number he dialed with his cell-phone records. It was his son's home number, all right."

Emily thanked her brother and went back inside to rejoin Holly in the library.

"How's it going?" Emily asked.

"I think I've found it."

Emily's eyes went to the computer monitor. A black lion stood on its hind paws with outstretched claws on a white shield dotted with what looked like drops of blood. And above it was the odd helmet.

She checked it against the faint imprint from the dagger. It was definitely a match.

Emily read the identifier at the top of the screen: *Fitzwalter family crest.*

WHEN BRAD FAILED TO REACH Emily by phone, he steered his car in the direction of the Botanical Gardens. On his way there, he punched in Ed's work number.

"I'm glad you called," Ed said. "I've been trying Emily's number for the past half hour and getting nothing but her voice mail."

"Yeah, I know the feeling."

"Things going okay between you two?"

Whereas Brad probably wouldn't have hesitated to share his original plan of becoming Emily's good friend with Ed, he didn't feel nearly so comfortable sharing his new plan with her brother.

"We're getting to know each other," he said carefully. "What's up with the case?"

"The results on Lester Toth's autopsy are in. You ready?"

"I'm hearing a drumroll in my head."

"He slipped and fell."

"An accident?"

"Coroner says he died when he hit the back of his head on a portable iron barbecue sitting in the corner of the kitchen. Flecks of the iron material were embedded in his head wound. Lab guys found his blood on it."

"What about the fight that took place in the kitchen?"

"Crime-scene crew don't think it was a fight after all. The back door was locked. Lester's body has no wounds on it—offensive or defensive—other than the one he got when he fell and cracked his skull. Only other fingerprints are those of his girlfriend."

"Then what happened to the kitchen?"

"Way they've reconstructed it, Lester got mad and started throwing the dishes at the walls and breaking things. Somewhere in his rage, a carton of milk got tipped off the table and spilled onto the floor. He stepped into the spilled milk and slipped, whacking his head on the iron barbecue. He was barefoot. Traces of the dried milk were found on the soles of his feet."

"Had he been drinking?" Brad asked.

"Coroner didn't find any alcohol in his blood."

Brad was trying to picture the scene. What could have made Lester so angry?

"At least it's good to know that we don't have a murderer running around out there," he said. "Any idea what happened to the time capsule contents?"

"No, but the crime-scene guys are sure Lester took them. They matched his fingerprints to those on the windowsill in Emily's office. They also found something very interesting in the bedroom of the girlfriend's apartment."

Brad waited through Ed's deliberate pause. "Okay, I'm hooked," he said finally. "What did they find?"

"Seems Lester was attempting to blackmail someone about what he pulled out of the time capsule."

AFTER SEEING to her duties in the Botanical Gardens, Emily returned to her office and printed out the time capsule file listing the names of the twelve men who signed the mayor's letter. She took it to the sundial in the center of the gardens and began to check the names with the corresponding carved initials.

"So this is why you're not answering your telephone messages," Brad said from behind her a few moments later.

She rose to see him smiling at her and found herself smiling back.

He looked freshly shaved and showered. As she mentally counted off the hours, she realized that he must have gotten off his last shift a mere forty minutes before.

"Are you busy?" he asked.

Despite the fact that he was committed to a killing schedule and was here to help her, he still made no assumptions that he had any right to her time.

"I was checking the initials on the sundial against the signatures on the mayor's letter," she said.

"Yes, I remember. There were twelve names on the letter and only eleven initials. So who didn't get to carve his initials into history?"

"Douglas Fitzwalter signed the mayor's letter but didn't initial the sundial."

"A Fitzwalter. That's interesting. What do you know about him?"

"I believe he was Serena Fitzwalter's older brother, but I'd have to check. While we're on the subject of the Fitzwalters, there's something I'd like to show you in my office."

As they started toward the museum together, Brad filled her in on his recent telephone conversation with Ed.

"Who was Lester trying to blackmail?" Emily asked.

"The crime-scene team couldn't figure that out. What they found in the wastebasket in the bedroom were words cut out of magazines and what appeared to be an aborted attempt at a blackmail note. It said, 'I have the time capsule's papers and I know what…'"

"Know what?"

"That's all it said, Emily. There was a large brown stain on the paper and the investigating team concluded that Lester spilled a drink of some kind on his first blackmail letter attempt and had to start over again."

"I'm relieved he wasn't killed. But someone must have those artifacts. Did Ed mention if he'd had a chance to check on the girlfriend's story?"

"She was out of town where she said she was. A neighbor watering the lawn next door saw her drive into her parking space. She came running out of the apartment a couple minutes later screaming. He called the ambulance and police for her. Doesn't look like she took what Lester stole."

"Any thoughts about who did?" she asked.

"Only that it had to be someone who knew Lester had them—and where he had them. And since the girlfriend has an alibi, I'm betting on the person Lester was blackmailing."

"Would he have been so stupid as to have told the person who he was and where he was staying?" Emily asked.

"I doubt he intended to, judging by the fact that the blackmail note was cut-up letters, clearly an attempt to disguise who it was from. But when the person he was blackmailing got in touch, Lester may have made a slip."

They entered the museum and Emily nodded at the security guard as they walked up the stairs to her office.

"So, he contacts the person to extort money," she said. "The person finds out who he is and somehow steals the stuff from him?"

"Possibly sometime later when Lester left his girlfriend's house to get food or whatever. When he returned home to find them gone, that could have been what caused his rage."

"That doesn't sound like him, Brad."

"What do you mean?"

"Lester was a lousy worker and obviously a thief. But when he didn't like taking my directions or completing an aspect of a job I'd given him, he'd simply ignore what I told him or the part that he didn't want to do. I never once witnessed his displaying the kind of uncontrollable rage that would have him throwing and breaking things."

"What do you think happened?"

"I haven't the faintest idea."

"You ready for my second piece of news?"

"Absolutely," Emily said as she unlocked the door to her office and stepped inside.

"Before I tell you, there's something else I'd like to attend to first."

Brad closed the door behind them, took her into his arms and kissed her.

"You taste even better than I remembered," he said a moment later. "And the way you feel in my arms…" He kissed her again.

After his second kiss, Emily had to put the desk between them before she could get the synapses in her brain to start firing again.

What she was feeling and doing was dangerous. But no amount of logical self-talk could take the edge off her inner glow.

"What was the second thing you wanted to tell me?" she asked, gesturing him to take a seat and trying her best to put her mind on something other than the man across from her.

Brad filled her in on his talk with Josh.

"Phoebe was probably on her way to visit Wayne, our historian," Emily said. "You remember. He suffered a stroke that morning."

"I checked, Emily. Wayne wasn't moved out of the ICU until the next day. Only family members would have been admitted to see him."

"But what would Phoebe have wanted with the skeleton? And how could she have hoped to carry it out of the morgue?''

''I couldn't even speculate.''

''Maybe she was visiting someone else at the hospital.''

''That's the most logical explanation. Any chance she'd tell you?''

''I never know how to approach her. When we were first introduced, I was excited to meet the woman who had written the advice column I used to enjoy.''

''What advice column?''

''You never read the 'Dear Miss Phoebe' column in the local newspaper?''

He shook his head.

''It was wise, very positive and quite witty. When I met her in person, I was surprised to find she comes across so...differently.''

''The aches and pains of age can sometimes change a person's personality.''

''I suppose,'' Emily conceded. ''Although I've never known anyone past seventy with fewer aches and pains than Phoebe. Except maybe Oliver. You should see how energetic he is when he's stomping around the golf course. Which reminds me. Did Ed tell you what Oliver said about that telephone call Phoebe overheard?''

When Brad shook his head, Emily filled him in on that and the information about the Smithsons buying the land around the oak tree at an auction.

''So that's cleared up at least,'' Brad said.

''Speaking of things being cleared up, this is what I wanted to show you.''

She pulled out the faint image of the Fitzwalter family crest from the dagger and then the copy Holly had printed from the computer.

''There's that Fitzwalter name again,'' Brad said as he studied the copies. ''We already determined that there were no Fitzwalters missing at the time the skeleton ended up in the time capsule pit. Now we find he was buried with a dagger that had a Fitzwalter coat of arms on it.''

"From everything I've read about those days," Emily said, "objects with a family crest stayed with the family. I'm getting more and more curious about who this guy was. Did you have a chance to take pictures of the skull?''

He pulled the camera out of his pocket. "From every angle. We're going to need the photographs of R. C. Cox and Lawrence Norland from the time capsule. Were there any of Douglas Fitzwalter?''

"Let me check.''

She went to the files and ran down the list of names. "Yes. Douglas Fitzwalter is on picture thirty-three.''

"Let's take it along, as well.''

"But the genealogy records showed Douglas Fitzwalter was alive in 1905," Emily said.

"I still believe the osteopetrosis makes that skeleton an ancestor of Leonard Landru," Brad said. "Which means the inherited disease could come from his Fitzwalter roots. Bones don't make mistakes. But the people who kept the Fitzwalter genealogy records might have.''

Emily nodded. After locating the photographs, she pulled them out and slipped them into a large envelope.

Brad got to his feet. "I've already talked to Harry. He's waiting for us. But before we go, I have a request.''

"What's that?''

"Ride with me.''

She shook her head. "You'll waste time bringing me back here. It could make you late for your next shift.''

"I'm not due in for another seven hours.''

"Seven *whole* hours," she said shaking her head. "You should be home right now sleeping.''

He moved beside her, wrapped a warm arm around her waist. "If that's an offer to tuck me into bed, you're on.''

She was so tempted to say yes, it scared her.

Bending his head he brushed her lips and said, "Don't be afraid of this.''

The last thing she needed was for him to start reading her mind. "I have two big brothers who legally carry guns for a living. What makes you think I'm afraid?"

His laugh was a husky rumble near her ear.

"Your other brother's name is Grant, isn't it?"

"Yes."

"What's he like?"

"He's the toughest homicide detective in the L.A. police department."

"If you're trying to scare me away, Emily, it's not working."

She sighed, grasping at the last straws of her good sense. "We'd better go, Brad. Harry's waiting."

IRENE MET EMILY AND BRAD at the door. She promised them that sandwiches and milk were on their way as she ushered them to the study at the back of the house where Harry waited in front of his computer.

He got up and fetched a chair for Emily so she could sit beside him.

"Has Brad explained to you how this kind of identification works?" Harry asked.

"He said that a photo of someone when they were alive can be matched to their skull bones after death."

"Good succinct explanation," Harry said. "Now let me show you the steps. First we need a clear picture of the skull."

Brad handed him the digital camera. Harry looked through the selection, chose one and loaded the picture into his computer.

"Now we need a photograph of one of the missing men."

Brad put Lawrence Norland's picture into Harry's scanner. When it appeared on Harry's screen, he deftly erased the enormous mustache from the man's face.

"Now what we need to do is be sure we size these two images so that they correspond," Harry said as he clicked the keys. A few seconds later the image of the skull took up the left half of the screen and the image of Norland's face filled the right.

Emily watched as he adjusted the widths and heights of the foreheads and chins until their sizes were approximately equal.

"Skull-face superimposition is based on the fact that although we all have the same basic features of two eyes, a nose and a mouth, each of us is unique in how our features are arranged," Harry explained. "Now we're going to see if these two fit."

He superimposed the image of the skull over the photograph.

"They don't," Brad said from behind them.

As Emily looked closer, she began to see what Brad meant. The eye sockets of the skeleton didn't match the eye placement in the photograph of Norland. Nor did the forehead or chin line up.

"Let's have the next candidate," Harry said.

Brad obliged by putting Douglas Fitzwalter's photograph on the scanner. A moment later it had replaced Norland's on the window beside the skeleton's skull.

Harry sized it as he had Norland's and then superimposed the image of the skull over the photograph.

"Still not your man."

"Damn," Brad said. "I would have sworn he was our best shot."

"Well, whatever the reason he was missing that day the sundial was set in place, it wasn't because he was lying in the time capsule pit," Emily said.

"Might as well try number three."

Brad put Cox's photo in place and Harry worked his magic with the computer program.

"The eyes are sitting in the center of the orbits," he said. "The nose is covering the nasal cavity precisely the way it should. And the teeth fit perfectly in the mouth.

Congratulations, Emily, Brad. You have identified your skeleton.''

"R. C. Cox, the traveling salesman," Emily said staring at the screen.

THEY WERE IN BRAD'S CAR and back on the road when Emily asked, "What would be the motive for murdering a traveling salesman?"

"Theft would be the first thing that comes to my mind," Brad said. "Although in this case, I'd be inclined to rule it out."

"Why?"

"Because of the gold coin I found with the skeleton. If someone were trying to rob this guy when they killed him, they would have taken the coin."

"Could one of his customers have had a bad response to the product?" Emily suggested. "Or he wanted his money back when it didn't work and Cox refused to give a refund? We could speculate all day and not come up with the right reason."

"Let's concentrate on what we know," Brad said. "This man had a bone disease that is shared by a Landru descendant. He was found with a Fitzwalter dagger. To me that says he was personally tied in some way to one— possibly both—families."

"A black sheep come to town under the guise of a snake-oil salesman using the assumed name of R. C. Cox?"

"Well, whatever his relationship to the families, his death wasn't something someone wanted known, otherwise we wouldn't have found Cox's skeleton buried with the time capsule."

Emily's cell phone rang. She answered it to find Dorothy on the other end of the line.

"Em…found…need to…"

"Dot, the reception's poor. You keep cutting out."

"Time…doorstep…come…"

"I'll call you back," Emily said. She ended the call, and then punched in Dorothy's number from her address book. After the fifth unanswered ring, she flipped her phone closed.

"We need to swing by Dot's place. I think something's wrong. Take a right at this next corner."

THERE WERE TWO PATROL CARS and another unmarked car in front of Dorothy's house when they arrived. She answered the doorbell immediately. The woman who stood before them didn't resemble the fun-loving lady Brad had met at the Founders Day Celebration. She looked worn and very worried.

"Dot, are you all right?" Emily asked.

"Yeah, fine," she said as she beckoned Emily and Brad inside. "I'm so glad you're here. Damn, I hate cell phones. I mean I love them because otherwise we'd have nothing, but I hate them when the reception is all shot to hell. The police are still in the back taking pictures of the stuff."

"Stuff?" Emily repeated.

"Sorry," Dorothy said. "I forgot you couldn't hear me. It's the contents of the time capsule, Em. When I got home from my cousin's today, I found them on the back porch."

"Dot, that's great!"

"Not so great. They were in trash bags."

"They're damaged?"

"I was afraid to look too closely for fear I'd tamper with evidence. Truth is, I don't know what condition they're in. But trash bags, Em. What idiot would put them in trash bags?"

Emily put her arms around her friend. Brad knew she was doing exactly the right thing. Dorothy's hands were clenching and unclenching, her pupils mere pinpricks. She was exhibiting all the signs of stress.

Brad followed them into the kitchen, where Emily sat

Dorothy in a chair and got her a glass of milk. She stood over her until she had drunk it. Resting back in her chair, Dorothy gestured to the other chairs at the table.

"Thanks, Em. I'm better now. Sit. Both of you. Please."

"Was there a note?" Emily asked as she did.

Dorothy shook her head. "They had those twist ties around the tops. For a moment, I thought someone had dumped their trash on our porch. Then I realized how stupid that would be. The alley right behind the house has plenty of empty trash cans. If someone wanted to dump something, they'd do it out there. That's when I decided to untwist one of the tops and look inside."

She exhaled. "There was one of those ancient phonograph records on the top. I picked it up without realizing for a moment what it was. Then I saw the old newspapers underneath. And the mayor's letter. That's when it hit me they were the things from the time capsule."

"Did you happen to notice if the box of *Ranger* letters was there?"

"I didn't see it, Em. Dean and Gerald are going to be so disappointed. I hope they don't take it out on each other. Ken tells me those two used to be such good friends when they were children. So much for sports teaching sportsmanship."

Holly came into the room and went over to her mother. "One of the detectives would like to talk to you again. They're going to take the time capsule contents in to be processed. He wants you to sign something."

Dorothy nodded and got to her feet. When she had left the room, Emily introduced Brad to Holly.

"I remember you from the ceremony," Holly said. "You're the one who knew the skeleton was old. Mom says you're trying to identify it so Emily can write an article for the newsletter, giving all the gory details. The Society eats that stuff up."

"But not you?" Brad asked, hearing an unusual note in the girl's voice.

"Right now I'm sick of everything to do with that stupid time capsule. I wish it had never been dug up."

"Is that because of your mom?" Emily asked.

Holly nodded. "She hasn't had a minute's peace. The phone keeps ringing and ringing. I got up to get a glass of water the other night and found her sitting in the kitchen trying to work on class notes at 2 a.m."

"Have you talked to your dad?" Emily asked.

"He's on his way home from work. I called a few minutes ago to let him know about someone dumping the stuff on us. He's going to take Mom to a B and B up the coast for the weekend to try to get her away from things for a while."

"Sounds like a great idea," Emily said. "Now what about you, Holly? How are you holding up?"

"I'm hoping it'll be better now that the news is reporting Lester's death was an accident. By the way, have you seen Josh? I called his number to let him know about stuff, but he didn't answer and—"

Before Holly could finish, Ed interrupted as he appeared in the doorway. "Dorothy said you were here, Em. This saves me a phone call."

"Is there something you need?" Emily asked.

"Yeah. You down at headquarters with the list of the stuff you cataloged from the time capsule."

"The list is back at the Heritage Museum. I'll have to swing by there. Why do you need it? Is something missing?"

"That's what we'd like to find out. Bring along two copies."

"Emily and I didn't get a chance to go through everything that was in the time capsule," Brad said.

"I know. But you got through most of the stuff that the mayor showed to the audience at the ceremonies that day, right?"

"Most of it," Brad confirmed.

"And that's the stuff people knew was there. So if we find the things on your list in the trash bags outside, at least we'll know no one's taken them."

"Do you suspect someone took some of the items?" Emily asked.

Ed's eyes skittered over to Holly before he answered his sister's question in neutral tones.

"Simply part of routine procedure to check these things out."

Brad was pretty sure there was more than routine procedure behind it.

On the way to the Heritage Museum, Emily told Brad she'd be driving her own car to the police station so he could take off for the E.R. when he needed to.

"You don't even have to be at the station to check out the items," she said. "You could go get some sleep or something to eat."

"Emily, I want to be wherever you are, even when it means one of your gun-toting brothers is our chaperone."

He could see her smiling out of the corner of his eye as he turned into the parking lot of the Botanical Gardens.

CHAPTER ELEVEN

EMILY WAS DISAPPOINTED when they arrived at the police station and learned that the criminalists wanted the list she and Brad had prepared, but not their help in going through the time capsule material.

She was told politely—but firmly—that the sterile gloves she had brought along and used on historical documents weren't good enough to protect any physical evidence from contamination.

Ed invited her and Brad to wait in his office while the criminalists checked the list against what Dorothy had found in the trash bags on her back porch.

"I didn't want to say anything back at the Mission place, but we found a woman's barrette on the porch between the trash bags containing the time capsule stuff," Ed said.

So that's why he'd given Holly that look back in the kitchen.

"It probably fell there before the trash bags were put on the back porch," Emily said.

"The barrette matched the one Holly was wearing in her hair today," Ed said.

"She has a dozen of those, Ed. So do I, as a matter of fact. It might have fallen out of my hair the last time I was on their back porch."

Her brother's face told her he wasn't sold on the explanation. "You have the extra copy of the list with you?"

Emily produced it and, at her brother's request, read off the items to him.

"I crossed off the pictures so your investigators wouldn't expect to see them among the other things," she said.

"And the rest are mostly letters and newspapers," Ed said. "Was it something specific in them that got Lester's attention?"

"Assuming that Lester used his key to the maintenance gate and was hiding somewhere in the trees during the ceremony," Emily said, "I imagine the letters from the *Ranger* crew would have struck him as the most valuable."

"I agree," Brad said. "Especially since Councilman Himlot was so vocal about his ancestor's letter being a family heirloom."

"Except Lester didn't only take the box of letters," Ed said. "He took everything from the time capsule he could get his hands on."

"Mayor O'Shea did emphasize that everything in the capsule was a treasure," Emily said. "Could be Lester decided as long as he was going to steal part of them, he might as well steal them all."

"Em, you worked with the guy. Do you think he took them purely for profit or for revenge over losing his job?"

"I wish I could tell you. The truth is, I never really knew Lester— I didn't even know he was stealing from the Botanical Gardens until Dot caught him in the act. He gave the impression that he listened and went along with instructions. But as soon as my back was turned, he did what he wanted."

"If he was the one who tried to get the skeleton," Ed said, "there might be at least a bit of revenge at play."

"Because the mayor described the skeleton simply as an interesting artifact?" Emily asked.

"Exactly. I can see Lester going after the contents of the time capsule to make a quick buck. But, unless he wanted revenge, I don't picture him taking a chance on getting caught stealing a bunch of old bones he couldn't sell.''

''At the moment I'm not nearly as concerned about Lester's motives as I am about finding out who put those items from the time capsule on Dot's back porch and why,'' Emily said.

''The person Lester was trying to blackmail?'' Brad offered.

''A logical, number-one choice,'' Ed agreed. ''And if anything is missing, that could tell us who, since he would have obviously kept anything that could incriminate him or cause him embarrassment. Or her embarrassment. This is an equal-opportunity suspect list.''

''In addition to the items on the list Brad and I made, we know the second page of the gardener's letter is going to be missing,'' Emily said. ''Her letter isn't something we had time to catalog. Have you learned how that last page of it came to be lying beneath Lester?''

Ed shrugged. ''Your guess is as good as ours. Leave that second copy of the list with me. The crime-scene guys are going to need to keep the other.''

She slipped it across the desk to him. ''Will you do me a favor and check to see if the first page of the gardener's letter was returned with the rest of the time capsule documents?''

''Are you asking this because you think it has something to do with the theft?''

''It's the botanist in me who's curious. The part that Oliver read talked about the plant's medicinal properties. I was hoping that the part he didn't read might go into more detail.''

Ed shook his head. ''Here I am working my tail off trying to solve a politically hot case and you're concerned about identifying a hundred-year-old weed.''

Emily smiled. She was used to her brother's gentle ribbing.

"You found nothing else that could have come from the time capsule in the girlfriend's apartment?" Brad asked.

Ed pulled out half a dozen sheets of paper from a file in his side drawer. "This is what the evidence gatherers listed as the contents. Nothing jumped out at me. If you see something, let me know."

He handed the pages to Brad. After he glanced through them, he shook his head at the question on Ed's face and turned them over to Emily. She gave them a cursory once-over.

"I don't recognize anything," she said, setting the sheets on top of Ed's desk and pushing them toward him. "When will you be able to give us the page from the gardener's letter?"

"It will be a while," Ed said. "Even though we've concluded Lester's death was an accident, the girlfriend's apartment is still a crime scene because of the theft, which means everything we found there is evidence."

"Would it be possible to get a copy?" Emily asked.

"Shouldn't be a problem," Ed said. "I'll swing by the evidence room later and have one sent over to you. Now, I know I originally told you that the skeleton wasn't our concern, but it's possible the attempt to steal it is connected with the theft of the artifacts, so maybe you'd—"

"Did you mention anything to Ed about Phoebe's visit to the hospital that night?" Emily asked Brad.

"What visit?" Ed asked, effectively answering her question.

Brad relayed his conversation with Josh.

"She might have simply been visiting a sick friend," Emily said, "which is why we didn't want to make a big deal out of it."

"Won't hurt to ask her about it," Ed said. "Now, getting back to the skeleton. How's that investigation coming?"

Brad told Ed how he and Emily had identified the skeleton as R. C. Cox, a traveling snake-oil salesman from the turn of the twentieth century, and that the dagger found with Cox had the Fitzwalter crest.

"Are you saying a Fitzwalter from 1904 killed him?" Ed asked.

"He was killed with a gun, remember," Brad said. "All we know for the moment is that a Fitzwalter dagger was found with him in the grave. And that there was a knife wound on his wrist."

One of the criminalists—wearing a hospital gown, hair cap and protective gloves up to his elbows—entered Ed's office. His clothing was stained with the perspiration that came from close work in restrictive garments.

"The box with the letters from the surviving crew of *Ranger* is missing," the investigator said. "And we didn't find the map of the Courage Bay community of 1904. Nor a copy of the newspaper with the date of the time capsule's burial. Other than that, what was cataloged appears to be intact."

"What about the condition of the items?" Emily asked.

"Hard to tell since I didn't see them before they were stolen," he said. "But my nonprofessional opinion is they don't look too bad."

Ed thanked him for the report and the investigator left.

"Any theories as to why those things are missing?" Ed asked.

"The map is a surprise," Emily said. "You've verified that the Smithson family acquired that land around the oak tree legitimately. I wonder if I overlooked something on the entries when we were doing the cataloging."

"You don't seem surprised that the *Ranger* letters were taken."

Brad looked over at her when she hesitated. "Have you told him about Dean Himlot and Gerald Fitzwalter?"

"No, but I'm sure Dot has."

"Dot has what?" Ed asked.

"Told you about Gerald's concern about getting those letters before Dean?"

Ed shook his head.

"And both of them having approached her to offer a reward?" Emily added, getting concerned at Ed's continuing head shake. "And how Gerald threatened to offer a reward on his own if the Society didn't?"

"Dorothy hasn't uttered a word about any of this," Ed said, looking anything but pleased.

Emily took a moment to fill her brother in fully on her conversations with Dorothy and Gerald.

"Dot's been tired and distracted," Emily explained. "It probably slipped her mind."

Ed wasn't convinced. "What about the missing newspaper?"

"I have no idea why it would have been taken," Emily said.

He looked at Brad.

"You've got me," Brad said as he got to his feet. "I have to report to the E.R. now. Walk me out, Emily?"

She nodded as she stood. "I have to be leaving, as well. Ed, you'll let us know when the time capsule's contents can be released?"

"Yeah, sure. And you'll let me know if you and Brad solve this damn case before I do?"

Emily smiled in understanding at her brother's look of frustration.

"When you finish your residency, will your hours get better?" she asked Brad as they walked out to the parking lot.

"Definitely shorter."

"And you'll stay at Courage Bay Hospital?"

"I've been offered a position at a major trauma center in L.A."

"A major trauma center must pay a lot more money than a community hospital," she said.

He nodded.

"And a position there would certainly carry more prestige."

Another nod.

"So the smart thing to do would be to take it."

"That would be the smart thing, yes."

"But you'd rather stay at CB because you like the people and know you're needed there."

"You're beginning to make me a believer in this psychic stuff."

He flashed her one of those smiles that had her smiling back.

"Brad, how can you face sixteen hours of work when you've had no sleep and the only thing you've had to eat is the sandwich and milk Irene prepared for us?"

"I like it when you worry about me."

"I don't."

He stopped, faced her and cupped her shoulders with his hands. "You don't worry about me or don't like worrying about me?"

She knew he wanted her to tell him how she felt. But there were a lot of very good reasons that kept her from doing that.

"Didn't your doctor ever tell you how important it is to eat and sleep on a regular basis?" she asked instead.

"Everybody knows doctors are a bunch of quacks. Besides, I'm disgustingly healthy. I never have to see one."

"Not even when you look in the mirror to shave?"

He chuckled as his hands slid down her arms. "Emily, you don't have to worry about me. I'll get something to eat in the hospital's cafeteria. When things are slow tonight, I'll grab some sleep in one of the empty rooms. Or I may simply lie there and think about you."

He kissed her lightly, then left to report in.

WITH EVERYTHING ELSE claiming her attention, Emily hadn't had an opportunity to go through the video of the news coverage that Ed had secured from the KSEA TV studio. Remembering she'd promised Wayne a copy, she took it home where she had a machine that could make one.

She watched the tape as she copied it. Unlike the edited version that had appeared on TV, this one included a lot of footage of the important dignitaries milling about before the ceremony and later the skeleton lying beside the time capsule in the pit.

Although the skeleton's outline was clear, it was partially buried in the earth. Even the close-up images revealed little but the white bones against the dark brown soil.

As Brad lowered himself into the pit, the camera followed his movements. At one point, it appeared he might be putting something in an evidence bag. But she couldn't see what it was because his body blocked what he was doing.

The next shot was of the mayor announcing to the crowd that the skeleton was an artifact and the ceremony would proceed.

Emily switched off the machine. Something about this coverage bothered her. She tried to remember the day of the time capsule's unveiling.

The police chief had been directing the news camera to take pictures over the pit. At one point, he'd waved the TV team behind the line of plainclothes police where everyone else waited. That was when he'd gone to confer with Brad and Ed.

As the three of them stood talking near the edge of the pit, Emily's attention had been diverted when Oliver approached to ask her if she'd seen Wayne, who he'd just noticed wasn't part of the crowd. The next thing she remembered was watching Ed coming toward her with Brad beside him.

She had a nagging feeling that she was missing something obvious. But the harder she tried to concentrate, the further it retreated. Putting the copied tape away, she switched on the local TV news to catch the weather report for the weekend.

KSEA's new meteorologist was a big improvement over the goofy guy they used to feature. Her forecasts were always right on. Assuring viewers that the Santa Ana winds had abated, she promised that temperatures would be dropping back into the lower seventies.

Emily was about to switch off the set when the news anchor reappeared on the screen and said, "And, finally, tonight we leave you with the kind of story we love to tell. The Courage Bay Clothing Drive for needy families reports tonight that it has received two hundred thousand dollars in anonymous cash donations. Looks like Christmas is going to come early for a lot of needy folks."

Emily switched off the set, smiling. If the news would report more good stories like that one, she'd watch it more often. Nothing was more uplifting than hearing about really nice people.

Which put her in mind of another one. She picked up her journal.

Dear Sprout,

Tonight, once again, the subject is your biological father.

There was a section of the sperm-donor questionnaire that dealt with some very probing, personal inquiries—so personal in fact that most of the sperm donors didn't answer them. He had the guts to answer them all.

One of those questions asked what was the most shameful thing that he had ever done. He wrote that he'd been goofing off with friends after school and later lied to his mother when she asked him why he hadn't completed his household chores. She'd believed him because she said she knew he always told the truth. He never confessed that lie to her. He wished he had. The shame that he didn't live up to the truthful person she trusted him to be still haunts him.

Most kids would have been happy to get away with the lie. Most wouldn't even have considered it a big deal. But it was a big deal to him then, and it remains a big deal to him now. Of all the things a man can show a woman, showing his true self is the most important.

I really like what he's shown me.

Sleep well, my little love.

Mom.

Emily put her journal away and switched off the light. But, as tired as she was, sleep eluded her. She kept thinking about Brad at work in the E.R. for so many hours yet to come.

It was a Friday night—a time he'd warned her was one of the hardest. She wondered what he would have to face. He'd told her he was strong, and she'd certainly seen the evidence of that strength.

But remembering the sadness on his features when he had gazed down at Samantha, she hoped he would not have to deal with a child in pain.

Not even Brad Winslow was strong enough for that.

BRAD WAS AT THE CHECK-IN DESK finishing a chart notation when a barefoot guy in pajama bottoms and no top burst through the door and ran up to him.

He was soaking with sweat, his eyes wild. "My wife's out in the parking lot having our baby."

Brad grabbed a gurney as he raced with the guy out the door.

A moment later he was lifting a woman in advanced labor out of the back seat of a beat-up Ford. The young man and his wife couldn't have been more than twenty.

And from the scared looks on both their faces, he had no doubt that this was their first child.

As they rolled her into the E.R., Brad learned from the husband that they were from San Diego, and his wife had been in for regular checkups there. She was healthy and her doctor had predicted no problems.

Pushing her into an open trauma room, Brad assured the young woman and her husband that she was doing really well and everything was going to be great.

He'd learned at the very beginning of his career that a patient's belief in a positive outcome could go a long way toward ensuring one.

"She's two weeks early," the husband said, clearly terrified.

"She's right on time," Brad reassured him.

At a signal from Brad, the trauma nurse immediately grabbed the phone to get the on-call doc from obstetrics to come in. After a quick examination of the mother-to-be, Brad knew the obstetrician would be too late.

The woman screamed as a contraction hit her. Her young husband paled and looked ready to hit the floor.

"Take her hand," Brad urged him. "Hold on tight. She needs you to be strong to help her through this."

The husband obediently grasped his wife's hand. In the next few minutes, Brad saw a boy become a man as the young father watched his baby being born.

The delivery was fast and, thankfully, without complications.

As Brad cradled the healthy newborn boy in the crook of his arm and gently cleaned the mucus out of his nose and mouth before handing him to his mother, it struck him that he was the first person on earth to hold this brand-new life.

The feeling was sweet and unbelievably joyful.

Ah, Emily, you don't know it yet, but when the time comes for my baby to be born, I'm going to be the one

*to deliver it. When my child opens its eyes, I'm going to
be the one to smile and welcome it into the world.*

EMILY'S NEW MAINTENANCE person had been sent from
heaven. Six-one with the arms of a weight lifter and the
sunny disposition of a Wal-Mart greeter, Helga Sorenson
had no problems showing up on time or sweeping the
Botanical Gardens and greenhouse pathways with a
broom. In two days she'd planted, fertilized and trimmed
up a storm—accomplishing more than Lester had in the
entire four months he'd worked for the city.

"With her here, you're not going to need me anymore," Josh said.

Emily glanced at the frown on his face. "Your part-
time job as my assistant in the Gardens and with the Society are guaranteed until the fall. You have my word on
it. After that…well…you're not really going to want to
stick around here after Holly leaves for Harvard, are
you?"

Josh's cheeks reddened. "I've got to finish planting the
new arbor," he said and took off down the path.

Emily watched him hurrying off, very much afraid that
he was going to end up with a broken heart.

It was late afternoon. She'd carried her cell phone with
her all day in case Brad called. He hadn't. Feeling both
disappointed and annoyed at herself for that disappointment, she headed toward the Heritage Museum.

Before she started up the stairs, the security guard in-
tercepted her, holding out a sealed envelope.

"A policeman dropped this by for you," he said.

Her name had been handwritten across the top.

Once she'd let herself into her office, she slit open the
envelope. Inside she found a copy of the second page of
the gardener's letter that had been found beneath Lester's
body.

Paper clipped to it was a scribbled note in her brother's
handwriting. It said that the first page of the gardener's

letter had not been among the returned time capsule documents.

The news perplexed Emily. Why would the person who had taken the time capsule contents from Lester have kept the first page of the letter? Who but a botanist like herself would be interested in such things?

Emily read the second page, which contained a sketchy drawing of the medicinal plant and directions to the place it had been found. The outline of the plant looked vaguely familiar. She was trying to place it when she suddenly caught sight of the signature at the bottom of the page. She stared at it in surprise and excitement.

A knock came on her office door. She called out for whoever it was to come in. Ken swung open the door and poked his head inside.

"Sorry to bother you, Emily, but the combination Phoebe gave me for the new lock on the supply-room door doesn't work. I must have copied down the numbers wrong. I need to get some film."

"I'll open the storeroom for you," she said as she got to her feet and came around to the front of her desk. "Time to replenish some of my office supplies anyway. Ever think of buying yourself a digital camera?"

"Digital. The very word conjures up distasteful images of fingers poking into places where they do not belong."

Emily smiled as they headed down the hall toward the supply room. "I take it you haven't kept up with the tide of technology?"

"Since you've introduced that metaphorical stream, I shall answer accordingly. I didn't miss the boat of tempestuous technological change—I saw it departing and decided not to catch it."

"I never realized you had such a facility with words."

"A good man should be as quietly competent and dependable as a good camera," he said, patting the one in the black case slung over his shoulder.

Emily was amused. "Ever think of writing a column for the newsletter?"

"No, thank you. If people don't like your news report or a photo, they simply glance past it. But if they don't like your opinion, they feel obliged to find fault—as if having access to the same twenty-six letters of the alphabet somehow imbues them with superior intellectual and emotional depth."

"Sounds to me like you've written more than news reports in your career," Emily said.

His only response was a shrug.

"Ken, you can't clam up on me now. I know you wrote stories and took photos for the local newspaper when Phoebe was a columnist. Did you secretly pen a manuscript in your spare time? Are you published under a pseudonym? Is it some exposé of political wrongdoing or some passionate tale of adventure that the literary critics have failed to appreciate?"

"If I tell you, will you promise to keep it a secret?"

"As long as it doesn't compromise the safety of our government."

He sent her an amused look and she grinned.

"It may have been Phoebe's picture and name on the column, but it was my artery that had been opened and was spilling forth on the page."

"You wrote the 'Dear Miss Phoebe' advice column in the local newspaper?"

"For nearly twenty years," he said.

"I read that column faithfully as a teenager. It was full of sane and very gutsy advice. Ken, you were my heroine! Of course, I thought you were Phoebe."

He smiled, clearly pleased. "Remember, you're not to say anything."

"Doesn't Phoebe want you to have the credit?"

"It's not that. She's told me if I wanted to own up to writing the column, that would be all right with her. Truth is, I couldn't have handled the face-to-face verbal combat that ensued when she met someone who didn't understand what I was trying to say or didn't agree with it.''

"Did that happen often?"

"Often enough. Phoebe was great—still is—treats them like a royal dismissing an ignorant peasant. I would have acted more like the ignorant peasant and gone for their kneecaps with my teeth.''

They had reached the door to the supply room and Emily punched in the code, making sure Ken saw what digits she was pushing and their sequence.

"You've never struck me as someone who could lose his cool,'' Emily said.

He shrugged. "Everyone has their hot buttons.''

"And yet I remember you once wrote that we should never let our identity get caught up in how we look or how our work is received. Otherwise, we'll only feel hurt, angry, even devastated when we don't get the response we want from others.''

"What did you do, memorize those columns?''

Emily chuckled as Ken followed her into the storeroom. "It's your own fault, Ken. You did too good a job of writing them.''

"They were a part of me—sometimes I think the best part. Problem is I've never been able to follow my own advice and separate who I am from the work I do.''

"When you figure out how to accomplish that, let me know,'' Emily said. "I could use some pointers.''

"I couldn't teach you a thing,'' Ken said. "I watched you the other night when Phoebe and Oliver were making complete jackasses out of themselves over the stolen time capsule contents. You, my dear, were a radiant example of restraint.''

"I doubt that restraint would have been nearly so radiant if I hadn't had such staunch and effective support.''

"Yes, Dorothy is special,'' Ken said, as he concentrated on rubbing a speck of dirt off his camera case. "Always has been.''

Actually Emily had been thinking of Brad's defense of her. But Ken was right. Dorothy had spoken out strongly on her behalf, as well.

"Five rolls, four hundred speed enough?" Emily asked.

He took the film from her outstretched hand. "Plenty. I'm in your debt."

"You can pay me back by letting me see a contact sheet of the photos you took at the Founders Day ceremony."

"They weren't that great."

"Even so, I'd really like to have a look."

He stepped forward, took her hand and blew a kiss across her knuckles. "I'm putty in the hands of a woman who not only appreciates what I wrote but can also quote my words back to me. Just don't tell Phoebe I've succumbed to your charms. She warned me not to share the pictures with anyone."

"Hello," Brad said from the doorway.

Emily started in surprise. "How did you get past the security guard?"

"He seems to have stepped away from his post. Am I interrupting something?"

Ken released Emily's hand and turned toward him. "Yes. I was about to ask Emily to marry me, and she was about to remind me I'm old enough to be her father. I'll get those contact sheets to you later," he called over his shoulder to her as he left.

Brad walked up to Emily and stood before her trying to look solemn despite the slight upper curve to his lip. "I can't leave you alone even for a little while without some guy trying to steal you away from me."

She smirked. "Yeah, that's what I do all day. Fight the men off."

He took her hands. "As long as you continue to fight them off. I missed you, Emily."

His kiss told her how much.

She understood the time was approaching when she was

going to have to decide how far to let this go. Logically, she knew what that decision should be. But every time Brad touched her, holding on to that logic became more difficult.

"Do you have any plans for the next few hours?" he asked, his tone suggestive of cool satin sheets.

Emily pushed the image from her mind. "Ed sent over a copy of the second page of the gardener's letter. It's back in my office. There's something in it that I think you'll find exciting."

He made no move to leave or let go of her hands. "There's something right here I find exciting."

His gaze traveled over her face, warm, caressing.

"It may be a key to what Lester was doing with the time capsule contents," she said, trying to hold on to some sense.

"Okay, Emily, I can take a hint. When I'm hit over the head with it."

He released her hands and followed her out of the storeroom. When she had closed and locked the door behind them, they started toward her office.

"So what is this exciting thing in the gardener's letter?" he asked.

"Remember when we were looking through the newspapers in the time capsule and I came across that article about the Kerr family having died in a fire?"

He nodded. "A houseguest went insane and set fire to their home."

"I know who the houseguest was," Emily said.

"Didn't her name appear in the newspaper article?" Brad asked.

"It said she was Agnes Hopper, a widow. But she wasn't just Agnes Hopper. She was also the gardener who wrote about finding the medicinal plant. Her signature is on the second page of her letter, the page Ed found beneath Lester's body."

"Interesting connection, but I don't see where the excitement comes in," Brad said.

"She signed her full name as Agnes *Smithson* Hopper."

"She was a Smithson?"

"The letter's on my desk. Come see."

Brad followed Emily into her office. But she didn't see the letter on her desk. Or anything else. The surface was clean.

"I don't believe this," Emily said. "Someone's taken it."

CHAPTER TWELVE

"YOU DIDN'T LOCK YOUR OFFICE when you and Ken went to the storeroom?" Ed asked.

Emily shook her head. "I was only going to be gone a couple of minutes. And the security guard was downstairs."

She had called Ed the moment she'd discovered the copy of the gardener's letter had been taken off her desk. The fact that Ed had arrived a few minutes later told her that he wasn't taking this latest theft lightly.

Brad walked through the open door to her office. "I checked with the security guard. He didn't see anyone unauthorized going up the stairs. Apparently he's been preoccupied part of the time policing a group of teenagers who were horsing around, trying to lift the glass off one of the museum's cabinets."

"Is that why he wasn't in position when you came up?" Emily asked.

Brad nodded. "He claims he saw me, but since you'd cleared me with him before, he assumed I wasn't a risk. I doubt he had his eyes on the stairs the whole time, however."

"Well, one thing's for certain," Ed said. "We now know Lester wasn't the only thief around here."

"I think this theft means more than that," Emily said. "The gardener's full signature was Agnes Smithson Hopper. According to that story I'd read in the copy of the missing *Bulletin,* she was the one responsible for the death of the Kerr family."

"Even so, you're talking about something that happened a hundred years ago," Ed said, not sounding too interested.

"I understand your interest isn't in history, Ed. But this is a historical society. And Oliver Smithson holds a prominent position within it. To the members here, these things are very important."

"What are you saying, Em?"

"It was the first page of the gardener's letter and that specific copy of the *Bulletin* containing the story of the fire that turned up missing from the time capsule contents Dot found on her back porch. The fact that the second page of the letter has been taken out of my office this afternoon can't be a coincidence."

"What's the tie-in?"

"If her maiden name was Smithson—" Emily began.

"You think Oliver is trying to keep us from finding out that some ancestor of theirs went wacko and did in a few neighbors?" Ed interrupted.

"I don't want to think that, but—"

"Em, if the person who returned the contents of the time capsule to Dot took that particular issue of the *Bulletin* and the first page of the gardener's letter to keep us from seeing them, why would they take the copy of the second page of the letter out of your office today? He or she must have realized we already *had* seen the information, not to mention that we'd have other copies floating around."

"I hadn't thought about that," Emily admitted.

"It's possible someone other than the person who returned the items from the time capsule took the copy of the letter from Emily's desk," Brad said.

She looked over at him. "Yes. That would make more sense."

"Since the security guard wasn't at his post near the bottom of the stairs and your door was open," Ed said, "anyone visiting the museum today could have walked up the stairs and taken the letter."

"Anyone could have," Emily said. "But unless someone understood the significance of the document they were reading, why would they have wanted to take it?"

"All right," Ed said. "I'll buy that. We're looking at someone who has a connection to the Historical Society or its families. So let's do this by the book. I'll get a team in here to check the place over."

"Is that really necessary?" Emily asked.

"Hey, you dialed my number, remember?" Ed said, looking and sounding more frustrated by the minute.

"What I meant to say is that various members of the Society are in and out of my office all the time. I'm not sure finding their prints here would mean anything. I don't want to waste your time."

"Let me be the judge of what wastes my time," he said. "You haven't touched anything since you came back and noticed the letter was gone?"

"Nothing," Emily said. "Not even the phone on the desk. I used my cell to call you."

"Good. Get out of here. I'll call you when you can come back. Considering the lateness of the day, don't figure on it being before tomorrow."

"I need to get something out of the files."

"What?"

"Copies of old newspapers Brad and I printed off microfilm."

"They may be gone, too, for all you know."

"I locked the file cabinet yesterday when I left and haven't opened it today. The only key to it is in my pocket."

"Show me which file cabinet but don't touch anything."

Emily led him to the file cabinet in the corner and pointed at a drawer. Ed examined the lock, took the key from Emily's hand and opened it carefully.

She poked her head inside. "Those are the copies I want. May I take them out now, Mr. Hard-Nose Detective?"

"Yeah, and then you may get lost, Dr. Pain-in-the-Butt."

Ed took the sting off his somewhat less than loving comment to his sister with a quick kiss to the top of her head.

Emily gave him a smile as she lifted the files from the cabinet and scooted out the door. She knew Ed was under a lot of strain with this case. It was getting as much publicity as a murder and everyone from the mayor on down was pressing for a resolution.

As she stood outside the office, she could hear Brad and Ed's mumbled voices from within but couldn't make out what they were saying. A moment later Brad joined her on the landing.

"You okay?" he asked.

"Fine. Why?"

"You seem tired."

"*You're* worried about *me* being tired? Now that's a laugh."

"Maybe you should call it a day."

She shook her head. "No, I'm fine. Besides, there's too much work to be done. I need to read more closely through the newspapers. And go through the Smithson genealogy files."

"Which are downstairs, right?"

"Right."

"Okay, but I'm carrying them."

They made their way to the basement for the records. Emily found the metal container with the Smithson label and Brad lifted it from the storage area.

"Let's see if there's one for the Kerr family," Emily said, as she paused to check.

"I was wondering when you were going to bring up Ken as a suspect," Brad said. "Especially since he was in the vicinity right before the letter from your desk disappeared.''

''I thought we were voting for whoever Lester was blackmailing,'' Emily said. ''What could Lester have possibly found to blackmail Ken about? His family wasn't one of the original ones in Courage Bay, so that lets out anything to do with the *Ranger* letters. From what Oliver read of the first page of the gardener's letter, there was nothing in it that would concern Ken.''

''Agnes Smithson Hopper was the one who caused the death of his family, remember? Besides, whatever Lester was using to blackmail someone could have been something in the documents we didn't catalog. No way to know how many of them may be missing.''

''Not a happy thought,'' Emily agreed. ''Well, Ken's family has no genealogy records down here. Not surprising, I suppose, since so many of his ancestors were wiped out in that 1904 fire. Let's go.''

When they'd climbed the stairs to the ground floor, the guard was escorting the last visitors out the door. The museum would be closing in a few minutes.

Emily hesitated, remembering they couldn't go back to her office. ''The library will be cleared out in a couple of minutes. Could you set the records in there for me?''

''I have a better idea,'' Brad said, as he headed toward the museum's back exit.

''Where are you going with the genealogy files?'' Emily called after him.

''I'm putting them in the trunk of my car.''

''Genealogy records are never supposed to leave the Heritage Museum,'' Emily said.

''Well, today they're going for a little ride with us.''

''Us?''

He was out the door and halfway to his car before she caught up with his long strides.

''What do you mean a ride with us? You have to report in to the E.R. soon.''

"Not for the next fourteen hours," he said as he opened the trunk of his car and slipped the box of records inside.

"You don't have to work on a Saturday night? How did that happen?"

"I put in an extra eight hours today taking care of the broken bones and black eyes of some overexuberant soccer players," he said. "This is my mandatory time-out."

He was smiling at her. And the implication of all that available time was beginning to settle in.

"Going to ride with me?" he asked.

She shook her head as she beat a retreat to her car. After setting the copies of the *Bulletin* on the passenger seat, she slipped behind the wheel.

He followed her and waited beside the driver's door until she lowered the window.

"I'm going to put together dinner for us tonight," he said.

"This is a joke, right?" she asked as she buckled up.

"You don't think I can do it?"

"I saw your kitchen, remember?"

"But you haven't seen my excellent selection of takeout menus. I can whip by a few of my favorite places and have a delectable assortment ready for you at my apartment in less than forty minutes. We can go over the genealogy records there."

"On your coffee table strewn with books? Or on your carpet strewn with body parts?"

He wore the confident expression of a man incapable of being distracted from his goal. "Since ambience is obviously important to you, we'll go to your place."

Alone with him at her place. He must have read what flashed across her face. Resting his hands on the edge of her open window, he met her eyes.

"Emily, we'll eat together, work together, and try to figure out these skeleton and time capsule puzzles together. And when the time comes, you'll be able to banish me to your couch if that's what you want."

He bent down to kiss her briefly before turning and heading back toward his car.

BRAD WAS SETTLED comfortably in one of Emily's chairs as he watched her finishing the remnants of the eclectic assortment of food he'd bought. He'd suggested they eat in her living room where they could spread out the records she wished to review. She'd not only agreed but now sat across from him on the couch, her shoes discarded under the coffee table, her feet tucked beneath her.

He liked the fact that she was at ease and informal with him. He also liked being here in her home and seeing all the effort she put into making it both beautiful and comfortable.

She was going to take care of their child with this same kind of loving attention.

Their child. He didn't know at what point the baby had changed in his mind from his to theirs, but he liked the new terminology.

Had it only been himself, he probably would have grabbed a hamburger tonight. But he felt both unaccustomed pride and responsibility knowing he was feeding her and their baby. So he'd carefully selected tonight's menu from several different delis that specialized in fresh fruit and salads as well as chicken and beef dishes.

She was studying the Smithson genealogy as she munched on a slice of apple. "I don't understand this. I can't find Agnes."

"How far back do the birth records go?"

"To 1868, when the Smithson family was still in Nevada."

"She might have been born before that time, since she was already a widow in 1904," Brad suggested.

"Possibly. But this genealogy purports to list all the Smithson family members alive as of that date—even those female members who married and had different surnames. She's not among them."

"If the Smithsons haven't been eager to have the story of Agnes Smithson Hopper causing the deaths of the Kerr family become common knowledge, it could be that one of them purged her name from the family records to prevent association."

"If they did, it would have to have been done a long time ago. All the entries on these records are carefully handwritten and there are no empty spaces between dates and events that would imply something had been deleted."

She put the Smithson records aside and munched the rest of her apple slice as a frown played across her forehead. "Every time I think we have a trail to follow, it seems to fade away."

"Did you bring the copies of the newspapers you printed from the microfilm in hopes we'll find a new clue?"

She nodded as she swallowed the last of her apple. "They may say something more about the fire. Want to help me look through them?"

He slipped beside her on the couch and took the ones she gave him. Focusing on them wasn't easy. Her thigh was touching his and the combination of fresh apple and her was proving to be an intriguing aphrodisiac. What's more, she was no longer moving away from him.

After staring at the same page for several minutes, the words finally started to register in his brain. He saw nothing about the fire. But a news brief did catch his eye.

"Emily, listen to this," he said and read the information aloud.

"'Douglas Fitzwalter is recovering from the effects of the serious injury that he sustained in an accident three weeks ago. For a time his life was despaired of, but now he is rapidly convalescing.'"

"What's the date on that newspaper?"

"Three weeks after the burial of the time capsule."

"So that's why he didn't get his initials on the sundial," Emily said. "He must have been injured right before the time capsule was buried."

"And quite possibly in an altercation with R. C. Cox."

"Which could have been when he lost his dagger," Emily said. "But why was he fighting with Cox? And who else was with him? And how did Cox's body get buried with the time capsule?"

"I wish I had the answers for you," Brad said.

She sent him a nice look before she went back to reading. Making an effort to refocus his attention, he scanned the headlines on the rest of the newspapers for any story that could relate to their puzzles.

"Here it is," Emily said a few minutes later.

Brad looked over to see her pointing at a short article. The headline proclaimed, Family Fire Tragic Accident. He read it aloud.

"'The fire at the Kerr home that resulted in the deaths of five family members and a friend last week was caused by a fallen candle. Agnes Hopper rushed in to try to save her neighbors and woke up six-year-old Gene Kerr, sending him for help. When the boy returned with another neighbor, it was too late. Agnes Hopper and the rest of the Kerr family had been overcome by smoke and perished in the conflagration. Gene Kerr, the only surviving member of the family, was sent to live with his aunt in San Diego.'"

"That's a completely different account," Emily said after he finished. "And no explanation as to why the story was changed. How strange."

"Some new fact might have come to light," Brad suggested.

"What do you mean?" Emily asked.

"That original story was printed the morning after the

fire, no doubt from first reports rushed to the newspaper that was being printed for inclusion in the time capsule.''

''You're saying someone didn't get the facts straight?''

''Only that it's possible. Gene Kerr was awakened in the middle of the night by smoke and fire and maybe even Agnes Hopper calling out. He had to be scared, disoriented. I've listened to some wild stories from young children brought into the E.R. under similar traumatic circumstances. What that youngster thought he saw and heard Agnes saying and doing could have been fueled by fear and imagination.''

''So what happened? Someone else who was at the scene came forward later to relate a different story?''

''That would explain this news brief. A home fire caused by a lit candle resulting in the death of a family and a neighbor trying to help them is far less sensational than a nice woman suddenly struck insane and running amok.''

Emily set the newspaper copies aside and rested the back of her head against the couch. ''If that's what happened, why did someone take the newspaper with the original story?''

''Assuming the newspaper was taken because of the fire story, it could be that whoever was trying to cover it up might not have been aware that a revised version had been published. This later copy of the *Bulletin* with the news brief we just read wasn't in the time capsule documents.''

''But this later version of the story has been in the archives for decades, available to anyone in the Historical Society,'' Emily said.

''Still, you only looked for the information recently.''

''I've been a member of the Society for a comparatively brief time. Since my family isn't part of Courage Bay history, I haven't made a point of going through the old records. However, the rest know about Dot's research. I can't imagine they didn't check through the microfilm for mention of their ancestors.''

"Okay, let's look at this from the other side. The families involved know about the revised story but not necessarily the original, since it only shows up in the *Bulletin* from the time capsule."

"Ken knew about the original story. Remember when he asked me if I'd seen it and said that I shouldn't let the story bother me because it didn't bother him?"

"How did he know about the original story, Emily? That copy of the *Bulletin* wasn't on the microfilm we reviewed."

"Since the history involved his family, I assume it was passed down to him. Which would also explain why he wasn't bothered by it. He knows about the second story of the fire that corrected the first."

"Maybe others knew about that original story and were more bothered by it than Ken. There was nothing in either of the newspaper articles that mentioned Agnes Hopper's middle name. Oliver Smithson was the only one who saw the second page of the gardener's letter with her full signature. Could be that's why he stopped reading it when he did, so her tie to his family wouldn't be known."

"But why? Even if he'd been told the original account of the story, surely he would have also been told that the fire was later ruled accidental. What would he be afraid of? Why take the gardener's letter and newspaper?"

"I'm stumped," Brad admitted.

She closed her eyes and let out an exhale of frustration. "This is like opening a mystery book in the middle. I get the feeling we're missing an important beginning. It would be nice to know if this was an Agatha Christie story, where the psychological makeup of the suspects would point us to the answer."

"Or a Sherlock Holmes tale," he said, "where the clues would be contained in the physical evidence."

Brad had been staring at Emily's profile ever since she'd closed her eyes. He didn't want to think about this puzzle anymore tonight. With the edge of his fingertips, he smoothed the tiny indentation of the frown drawing her eyebrows together. Then he traced the hollow beneath her cheek and the soft curve of her chin.

"What are you doing?" she asked, her eyes still closed, her lips lifting at the edges.

"Being too subtle, obviously."

He kissed her forehead, the tip of her nose, her lips.

Her eyes opened—large and lovely—and stared into his.

"Are you trying to seduce me?"

"Could I?"

"Not a chance."

"Damn, I didn't think so."

Her smile came and went very quickly. The seriousness of the look that replaced it gave him pause.

"Brad, I really need to take this slow."

"Slow," he repeated. "Got it." He kissed her neck, very slowly.

Her resulting sigh was a little bit shaky. "I can't afford any complications in my life."

"No complications," he repeated. "Got it."

His arm circled her waist as he gently nibbled on her ear.

The pulse in her neck was throbbing. "You're making love to me."

"Yes, Emily. Nothing complicated about that."

The sound that escaped her throat was low and breathy. "You told me I could banish you to the couch."

"I'm already on the couch," he whispered near her ear. "Stay with me here."

"This is not a very big couch."

"One of its best features." He brushed kisses down her neck and she let out a delicious little moan.

"Your feet are going to hang off the edge."

"We'll watch them dangle together. They'll be our comic relief."

"Brad, it's time I went to bed."

As hard as it was, he made himself stop. He'd told her she could banish him to the couch. She had to know that when he gave his word, he meant it.

He rose, bringing her with him. Holding her hands within his, he planted a soft kiss inside each palm. "Do I let myself out or is the couch an option?"

She looked him in the eye and smiled. "Your feet won't dangle off the edge of my king-size bed."

One very long second passed before the message in her words fully sank in. He held her gaze as he bent down to kiss her, first lightly and then not lightly at all.

Her arms circled his waist. She was with him. And that was the last coherent thought he had for a long time.

EMILY LAY ON HER BACK IN BED staring up at the blackness of the ceiling. She could feel the warmth of Brad beside her, his breath against her cheek.

His slow, deep breathing told her he was asleep. By all rights she should be, too.

Her body was heavy with that lovely lassitude that resulted from being well and truly loved. When it came to a woman's anatomy, this doctor most definitely knew what he was doing.

Resisting him tonight had not been possible. And she very much doubted she'd be able to resist him tomorrow. But she could and would resist ascribing more meaning to this than was there.

Every time she began to care for a guy her expectations would fly off to some mythical cloud nine of romantic perfection—only to plummet back to earth shattered into a million pieces when reality finally set in.

That was not going to happen this time. She was taking this slow. This was going to be uncomplicated.

They were simply two people enjoying each other and

the time they shared. No expectations whatsoever. When one had no expectations, one was never disappointed.

She closed her eyes and went to sleep on that peaceful thought.

BRAD STEPPED OUT of Emily's shower to find a new toothbrush—still in its wrapping—with a tube of toothpaste beside it next to the sink. There was also a razor with a fresh blade.

His reflection in the mirror smiled back at him. He couldn't remember ever feeling this good. When he exited the bathroom a few minutes later, he smelled coffee and heard the comfortable clatter of breakfast dishes coming from down the hall.

Great smell. Great sounds. Great woman.

He'd flung his clothes on the floor in his considerable haste of the night before. She'd picked them up and laid them neatly over a chair.

Probably thinks I'm a slob, he mused as he got dressed. *And she still likes me.* The thought made him grin.

He sat on the edge of the bed, pulling on his socks and shoes. She wanted to take this slow. No problem. He could do slow.

Over the next few months he'd start to drop hints about his moving in when the baby came. His hours would be fewer and more regular. He'd be a big help to her. When the baby woke up during the night, he could be the one to get up and take care of it. Yes, lots of selling points there.

Breast-feeding was very important for a baby. None of this formula in a bottle stuff. He was going to have to talk to Emily about this. She was a smart, reasonable woman. Once she knew the facts, she'd do the right thing.

They had a lot to talk about. Might be a good idea for him to move in before she had the baby. Yes, that made more sense. He needed to be on hand to take her to the hospital when the time came. And welcome their baby into the world.

Slow. That was the way to approach her on this stuff. One small step at a time so he didn't scare her. Last night had been groundbreaking—not to mention ground shaking. But he didn't kid himself. She could still back off if he wasn't careful.

No complications she had said. No problem. He'd keep it uncomplicated.

Next month after the exams were over, he'd start laying the groundwork for his moving in. Bring a few things over for the nights they spent together. Get her used to the idea.

All he needed was a bit of closet space, an extra drawer. Her home was very neat. He suspected her storage areas would be, as well. He pulled open the nightstand to see if it offered any room.

Exactly as he thought. Not cluttered at all. Only a box of tissues, a scrapbook and a pen. Curious, he picked up the scrapbook and opened it to the first page.

Dear Sprout,

Today I learned you are a part of me. I don't have the words to tell you how wonderful it feels to know that we are one. How much sweeter my days on this earth have become. How the rhythm of my life has finally found its perfect beat.

Not a scrapbook, but a journal. Emily was writing to her baby.

As Brad flipped through the pages, he could see that she had done so nearly every day since she'd learned she was pregnant, sharing her hopes and dreams and so much love for the tiny life she carried.

She hadn't spoken to him about the baby. He had no idea she felt this deeply. Ed had told him that Emily was thrilled to be having a child. He didn't understand how thrilled until he read these loving thoughts.

He was trespassing on her privacy and he knew it. He should close the journal and put it away. But he kept on reading because he was captivated by the beautiful words, the heartfelt emotions that poured out from the sweetness inside her.

Still, not even those prepared him for her latest entries—the ones full of him.

EMILY NORMALLY DIDN'T go to the trouble of making coconut-cream muffins from scratch. But she loved the aroma that filled the house when they were baking. And there was a reason to make the effort this morning. She had a guest to share them with.

She checked the clock. They had slept in and then some. By her calculations, Brad should have another hour before he needed to leave to check in at the E.R. Time for a nice, leisurely Sunday breakfast.

Once the muffins were in the oven, she squeezed the oranges. Nothing like fresh-squeezed orange juice. Well worth the effort. She was humming by the time she began to assemble the ingredients for their omelettes.

This felt comfortable. Finally, an open, companionable, manageable relationship with a man. Free of all those unsettling and unsavory emotional complications that were inevitable when one led with one's heart instead of one's head.

She was facing the counter, cracking the eggs into a mixing bowl when she heard him enter the kitchen. A moment later his two strong arms circled her waist, his hands spreading over her tummy, bringing her back against him.

"Hi," she said over her shoulder. "Breakfast will be ready in a few minutes."

He took an egg out of her hand, set it on the counter and turned her toward him. The smile on her face stilled when she saw the intensity of the look on his.

"Brad?"

His answer was a kiss. Not a sweet kiss. A desperately passionate kiss that lasted a very long time and left Emily dizzy and breathless. And made her wonder how the man who had made such extraordinary love to her in bed a mere hour before could possibly possess the energy or stamina to execute such a kiss.

He held her close to him afterward, fiercely close. It was a good thing. Emily wasn't sure she could have stood on her own.

A moment ago she'd been congratulating herself on the uncomplicated relationship she had with this man. This did not feel uncomplicated.

This felt dangerous.

There was a buzzing going off inside her head. It took a moment for Emily to realize that it was the oven timer.

"The muffins," she mumbled into his shoulder.

He said nothing, made not a move to let her go.

"I have to take the muffins out of the oven."

Still nothing. And the timer kept buzzing.

"Brad?"

Finally, he released her and stepped back.

Emily grabbed an oven mit and hurriedly pulled out the muffins. Her hands were shaking. She set the pan on the counter, closed the oven door and sank onto the nearest chair.

She watched him pour himself a cup of coffee and drink it down in one gulp.

"What was that?" she asked, when she finally had enough breath to do so.

He refilled his cup and faced her. "I don't want to take this slow, Emily."

She stared at him, newly shaken by the emphatic delivery of those words.

"I'm well aware that your life plan no longer includes a man. But I'm here. And I'm staying."

He was looking at her straight. She didn't know if she was thrilled at the implications of his message or scared to death, but suspected she was both.

She swallowed hard, took a deep breath. "I told you last night that I'm not looking to complicate my life."

"You've had two lousy relationships with men. I can understand why you'd rather stay alone than risk another one. But you're going to like our relationship, Emily. I haven't had a vasectomy, nor am I hiding a wife and kids in another state. And I plan to complicate the hell out of your life."

She stared at him, wondering if she could possibly be interpreting what he was saying correctly.

The doorbell rang. It took an extreme effort of will for Emily to get her numb brain and body sufficiently animated to go see who was there.

CHAPTER THIRTEEN

EMILY SAW HER BROTHER'S FACE through the peephole. It wasn't unusual for him to pay a visit on the weekend. But his timing this morning left something to be desired.

"Hi, Em," Ed said, as he brushed by her on his way inside. "Was in the neighborhood so I thought I'd drop by for some coffee. Is that Brad's car I saw outside?"

"We were about to have breakfast."

"And you made coconut-cream muffins," he said, sniffing the air appreciatively. "Now I remember why you're my favorite sister."

"Because I'm your only sister," she called after him. He was halfway to the kitchen. By the time she got there, Ed had poured himself a cup of coffee and was taking a seat next to Brad at the table.

If Ed thought it strange to find Brad here, he gave no indication. Emily was glad she'd furnished Brad with a fresh razor. He was shaved, his hair in perfect place. He looked far more like a man who had stopped in for breakfast than one who had spent the night.

She went back to the mixing bowl and set about finishing the omelette.

"You look dressed for work," Brad said to Ed. "I thought Sunday was your day off."

"Chief called me in. Things have been hopping on the case. You're not going to believe the latest."

"Try me," Brad said.

"Councilman Himlot came into possession of some of

the stolen letters written by the crew members of the *Ranger*," Ed said.

"From the way you phrased that, I take it you don't suspect he took them."

Ed shook his head. "When he came out of church this morning, he discovered a packet of *Ranger* letters had been left on the driver's seat of his car."

"And he immediately went through them looking for his ancestor's letter," Emily guessed as she grated cheese.

"Which he didn't find," Ed confirmed. "He also didn't find the Fitzwalter letter among the bunch. He was hopping mad. Wanted the chief to get a warrant to search Fitzwalter's home and car."

"If Gerald Fitzwalter had taken the *Ranger* letters, why would he give any to Dean Himlot?" Brad said.

"That's what the chief tried to get through Dean's thick skull. Our councilman finally listened to reason and quieted down."

"Since Himlot was given some of the *Ranger* letters, is it possible that Fitzwalter was given some, as well?" Emily asked.

"You ever get tired of botany, you can join me in the detective unit any day," Ed said. "Fitzwalter's call came in soon after Himlot's. Gerald found a bunch of the *Ranger* letters—as well as the original box they were in—on his doorstep this morning."

"Let me guess," Brad said. "Neither the letter from his ancestor nor Himlot's was among them."

"Not bad," Ed said. "How did you figure that?"

"I'm getting the feeling that someone is playing a game with those two. And maybe the rest of us."

"Have any idea who?"

"Number one on my list would be the person Lester tried to blackmail, and who later ended up taking the artifacts from him."

Ed nodded. "That's the way the chief and I see it, too.

We think that this guy—or gal—is now returning the stuff in his or her own sweet time and way."

"You realize there's one thing that's not going to be returned," Emily said.

"Yeah. The item that was being used to blackmail. So, what's your pick? The two missing *Ranger* letters, the map, the copy of the Bulletin or the first page of the gardener's letter?"

"It could be something that Emily and I never got a chance to catalog," Brad said.

"And even if it's something we did catalog," Emily said, "I think the person being blackmailed might hold back on one or two other items to confuse matters, don't you?"

"If that turns out to be the case," Ed said, "there's a good chance we're never going to know what the blackmail was all about."

On that disturbing note, Emily served their breakfast. They grew quiet as they ate.

Ed's cell phone rang as they were finishing their coffee. He looked at the calling number. "It's the chief," he said. "I'd better take this outside."

He went out the back door into the yard, closing the door behind him. As much as her brother had shared with them about the case, it was clear to Emily that he wasn't sharing everything.

"Time for me to leave for the E.R.," Brad said as he rose. He took her hand, drew her to her feet and led her to the front door.

"I'll call you as soon as I get off work," he said. "Try not to figure out all the answers to our mysteries before then. I'd like to think that you need me as much as I need you."

He kissed her again with that same kind of passionate desperation that drained all the feeling out of her legs, the air out of her lungs and every single thought from her head.

As she watched him walk to his car, she leaned against the door frame, grateful for its support.

"So, what's going on?" Ed's voice said from behind her.

Emily didn't think he'd seen the kiss. If he had, he wouldn't have to be asking that question.

"What do you mean, what's going on?"

"Last time you made coconut-cream muffins for a guy you were married to him. What's with you and Brad?"

"Go to work," she said, pushing him gently out the door. "I'm sure a big, important Courage Bay detective has a lot more important things to attend to than interrogating his favorite sister."

WHEN BRAD ENTERED the physicians' lounge, he found Ed waiting for him.

"Nurse told me you were here," Brad said as he headed for the coffee machine. "Waiting long?"

Ed glanced toward his wristwatch. "Over an hour. What in the hell have you been doing?"

"All the wild, exciting things that make Sunday afternoons in the E.R. so much fun."

"Such as?"

"A man yawned too loudly in church and dislocated his mandible. After getting his jaw back together, I had to remove a bug from a two-year-old's ear and then drain a felon."

"Drain a felon?" Ed repeated. "Jeez, I thought we cops were tough."

"A felon in this case being an infection of the distal pulp of the finger," Brad said as he picked up the plastic cup full of the dark stuff that had the nerve to call itself coffee. From now on he was going to be bringing a Thermos of Emily's superb brew to work. She'd already spoiled him. The thought made him smile.

"You seem happy about this felon draining," Ed remarked.

"A job well done always leaves a good feeling," Brad said as he took the chair opposite his friend's. "I'm surprised you hung around so long. Thought you'd be busy on the case, what with all the new developments of the *Ranger* letters showing up and the call from your chief at breakfast."

"Speaking of breakfast."

Yeah, Brad figured that was why Ed had been hanging around waiting to talk to him.

He sipped the awful coffee and set it quickly aside. "Emily's a great cook."

"You weren't there for her cooking. The hood of your car was cold."

That's what he got for romancing the sister of a detective.

"What's going on, Brad?"

"That's between me and Emily."

"Wrong. It's never been just between you and Emily. I'm the one who started this mess, remember?"

"Are you asking me what my intentions are toward her?"

"Of course I'm asking you about your intentions. I'm her brother, damn it! A couple of weeks ago you didn't even know her. And now you're spending the night?"

Yeah, that was kind of mind-blowing.

"This is totally out of character for Emily," Ed said. "Hell, she didn't even let the jerk she married kiss her until they'd been dating three months. Why is she with you? Does she know you know about the baby?"

"Not yet," Brad said, trying not to smile. So, her making love with him had been special for her. He figured as much, especially after reading those things she'd written about him in her journal.

"When are you going to tell her?" Ed asked.

"I'm not. She's going to tell me."

Ed frowned. "Run that one by me again."

"Emily likes me. A lot. When the time comes that she knows she can trust me, she'll tell me."

"What are you going to do then?"

"Let her know how happy I am she's having my baby. How much I want to be a part of its life. Once she understands that, she'll accept me as the baby's father. I'm going to be a good father, too. It's not a decision she'll ever regret."

"You're sure this is going to happen?"

"I'm going to do my best to make it happen."

"Brad, I swear to God, if you hurt her—"

"Ed," Brad cut him off sharply, "believe me. I wouldn't hurt Emily for anything in this world."

His friend looked at him squarely for a long moment before a small smile of understanding circled his lips. "No, I don't believe you would."

WHEN EMILY EXITED her front door Sunday afternoon to reset the timer on the sprinkler system for her plants, she was surprised to see an agitated Holly charging up the walkway toward her.

"Did you put this in our mailbox?"

Holly was waving a letter-size envelope in her hand. Emily beckoned her inside and closed the door before taking the envelope out of Holly's hand. *Dorothy Mission* was typed on the front. She pulled out the single sheet of paper within. The message on it was also typed.

I understand what you took, and I think I even know why. Don't worry. If that's the way you want it, no one else will ever know.

"Did you?" Holly asked. "Please tell me."

Emily shook her head. "When I have something to tell your mother, I don't do it with anonymous notes. You say you found this in your mailbox?"

Holly began to pace. "Mom always brings in the mail, but she's away with Dad at that B and B for the weekend. When I went out to the box this morning to see if we had any letters delivered yesterday, I found that stuffed between a couple of bills."

"The envelope was sealed?"

"Yeah. Do you have some coffee?"

That was when Emily saw what she had missed before. Holly wasn't only agitated. She was scared.

"Come into the kitchen and I'll make a fresh pot. There's a coconut-cream muffin left over from breakfast if you're hungry."

Emily waited until Holly had drunk two cups of coffee filled with milk and sugar and munched down the muffin before asking the question that was foremost on her mind.

"What is it you think your mother has done?"

Holly slumped in her chair. "Mom didn't do it. I did."

"What did you do?" Emily asked.

"I found the garbage bags filled with the time capsule contents on our back porch before Mom came home. I didn't know what they were so I opened them. It was sitting on the very top—staring me right in the eyes. I was so shocked that all I could think about was that Mom didn't deserve the grief."

"What was it you saw that would have caused her grief?"

"A newspaper story about a woman going insane and killing a whole family. Her name was Agnes Hopper. Hopper is my maternal grandmother's maiden name. We're directly descended from Agnes."

Emily gave herself a moment to come to terms with that bit of news. "Holly, I've heard of Agnes Hopper," she said carefully. "I was under the impression that Agnes's maiden name was Smithson."

Holly shook her head. "Agnes did marry a Smithson when she was around twenty. But he died in some kind of an accident a year later and they never had any kids."

That would explain why Emily hadn't found Agnes in the Smithson family genealogy. She hadn't been born a Smithson. When their genealogy records were prepared, she must have already been widowed from her Smithson husband.

"Elias Hopper married Agnes a few years after her first husband died," Holly went on. "They had a couple of kids before he kicked and she ended up a widow again. He was a lot older than she was. Elias was my great, great, great grandfather. It's all in our genealogy records."

The one set of records Emily had not looked through.

"Mom doesn't know Agnes went insane. She thinks…"

"What does she think?" Emily prodded when Holly hesitated.

"That Agnes was some sort of heroine. When I was a kid she showed me a copy of the *Bulletin* she'd saved on microfilm from that time. It gave an account of Agnes dying in the fire at the Kerr home while she was trying to save her neighbors."

The story she and Brad had read the night before.

"Mom was so proud of Agnes. If that article I read in the *Bulletin* was circulated among our family and the Society, she'd be so ashamed. I couldn't let that happen. Can you understand?"

"I can understand that the desire to keep someone you love from hurt can make finding that line between right and wrong very hard sometimes. But, Holly, that article you read in the *Bulletin* from the time capsule was dated before the article your mother found. There's a good chance that the first story wasn't accurate and the second one describing Agnes's heroism was."

"You mean it was meant to correct the first? But why didn't it say that?"

"I don't know. It might simply have been the way they did things in those days. What happened to the copy of the *Bulletin* with the fire story?"

"I hid it. I wanted to burn it—I nearly did—but I couldn't bring myself to. Guess I got some of Mom's historical-preservation genes after all. Are you going to tell your brother?"

"I'm going to let you do that," Emily said.

"What if I don't?"

Emily smiled at her. "You will. During the past ten years your mother and I have been friends, I have watched you grow into a strong young woman. You are very much like her. I have never once seen you shrink from facing either the hard facts of life or the consequences of your actions."

Holly let out a sigh. "You're already far too good at this mom stuff. Your kid's never going to be able to get away with anything."

Emily chuckled.

"We still don't know who sent this note," Holly said as she stared at the envelope lying on the table beside her coffee cup.

"Since our fingerprints are all over it, it might be difficult for the police to decide," Emily said.

"You think I should give it to them?"

"What do you think, Holly?"

"I don't want to get whoever it was into trouble. They knew what I did and said nothing."

"Have you forgotten the envelope was addressed to your mom?"

"That's only because they assumed she was the one who got rid of the newspaper. When I opened the first trash bag and saw what was inside, I pulled all of them into the house so no one would see me."

"You went through the other things?"

"Only the newspapers. I had to be sure that it was the only story that talked about the fire Agnes started. When I didn't find any others, I put all the rest of the stuff inside the trash bags and dragged them back onto the porch so Mom would find them there."

"Still, the note in your mailbox said the writer knew what your mother had done and why. How did that person know what had been done, Holly?"

"Because they read the newspaper article about Agnes Hopper, and when the TV news reported that issue of the *Bulletin* was missing, they thought Mom had taken it. There are people in the Society who know my grandmother's maiden name was Hopper."

"No doubt. But who knew about the newspaper article that mentioned Agnes?"

Emily watched the rest of the truth dawn on Holly's face, the truth that her guilt had blinded her to from the moment she'd picked up the envelope.

"Oh my God. It had to be the person who returned the items to Mom. The one who took them away from Lester. The one who kept all that other stuff. That's the only person who would have had a chance to read that newspaper article!"

"THANKS FOR BRINGING Holly in," Ed said.

"You won't charge her, will you?" Emily asked as she took the chair in front of his desk.

"She came forward voluntarily. Handed over what she took. Seeing as she's still a minor, I'm sure the D.A. will let the matter slide. I'll tell the reporters that the missing newspaper from the time capsule was turned in by an anonymous source."

"You're a pretty nice guy for a brother," Emily said. "You ever get a chance to talk to Phoebe about visiting the hospital the night someone tried to steal the skeleton?"

"She says she was dropping off a fruit basket for the guy who had the stroke. Left it at the nurses' station."

Emily supposed that was plausible. "Was the call from your chief this morning about the case or can't you talk about it?" she asked.

"He wanted to tell me that the only fingerprints found

on the box of *Ranger* letters put on Fitzwalter's doorstep were Gerald's. I would have told you this morning but you shoved me out of the door so fast, I didn't have a chance."

Ed looked at her pointedly.

"Brad's simply helping me with the skeleton," she said. "And he's been very supportive since the theft of the time capsule contents."

"He's a damn good guy—as I think I've mentioned on one or two occasions before. I'll see Holly home after her statement is completed and she has a chance to sign it. You don't need to stick around, if there's someplace you want to go—or someone you want to talk to?"

"Thanks," Emily said, refusing to be baited. "There is work I need to catch up on."

Her brother's look was a bit too smug as she left his office.

Was she that transparent? She did want to talk to Brad and tell him about Holly having taken the copy of the *Bulletin.* And see him. But he was at work. And dropping in on an E.R. doctor at work wasn't the same as dropping in on a research scientist or a computer programmer.

I'm going to complicate the hell out of your life.

He already had.

The TV tape she had promised Wayne and the Smithson genealogy records were in the trunk of her car. After dropping off the TV tape at Wayne's home, she headed for the Heritage Museum, eager to get the genealogy records back where they belonged before someone noticed they were missing and raised an unnecessary alarm.

Besides, she needed something to distract her mind. As she drove to the Botanical Gardens, she could feel the restless excitement and euphoria that only one emotion could bring to a woman.

She'd fallen for Brad Winslow.

For days she'd been telling herself to slow down, that it was happening too fast. But it hadn't been that fast. The truth was that she'd started to fall for him the moment she read his sperm-donor questionnaire. And read it again and again, her heart beating faster, harder, happier each time.

Even then on some level she'd known that she hadn't only found the right sperm. She'd found the right man.

At what point she could have stopped this from happening—if she could have stopped it from happening—she didn't know.

But what she did know was that a deeply buried part of herself—some foolish part that still believed in romantic love, no matter how much sense she'd tried to drum into it—had wanted this very much. Quite possibly even from the moment Ed had first told her about Brad.

I'm here. I'm staying.

That was what he had said. He was planning on being a part of her life. And he didn't even know that the baby she carried was his. She couldn't wait to see his face when she told him.

She was coming out of the basement of the Heritage Museum after returning the records when she glanced up and noticed Ken at the top of the landing.

"There you are," he said, greeting her with a smile.

"How did you know I'd be here?" she asked, as she climbed the stairs.

"I saw your car in the parking lot. When I knocked on your office door and you didn't answer, I figured you were in the library or down in the basement. Wanted to give you these."

Emily saw Ken was holding out a large manila envelope.

"It's those contact sheets I promised you from Founders Day," he said, answering the question that must have been on her face.

Reaching him, she took the envelope. "Thanks for remembering."

"Don't expect too much. I shot six rolls of film and

only got four decent photos for the newsletter. The next issue will be totally devoted to the time capsule. Speaking of which, I'll need your article on the skeleton by Tuesday.''

"We may not have all the answers by then.''

"Not a problem. This issue of the newsletter will be an overview of the Founders Day events and what was found. The more in-depth articles will follow when the police return the artifacts to us. Which reminds me. What was it that was stolen from your office yesterday?''

"A page from the gardener's letter that Oliver read on Founders Day.''

"The police are letting you look at the time capsule documents that were returned?''

"This was the second page of the letter—the one that was found beneath Lester's body.''

Ken nodded. "Something about it interest you?''

"I was curious about the medicinal plant she described.''

"You figure out who took the letter from your desk or why?''

She shook her head as they went through the back door toward the parking lot. "It makes no sense that someone would. It was only a copy. Ken, did you see anyone suspicious lurking about that day you came to get the film?''

"Police asked me that, as well. You, me, Winslow— we were the only ones on the top floor, far as I know. And I'm assuming from the way you look at him that the good doctor is above suspicion?''

Emily answered Ken's speculative look with a smile.

"Yes, I can see he is,'' Ken said. "Strange that anyone else would be interested in that plant. Unless Oliver is in financial trouble and decided it was an undiscovered medicinal wonder that his family's pharmaceutical company could cash in on?''

Emily knew Ken's comment was meant to be a joke. But remembering the conversation she'd overheard between Oliver and Wayne at the hospital, she didn't feel quite like laughing.

"The gardener drew a rough sketch of the plant," she said. "Before I had a chance to take a really good look, the page disappeared. Next time I see my brother, I'll have to ask him to get me another copy."

"When you do figure out what the plant was, let me know. I'm officially recruiting you to write an article about it."

They had reached their cars and Emily turned to him. "Ken, is this the first newsletter to highlight the year 1904?"

"I believe it is."

"What do you know about the families who were living in Courage Bay then?"

"I've heard and read various things about them over the years. Any family member in particular who interests you?"

"Douglas Fitzwalter."

"Serena's older brother. Yes, I remember reading about him, although offhand I can't remember the specifics. What do you want to know?"

"I came across an article about him in one of the old *Bulletins*—something about a serious injury he'd sustained around the time capsule's burial. Ring a bell?"

He shook his head. "I'm a writer and photographer— not a die-hard historian like so many others in the Society are. You should ask Phoebe."

"Maybe Gerald would be a better source."

"Gerald? That's a laugh. He could be directly descended from this Douglas guy and not know it."

"You're kidding."

"Gerald's a good guy, don't get me wrong. But he's not a historian—not even when it comes to his own family tree. His main interest in the Society is attending the social functions and making business contacts. Phoebe's the virtual encyclopedia on this stuff. And she considers herself as much a Fitzwalter as a Landru. She inherited all of Serena's diaries when the old girl passed.''

''I didn't know there were diaries.''

''They line two floor-to-ceiling bookcases in Phoebe's library at home,'' Ken said. ''Serena was nothing if not prolific. From the dates on the outside, she must have started writing them when she was thirteen and didn't stop until she passed in her sixties.''

''Firsthand accounts by a woman of the time. Those diaries could be invaluable. Why hasn't Phoebe mentioned them?''

''I asked her once why she didn't donate them to the Society like she has her family's pictures and correspondence. She told me the diaries were personal, private reminiscences of her grandmother and not meant for the eyes of anyone outside the family. Said she'd drawn up her will with the provision that her grandmother's diaries would be cremated with her when she goes.''

''She's shared so much of her family's history. Why not the diaries?''

''Only one explanation, Emily. There must be some really scandalous stuff in them.'' Ken seemed amused at the thought. ''Makes you want to read them even more, doesn't it?''

IT WAS A SLOW NIGHT. Normally, Brad would welcome the extra time to catch up on paperwork or sleep. But he was too restless to be satisfied with either.

He'd tried Emily's home and cell numbers several times. He'd even tried her office number on the chance that she had decided to go there. But all he got for his efforts were voice-mail options and unanswered rings.

Damn, he really wanted to talk to her.

He wished he could walk up to his boss, tell him he needed some time off to take care of personal business and go find her.

But an E.R. doctor couldn't do that. Feeling frustrated

and not knowing what else to try, Brad punched in Ed's number at home. His friend answered on the second ring.

"So, you haven't heard from Emily, huh?" Ed baited him. "Maybe my sister doesn't like you quite as much as you thought."

"She knows that unlike her brother—the detective who sits around on his butt all day wasting taxpayers' money—an E.R. doctor is busy saving lives."

"That right? Well, if I were you, I wouldn't be making snide comments about the police officer who one day might be all that stands between you and a gunslinging psychopath."

Brad grinned. "And if I were you, I wouldn't be giving the runaround to the doctor who could be opening up your chest with a scalpel to dig out the bullets from the gun of that psychopath."

Ed laughed. "Yeah, I've heard from Emily. We were at the station together a few hours ago."

Ed filled Brad in on the visit he'd had from Emily and Holly earlier that day.

"So Agnes Hopper was Dorothy's ancestor," Brad said, surprised.

"Yeah. You never know who is related to who around here. We didn't get any prints but Emily's and Holly's off the weird note stuffed into Dorothy Mission's mailbox."

"What about the trash bags?"

"In addition to Holly and Dorothy's prints there were a couple of unidentified smudged partials on the bags. Not good enough to run through the system."

"Did you get anything from Emily's office?"

"Nearly everybody's prints including yours. She was right. Too much traffic in and out to be of any help."

"Do you know where Emily is?" Brad asked.

"If she's not at home at this time of night, my guess would be she's visiting friends. And considering everything that's been happening today, those friends would probably be—"

"The Mission family," Brad finished and got the number from Ed.

"THANK YOU FOR BEING THERE today for Holly," Dorothy said. "And helping her to make the right decisions."

Emily was sitting across from Dorothy in the living room, while Ted and Holly were in the kitchen cleaning up the dinner dishes together. From the sounds of it, they were having a good time splashing each other with water and generally horsing around.

"She made all the right decisions on her own, Dot, thanks to the way her parents raised her."

"You're a good friend, Em."

There was a weariness to Dorothy's voice that concerned Emily. Despite the fact that she and Ted had returned from what was supposed to have been a relaxing stay at a B and B, Dorothy did not look very rested. The worry lines of the past week were still etched across her forehead.

"I don't know what to make of that newspaper article Holly read," Dorothy said. "How can the two stories about the fire be so different?"

Emily told Dorothy about Brad's suggestion that the six-year-old Gene Kerr may have been confused about what he heard and saw.

"Now that makes sense," Dorothy agreed. "Between you and me I'm glad that issue of the *Bulletin* wasn't one of the newspapers I came across while I was doing my doctoral thesis. That original story would have devastated me. Not to mention Ken."

"Ken?"

"He was working at the newspaper at the time. It was still housed in the old *Bulletin* building. He helped me copy the old papers in the basement archives onto microfilm."

"I didn't realize you two knew each other before he joined the Society."

Dorothy glanced toward the kitchen and lowered her voice. "We knew each other...quite well. The day he came across that news brief about his ancestors and mine, he put it on microfilm for me and printed out a copy. That's when he told me that Gene Kerr—the boy who escaped the fire—was his father. He said if Agnes hadn't awakened Gene that he would have died, too. Ken gave me a big hug and laughed about how we were linked by destiny to be together."

"You were romantically involved?" Emily asked.

Dorothy nodded. "He was older, fun, witty. I enjoyed his company. So many of the guys my age had no conversational skills or anything else to recommend them. But then I met Ted, and, well, as they say, the rest is history."

Emily wondered if it was history for Ken.

"So how's it coming with the skeleton's ID?" Dot asked.

"Brad and I have been able to identify him as R. C. Cox, a traveling snake-oil salesman from the time."

"Ah, so it *is* Brad now. No wonder you're glowing."

"Dot, you know perfectly well that's the pregnancy hormones."

"You were pregnant for eight weeks without so much as a glimmer. Now after a couple of weeks with Brad you're suddenly the Magic Castle at Disneyland. I rather doubt the hormones at work here have anything to do with pregnancy."

"The dishes are done, Mom," Holly said as she came bouncing into the room, saving Emily from having to respond. "Dad wants to know if you'd like a brandy and Emily would like a soft drink."

Before Dorothy or Emily could answer, the phone rang.

"I thought your father was going to leave that damn thing disconnected tonight," Dorothy said, the stress that had been so much a part of her over the past week rising once again to the surface.

"I plugged it back in, Mom," Holly said with an apologetic shrug. "I'm expecting a call."

Ted poked his head into the room from the kitchen. "It's Josh, Holly. He said you left him a message."

Holly left to take the call.

"Maybe Holly likes to talk to Josh precisely because he has nothing to say back," Dorothy commented with a shake of her head. "That way she can talk to her heart's content without fear of being interrupted."

Emily smiled as she checked her watch. "Every woman's dream. I'd better go home and check my messages. I left my cell on the kitchen counter, and I've been gone all day."

"So how many times do you think he's called?" Dot asked.

"He's a very busy E.R. doctor. He doesn't have time to call."

"Amazing how you knew exactly who I was talking about. Come on. Give me some of the good stuff."

Emily sent her friend a smile. "Dot, I feel like I've known him forever. And yet every time I'm with him, it's new and exciting."

Dorothy beamed back. "Em, I'm so happy for you."

WHEN EMILY FINALLY ANSWERED her phone at home, Brad let out a sigh of relief. "I was getting ready to call your brother and ask him to put out an APB."

"You've been trying to reach me?"

"Only for the past two or three hours. Please, don't leave home without your cell phone again."

"How did you know I had?"

"I just got off the line with Dot. She told me to tell you that the Magic Castle at Disneyland has a special fireworks display tonight, whatever that means. Is it too late or can I talk you into coming down to the E.R.?"

"Now? I thought you told me to never come down to the E.R. at night?"

"You listen well."

"Depends on who's talking."

He grinned at her using his words on him. "I'd like to show you something."

"Actually, there's something I'd like to show you, as well," Emily said.

"Good. How soon can you be here?"

"Give me forty minutes."

CHAPTER FOURTEEN

BRAD WAS WAITING near the entrance of the E.R. when Emily arrived. To her surprise, he whisked her toward the elevator without a word. They entered with several other people and rode up to the floor that housed the ICU. Stepping from the elevator, he led her to the open doorway of a familiar room.

Samantha was sitting up in bed giggling at something the bedraggled man seated beside her was saying.

"When did it happen?" Emily asked.

"A few hours ago," Brad said. "The nurse said Samantha opened her eyes and the first thing she did was smile at the roses beside her bed."

Brad took Emily's hand and interlaced their fingers. "She insisted the nurse move the flowers closer so she could smell them."

Emily's eyes went to the vase sitting on the table beside the hospital bed. The buds had fully opened, providing a bright splash of color in the room.

"Is Samantha going to be okay?" she asked, fighting the lump in her throat.

"She doesn't remember the accident, which, all things considered, is a blessing. Other than that she's one hundred percent. Her father will be able to take her home in a few days. That's him with her. He only looks like a street person because he's refused to leave her side for the past three days and nights."

"Sounds like exactly the kind of dad she needs. I have a feeling you're going to be like that with your children."

He tugged her into a nearby storage room, closed the door and kissed her. It was another one of those kisses that had the earth disappearing beneath Emily's feet.

Abruptly, he pulled back. She was confused until she heard the faint crackle of the PA system in the hall. "Dr. Winslow to E.R. Dr. Winslow to E.R."

Because there was no ready elevator on the floor, they took the stairs down to the E.R. As he hurried toward the nurses' station, Emily marveled as all vestiges of the man who had kissed her so hotly disappeared into the countenance of a stoic doctor.

"What do we have?" he asked.

"Twenty-three-year-old male. Sucking stab wound, right anterior chest. Another superficial wound left thigh. ETA any minute."

"Where's Alec?"

"Curtain three. Drug overdose."

He nodded and grasped Emily's arm, moving with her out of earshot of the duty nurse.

Taking Emily's hand, he pressed something into her palm and closed her fingers around it. "This is an extra key to my apartment. I'll call you there as soon as I can."

"Your apartment."

"It's much closer than your place. Spend the night. I'll serve you breakfast in bed tomorrow morning when I get off shift."

"Brad, I—"

"It's either that or I'll be banging on your door at 6 a.m., waking up your neighbors and every barking dog within ten blocks," he warned. "You're dealing with an obstinate and pigheaded man here, remember."

The ambulance bay doors burst open and the paramedics ran in, pushing a gurney on which lay a groaning man covered in blood.

Brad gave her a gentle shove toward the door. "Go, Emily. I'll call you."

He rushed to join the paramedics as they rolled the

gurney toward the nearest trauma room, exchanging a barrage of cryptic questions and answers that Emily understood were an assessment of the critically injured man's vital signs.

This was the place Brad called home—where the heartwarming and heartrending existed side by side. She stood there silently taking it in, wondering at the strength that enabled him to do what he did, before letting herself out the door.

HIS LIVING ROOM MIGHT look like the set for a Hannibal Lecter movie, but Emily found Brad's bathroom to be clean and orderly. She wasn't surprised. He'd left her bathroom that way, as well. She didn't know a lot of guys who wiped down a shower after they used it.

This doctor training was good stuff for a man. When Emily walked into Brad's bedroom, she found it was also quite neat. Her eyes immediately went to the two framed photographs on his dresser. She picked up the first—a shot of an older woman, her arms around two teenage boys, one of whom Emily recognized as Brad.

She had no doubt that the woman was his mother and the older teenage boy, his brother—the one who had taken care of Brad when their mother died. He had a nice look to him.

In the second picture, Brad was standing in what appeared to be an anthropological excavation site, his arm around a young woman. She had soft black eyes and a face full of sunshine.

Emily slipped the photograph out of the frame, turned it over, read the words written on the back.

This was Julie's favorite picture of you two. We know she would have wanted you to have it.

So, her name had been Julie. Replacing the photograph in its frame, Emily studied the woman's delicate face, and the smile Brad had worn when he looked at her. The fact that he still kept their picture on his dresser was not lost on Emily.

She put both photographs back exactly where she had found them and sank onto the edge of the bed. She had been falling for Brad for some time now. But this had been very quick for him. Too quick?

His phone rang. She started to reach for it, but had second thoughts and withdrew her hand. This was his place, not hers. What had possessed her to come?

Her cell phone rang seconds later. She pulled it out of her purse and answered.

"Just wanted to make sure the key worked okay," Brad's warm voice said in her ear. "And that you didn't trip over any body parts."

He sounded so calm and sure.

"Emily, everything okay?"

"The key worked fine and all body parts are safe and sound."

"Glad to hear it. That was me who called on the land line a moment ago. Feel free to answer when it rings."

The picture of Julie looked down at her from the top of the dresser. "What if it's a woman from your past?"

"You're the only woman in my life now, Emily."

She smiled, kicked off her shoes and stretched back on the bed.

"Things became so hectic right before you left," he said, "that I never got a chance to ask what it was you wanted to show me."

"There is no dagger," she said.

"No dagger?"

"In the contact sheets Ken gave me. He said he used six rolls of film. I have six contact sheets, each one representing a roll of film. And not one of them has an image of the dagger that you found in the pit with the skeleton— or anything else you found."

"You seem to think that's important."

"Phoebe told me that Ken had photographed the dagger

in the pit. That's how she knew the dagger was with the skeleton. But Ken didn't get a picture of the dagger. And we didn't mention it was found with the remains. Nor did the TV film footage show it. So how did Phoebe know that the dagger was there?''

"That's a very good question.''

"Ken says Phoebe has Serena Fitzwalter Landru's diaries. Apparently Serena was a prolific writer and her diaries date from before the burial of the time capsule. Despite everything that the Landru family has shared with the Society, Phoebe is adamant that she'll not share her grandmother's diaries. I have a strong suspicion that there's something in them about R. C. Cox and how he ended up in the time capsule pit with a Fitzwalter dagger.''

"If Phoebe learned about the dagger from Serena's diaries, do you know what that means?''

"That the skeleton in the pit came out of Phoebe's family closet,'' Emily said.

"Shall we go see Phoebe tomorrow and get the straight scoop?''

"We'll need a plan for how to approach her. Phoebe has kept quiet about these things her entire life. And if what Ken says is true, she intends to take them with her to the grave. I don't see her suddenly opening up to us.''

"I already have a pretty good suspicion of what happened, Emily. And as smart as you are, I'm sure you do, too. Let's tell her what we know in a way that leaves her with the impression that we have the important answers.''

"And all we want her to do is fill in a few of the superficial details,'' Emily said, catching on. "So we put Plan Phoebe into operation immediately after breakfast tomorrow?''

"Not *immediately* after breakfast,'' Brad said. "I don't intend to get out of bed quite that quickly.''

Emily smiled at the message. Breakfast was getting to

sound better by the minute. "Your bed is firmer than mine."

There was a definite pause on the other end of the line. "Okay, I can see right now that we're going to need some ground rules. Rule number one. Never tell me you're in my bed when I can't join you there for another eight hours."

She smiled. "Did I say bed? I meant couch. Very firm couch you have."

A pause. "No, that's not going to work, either."

In the background she could hear him being paged.

"I have to go," he said. "Quick. Give me another image—any image—that doesn't involve you being either supine or prone."

"Okay. How about I've taken off all my clothes and I'm getting ready to step into your shower?"

He let out an exasperated breath. "I'm going to get you for this."

Emily was laughing hard as she hung up the phone. And feeling a whole lot better. Amazing what a call from her doctor could do.

AFTER TALKING IT OVER, Brad and Emily had decided he should contact Phoebe to set up their meeting. His knowledge of forensics gave him the authority to deliver the information they had uncovered.

Her home was in an upscale neighborhood with the kind of expansive grounds that required weekly tending by professional gardening services. Phoebe opened the door to them and, without so much as a word of welcome, led the way into a large living room.

The walls were mahogany panels. The shiny wood furniture, upholstered in soft brocade, looked expensive and antique. After gesturing toward two uncomfortable-looking chairs, Phoebe alighted on the one opposite, projecting the haughty disdain of disturbed nobility.

"Dr. Winslow, I have a very busy schedule today,"

she said. "I would appreciate it if you would get to the point and tell me what it is you chose to make such a mystery about over the phone."

She was a tough old gal, but Brad sensed a real concern behind her projected impatience.

"Emily and I thought that you would prefer to tell us in person what you would like us to do with the remains of your grandfather, R. C. Cox."

She stared at him for a long moment—not moving so much as an eyelash—before finally exhaling a soft, stricken sigh. Her firm shoulders slumped as though keeping them straight another second had suddenly become too exhausting a task.

"How did you find out?" she asked in a voice that was barely an echo of her normal hearty tone.

"His bones told us who he was," Brad said. "We matched them to his picture and to your family's genes."

"Genes?" she repeated.

"Cox had a rare bone disease," Brad said. "The same rare bone disease your father inherited from him. Your nephew came into the E.R. last year and was diagnosed with it, as well. Cox's bones also told us about the men he fought with before his death."

Phoebe wrapped her arms around her waist and held herself tightly as though cold. She stared past them. Whatever internal image she was seeing wasn't pleasant.

"We know Serena wrote about what happened in her diaries," Emily said, her voice soft. "And that you've read those diaries. We understand why you haven't said anything about this. Serena was a simple, small-town girl, barely seventeen. Cox was far more sophisticated, from a big city and at least twenty-five, -six?"

"Roscoe Cox was thirty-one," Phoebe said in syllables of ice.

"How did he seduce her, Phoebe?" Emily asked, coming forward in her chair, her tone full of the kind of concern that Brad knew could not be faked. "What lies did he tell her?"

"The same lies men have been telling women for ages," Phoebe said, as her eyes turned to Emily. "That he loved her. That he wanted a life with her. When she ran to him with the news that she was pregnant, she thought he'd be happy. That they'd get married as he'd promised."

"That's when she learned he wasn't going to keep that promise," Emily guessed.

"He told Serena that he already had a wife in San Francisco and he was leaving town to return to her," Phoebe said. "He warned her that if she claimed the baby she carried was his, he'd tell everyone that she knew he was married all along and pushed herself on him anyway."

"And that's when Serena's brother, Douglas, decided to have a talk with Cox," Brad said.

"Douglas found her crying," Phoebe said, as she turned her eyes to Brad. "When he coaxed the truth out of her, he became furious, grabbed his dagger and took off after Roscoe. Douglas was short, slender—no match for the big, burly Roscoe. Fearing for her brother, Serena ran to his good friend, Norman Landru, and told him. Norman promised her that he'd follow her brother and keep him safe from harm. He came upon them as Douglas drew his dagger and challenged Roscoe to a fight. Roscoe pulled out his gun and shot Douglas."

"Douglas was badly injured," Emily said, remembering the article that referred to his being wounded. "That's why he wasn't on hand to help bury the time capsule and carve his initials on the sundial."

Phoebe nodded, accepting Emily's knowledge without further question. "Norman slashed Roscoe's wrist with his knife, got him to drop the gun. But when Norman went over to help Douglas, Roscoe lunged for the gun. Norman wrestled him for it, wrenched it out of his hand. Then he shot Roscoe, killing him."

From having read the knife wounds on the skeleton, Brad didn't doubt that Phoebe's story fit the facts.

"The bullet had hit Douglas in the stomach," Phoebe continued. "He was bleeding badly. Norman carried him in his arms to the doctor's house two miles away. They told the doctor that Douglas's gun had misfired. Then Norman went back for Roscoe's body. He couldn't leave it for anyone to find, not with the bullet hole in its head."

"I take it that neither Norman nor Douglas was prepared to tell the sheriff why they had confronted Roscoe," Brad said.

"Of course not," Phoebe said, as though that should be obvious. "Serena's reputation was at stake. In those days, a woman was only as good as her reputation."

"Where had the fight taken place?" Emily asked.

"The outskirts of town. Once Norman had returned to the scene, he picked up Douglas's dropped dagger and Roscoe's gun, but realized that he didn't have a shovel to dig a grave."

"That's when he thought of the pit that had already been dug," Emily guessed.

Phoebe nodded. "It was almost dawn. In a few hours Norman was to join the others in burying the time capsule and setting the sundial over it. He dragged Roscoe's body to the hole and dumped it in. Then he covered the body with a layer of dirt."

"That's when Douglas's dagger must have fallen out of his pocket," Brad said.

"How did you know it was his dagger?" Phoebe asked. "When I looked at it, I saw no distinguishing marks at all."

"The magic of computer enhancement," Emily explained.

Phoebe shrugged, clearly not understanding the process and not caring to.

"The rainy, overcast day helped to hide Roscoe's body

when the capsule was later lowered into the pit," she continued. "No one suspected it was there."

"And Cox's wagon and team of horses?" Brad asked.

"After towing the wagon to the mountain pass and dumping it off a cliff, Norman let the horses go free to range over the hills. He figured when the wagon was found—and Roscoe and the horses were missing—that everyone would assume he'd continued his journey to San Francisco, which they did."

"Serena must have been very appreciative of all that Norman had done on her behalf," Emily said.

"He saved her brother's life and protected her name. Norman had loved her for some time—had only been waiting until she was eighteen to court her properly, openly, like a man of honor. When he asked her to marry him, he promised that he'd bring up her child as his own. He kept that promise. Serena grew to love him dearly."

Phoebe lifted her head to stare up at a portrait on the wall behind them.

Brad glanced over his shoulder at the painting. It predated the one in the museum by a few years. Serena was holding her new baby in this portrait and smiling. Norman was standing behind her, his hand resting on her shoulder, wearing the kind of look only a man very much in love with his wife and new baby could.

Unlike the more formal portrait in the museum, this one revealed the feelings that flowed between husband and wife.

"Norman didn't simply love, protect and marry my grandmother," Phoebe said. "He raised my father to be an honorable man who kept his word and did right by his employees. It was Norman who bounced me on his knee when I was a child and told me how much he loved me. Had I found such a man, nothing and no one—not even an ill father—could have kept me from him."

Brad watched Phoebe as she said those words. Her back had straightened, and she had once again assumed the look of someone certain of her breeding. But the woman before him knew her pride and strength had not been a product of her genes. It had been a direct result of feeling valued and loved.

"When do you hand in your article for the newsletter?" Phoebe asked Emily.

"Ken told me he needs it by tomorrow. I'll make a copy for you and drop it by so you'll know what to expect. You will not be disappointed."

Phoebe got the message Emily was sending. The smile that drew back her lips lightened her face and reached into her eyes. "As I've said before, Emily, you have nice qualities."

"What would you like me to do with the remains of Roscoe Cox?" Brad asked.

"I do not care what you do with his bones. He means nothing to me or my family. *My* grandfather's remains are buried in our family plot."

"I understand," Brad said.

"PHOEBE WAS THE ONE who tried to break into the morgue, wasn't she?" Emily asked once they had left her house and were on the road.

"I'm sure she was," Brad said. "Only she wasn't after the skeleton. She was after the dagger. Are you going to say anything to Ed?"

"No point. Even if he could prove it, which I doubt, I don't see what would be gained from bringing Phoebe up on charges for an attempted B and E."

"Tell me what you're going to write in the newsletter article."

"You've identified the skeleton as R. C. Cox, a traveling snake-oil salesman. That's all it has to say."

"Nothing about his tie-in to the Landru family?"

"As far as Phoebe is concerned, he has no tie-in. I'm ready to support her decision not to claim him. How about you?"

"The man lied to and seduced a seventeen-year-old girl, then wouldn't acknowledge her child as his. He shot and no doubt would have killed her brother if Norman hadn't taken action. He has no right to be called an ancestor. No such man does."

"I knew you'd feel that way. Any suggestions as to how I'm going to explain his cause of death?"

"We know he was shot with his own gun and that he peddled a concoction that no doubt contained fifty-percent alcohol. He could have gotten drunk, accidentally shot himself in the head and then wandered off dazed from his head wound until he fell into the open time capsule pit."

She laughed. "You have a very inventive mind. I should let you write this article."

"In the mayor's letter from 1904, it asked that their history be recorded with a light and understanding hand. I can think of no one better qualified to do that than you, Emily."

She smiled at him, a lovely smile that warmed him from the inside out.

"This feels good," she said after a moment.

"Having solved the mystery of the skeleton or going back to my place to make love?"

She leaned over and kissed his cheek. "Both."

As EMILY WAS STEPPING OUT of her shower, the telephone rang. She grabbed a towel and quickly wrapped it around herself. After spending most of the day at Brad's apartment, and knowing he was at work tonight, she didn't think it would be him calling.

But even the thought that it might be made her dash for the phone on the night table by her bed.

"Have you seen them?" Ed's voice boomed in her ear.

Emily fought down her initial disappointment as she tried to make sense of her brother's words.

"Seen what?" she asked as she sat on the bed and started to dry herself.

"The Fitzwalter and Himlot *Ranger* letters."

"You've found them? Where?"

"Copies of both letters were printed in the Society's newsletter right next to your article on the skeleton."

It had been several days since she'd submitted her article.

"I didn't even know the newsletter was out."

"You might have heard if you'd been at your office or home today. Where have you been?"

Emily had no intention of telling her brother she'd spent the day with Brad—or how they'd spent it. "Here and there," she said. "Where did you get a copy?"

"Mayor sent his over to the chief this afternoon. The editor of the newsletter printed a statement that copies of the Fitzwalter and Himlot letters were received anonymously with the request that their contents be included in the time capsule issue."

"Ken has had copies of those letters and not said a word? Have you talked to him?"

"He isn't answering his phone. Nor his door."

"Ed, what did the letters say?"

"Remember the story about Himlot saving a fellow crewman by grabbing a sail and smothering the sailor's clothes that had caught on fire?"

"Yes, of course."

"Well, according to the letter Fitzwalter wrote, *he* was the sailor Himlot saved. Fitzwalter described the scene in vivid detail. The wind screaming in his ears, the lightning slashing through the hull at his back. His clothes suddenly on fire. And then, while others fled from the flames, Himlot running to his rescue. The Fitzwalter letter said that he wanted history to have a record of the bravery of his fellow crewman and friend."

"Dean Himlot must be elated."

"There's more. Remember the story of Fitzwalter keeping an injured crewman afloat in the sea until the Indian boats came to rescue them? Well, it turns out that injured crewman was Himlot.''

Emily laughed as she rubbed her shoulders with the towel. ''No, this is too good to be true.''

''As he was weaving through the burning rubble of the sinking ship, Himlot grabbed a piece of iron pipe that had fallen in his way. The pipe was so hot it seared his hands. Fitzwalter helped him overboard and kept him afloat when he passed out from the pain of his injuries, until the Indians came to rescue them. Himlot explained it all, along with his poor penmanship, caused when those burns fused his fingers.''

''So it ends up they saved each other,'' Emily said. ''What a great story for Courage Bay history. What I like most about it is the fact that each man wrote about being rescued and gave credit to his rescuer. Neither boasted about having been a hero.''

''Gives you a good feel for the kind of real heroes these men were.''

''I hope Dean and Gerald are taking notes.''

''It'll be interesting to see how they respond when the news picks this up.''

''Brad said someone was playing a game with these two, giving each of them some of the *Ranger* letters—but not the ones they really wanted and were so worried about,'' Emily said. ''And all the time the guy, or gal, knew how it would end. I wonder who it is?''

''Em, hold on. My other line is ringing.''

While Ed had her on hold, Emily returned to the bathroom to hang up the wet towel and brush her hair. On her way back to the bed, she pulled out a nightgown from the dresser and slipped it on.

''Sorry to be so long,'' Ed said in her ear. ''Ken turned himself in.''

''He's there now?''

''Yep. With the copies of the Himlot and Fitzwalter letters.''

"How did he receive them?"

"According to him, they showed up on his doorstep a couple of days ago with the note that instructed him to publish them in the newsletter. Note also said that the originals would be returned to the Historical Society at a later date. Ken claims that his deep belief in freedom of the press made him comply with the note's request."

"Are you going to charge Ken with withholding evidence?"

"I don't know. He was wrong not to tell us about getting copies of the letters. But, to be honest with you, everyone here is so relieved at what's in those letters, I think it will blow over."

"Now we're only missing the map and the first page of the gardener's letter. Think we'll get either of them back?"

"I wouldn't take any bets. This has been the craziest damn case I think I've ever worked."

"I'd like to have another copy of the second page of the gardener's letter. And the tin of seeds."

"A copy of the letter, no problem. But the tin of seeds is still evidence. It will be released to the Society when the time comes."

"Have your criminalists processed the tin for fingerprints and such?"

"Yes."

"Can you tell me what they found?"

"Lester's fingerprints are on the tin, as they are on nearly everything else, but no surprise there. It's also empty."

"Empty?"

"The guys tell me the original seal was probably pretty tight, but that the tin had recently been pried open. Either Lester or the person who took the tin from him emptied out the seeds."

"If I swing by your office on my way to work tomorrow, could I get another copy of that second page of the letter?''

"So you're going to be at work tomorrow?"

"Yes."

"And answering your telephone?"

"Yes, of course. What's this about?"

"This is about not being able to get ahold of you or Brad all day. Odd both of you suddenly disappearing off the face of the earth at the same time, wouldn't you say?"

"Good night, Ed. See you tomorrow."

As Emily hung up the phone, she was smiling. Ed wasn't dumb. She had no doubt that he knew about her growing relationship with Brad. But confirming it for him was not something she felt inclined to do at the moment.

There would be time later.

Right now there were other things occupying her mind. And foremost on the list were the missing items from the time capsule. To the map and the first page of the gardener's letter, she now had to add the seeds in the tin.

She thought about Ed's comment concerning the case. There was a craziness to some of the unexpected things that had happened. But they had also found a definite order behind some of the other things when they had studied them long enough. The skeleton was proof of that.

Maybe what she needed to do was sit down and list what they knew and didn't know and calmly think through everything to see if she couldn't find some hidden logic in the missing pieces.

She yawned. A good plan, but tonight was not the time to execute it. She was tired and her brain too muddled to think clearly. Tomorrow, she'd tackle the task.

Still, there was one thing she wasn't too tired to do.

It had been days since she'd written in her journal. She opened the drawer of the nightstand and drew it out.

There was so much she wanted to tell Sprout about Brad. How he'd saved Samantha. How he'd figured out who the skeleton was. A lot had happened. Propping up her pillows behind her, she got comfortable and opened up the journal to the spot where her bookmark identified her last entry.

But the bookmark wasn't at her last entry. It marked an entry several pages earlier. Emily frowned, the displacement bothering her tidy soul. She was a creature of habit in many things. Writing in this journal was one of those things.

Had she been interrupted during her last entry and unthinkingly shoved the bookmark in the journal and closed it? No. That didn't make sense. Even if she'd been distracted, she would have put the bookmark on the page she'd been writing on.

Someone else had to have moved it. There had been only one other person in her bedroom.

Emily sat straight up as the implications sank in.

Brad had read her journal. He knew she'd selected his sperm.

No wonder he'd come into the kitchen that morning after they'd made love and kissed her as he had. No wonder he didn't want to take things slow. No wonder he was so adamant that he was going to stay around. He'd just found out that the baby she was carrying was his!

And in all that time they'd spent together since, he hadn't said a word about knowing.

The tender, loving feelings she thought he had for her. They weren't for her. They were for the baby she carried.

Emily closed her journal and put it away. She couldn't write to Sprout tonight. Not with a heart full of fallen expectations.

CHAPTER FIFTEEN

"I DIDN'T KNOW WE HAD a celebrity in our midst," Alec said.

Brad completed a note on a patient's chart before glancing at his friend. "Who would that be?"

Alec was holding the Historical Society's newsletter in his hand. He referred to it as he read, "'According to an in-depth forensic analysis conducted by Dr. Brad Winslow, an emergency room physician on staff at Courage Bay Hospital, the one-hundred-year-old skeletal remains found with the time capsule are those of a traveling salesman.'"

"Let me see that," Brad said, reaching for the newsletter. As his eyes scanned the article, he found his name mentioned at least three more times. He should have known that Emily would give him the credit.

"Didn't realize you had spent so much time with Dr. Barrett studying that skeleton in the morgue," Alec said. "I'm obviously not giving you enough patients to treat."

Brad ignored his friend's ribbing as his eyes scanned the other article on the page. "When did this come out, Alec?"

"Found it in my mailbox before I came in tonight. What do you think of the Himlot and Fitzwalter letters?"

Brad took a few moments to read them. "They sound like scenes out of a historical novel—a surprisingly well-written one."

"Himlot and Fitzwalter are being interviewed early tomorrow morning about their ancestors' letters. If things are quiet, we can watch it on the TV in the lounge.''

Brad's attention went to a note at the bottom of the page. He reread it to make sure it said what he thought.

"Alec, I'd like to borrow this newsletter for a minute."

"Sure. Where are you going?''

Brad was already on his way to the privacy and quiet of the physicians' lounge. "I need to talk to someone,'' he called over his shoulder. "Be right back.''

He let himself inside and closed the door. But when he dialed Emily's home, the phone just rang. He checked his watch. It was after ten. She was probably in bed, trying to sleep. Not something either of them had done much of during his last day and a half off.

He smiled as he hung up the phone. She and the baby needed their rest. This could wait.

WHEN EMILY ARRIVED at her office the next morning, she found Dorothy standing outside the door. Her friend looked worn and very weary.

"Aren't you supposed to be in the monthly management board meeting?'' Emily asked after greeting her.

"It's been delayed. Chief Zirinsky called a couple of minutes ago to say that the police are releasing the returned time capsule contents to us. They should be arriving within an hour or so. We decided to wait to convene until they're here so we can look through them.''

"In the meeting room?''

"The thermostat's been turned down and the drapes drawn. Phoebe's in the storeroom getting us all gloves. The board is planning to make a day of it to get the cataloging completed. Oliver called Wayne. He's on his way over with his laptop to add the rest of the items to the list you and Brad began. Ken will be on hand to take pictures to put in the next newsletter. Josh has agreed to help Wayne carry the items down to the basement vault. Do you mind?''

"Mind? Why should I mind?"

"You've been cut out of things."

"It doesn't matter. Really. My enthusiasm for the process has definitely waned."

"Thanks for taking it that way, Em. I was going to fight Oliver over the plan, but to be honest, I didn't feel up to it this morning."

"Are you okay?"

"Yes. No. Can I talk to you?"

"Of course. Come inside."

Emily opened the door and closed it behind them.

"I tried calling you this morning," Dot said. "I didn't get an answer."

"Sorry. I muted the phones last night to get some sleep and forgot to turn them back on."

Emily took a seat behind her desk and beckoned Dorothy to take the chair opposite. "What's up?"

"You know about the Fitzwalter and Himlot *Ranger* letters being published in the current newsletter?"

Emily nodded as she pulled her issue out of her shoulder bag and held it up. "I haven't had a chance to read my copy. I got home too late to go through my mail. But Ed filled me in when he called last night."

"Dean and Gerald were on TV this morning," Dorothy said.

"I watched the interview. Each of them holding up their copy of the newsletter, looking proud enough to bust. When they broke down and hugged each other, I began to think there might be hope for world peace after all."

Dorothy sighed, hard and deep. "It's not true."

"What's not true?"

"The letters. That's not what they said."

"Dot, how do you know?"

"Because I read them."

Emily came forward in her chair. "When?"

"Right after you left the office that night they were stolen. I came up here and let myself in."

"But the door was locked."

"You don't remember making me a key last winter when they were painting my office at school and I needed a quiet place to grade tests away from the fumes?"

"Now I do. Dot, you can't be telling me it was you and Lester—"

"No! I did not take the letters nor did I have any part in Lester's theft. I only came up here to get a photograph of them, which I took with my digital camera. I was in and out of the office in maybe fifteen minutes."

"You photographed the Fitzwalter and Himlot letters and left?"

"I photographed all of the *Ranger* letters. If it had only been you up here, I would have simply told you what I was going to do and why. But Brad was here, and as much as I liked him right off, I didn't really feel comfortable revealing my reasons in front of him."

"What were your reasons?"

"Dean's anxiety regarding his ancestor's letter at the ceremony was out of character. He seemed to suspect that something might come out in that letter that could be distressing. I wanted to be adequately prepared to do damage control with the media, if it came to the worst."

"The worst being that his ancestor wasn't a hero?"

Dorothy nodded. "Councilman Himlot is a valued member of our community as well as our Society. I only wanted to save him embarrassment. But since I was photographing that letter, I decided to shoot the rest of them and be the first to see how close they were to the accounts that were passed down. But it was never my intention to allow someone to tamper with history."

"And you're saying someone has?"

"Yes."

"If the content of the letters was not what was published in the newsletter, what did they say?"

"Himlot's letter made no sense, Em. I pored over it for days. In Fitzwalter's letter it says that Himlot was struck on the head by falling debris as he attempted to leave the ship and was never mentally right again.''

That certainly fit in with what Emily had observed in her brief perusal of the letter. "Did Fitzwalter keep him afloat until the Indian boats rescued them?"

"According to Fitzwalter's letter, he and Himlot were the last of the crew to get off the ship. An Indian boat was already alongside. It took them directly onboard. For them, there was no struggle in the water. The only heroes in Fitzwalter's account were the Indians.''

"So the versions passed down from their ancestors and the letters published in the newsletter were fiction.''

Dorothy nodded. "A lot of the other letters do describe brave acts by other *Ranger* crewmen. But the heroes weren't Himlot and Fitzwalter.''

"Amazing. For generations their descendants have been misled.''

"Or, in Dean Himlot's case, perhaps they knew or suspected the truth and deliberately let the myth be passed on. When the time capsule contents showed up on my back porch, the letters were the first items I looked for. But the box containing them wasn't there. I didn't know if they'd been destroyed or if they'd turn up at any moment to devastate both Dean and Gerald.''

"No wonder you haven't seemed yourself lately.''

"I've wanted to explain all this to you, Em, but I didn't know how. When everything was stolen, I was afraid to tell the police that I'd let myself into your office. I was already worried that it might be Lester who had taken the artifacts. If they knew that I'd been in your office, they might think I was in on it with him.''

"Have you told anyone else?''

"Not even Ted.''

"Well someone knows the truth about the letters. Who gave those phony ones to Ken?''

"It had to be the person Lester was trying to blackmail," Dorothy said. "Logically, you know who that means."

"Dean Himlot or Gerald Fitzwalter," Emily said. "Or both of them."

Dorothy nodded. "If I come forward and present the copies I made of the real *Ranger* letters, I could end up hurting a lot of people. No, correction. I *will* end up hurting a lot of people. Everyone seems so happy with what those phony letters say. Em, what would you do?"

She let the choice bounce around in her head.

"I think I'd sit tight for the present, wait to see if the missing map and first page of the gardener's letter are returned. Ed says that the seeds in the gardener's tin are gone, too."

"Is there a connection between those missing items and the falsified *Ranger* letters?"

"I don't see how there could be. But then, every time we turn around, the things from the time capsule present us with something else unexpected."

The phone on Emily's desk rang. Instead of answering it, she leaned over and switched off the ringer.

"Why did you do that?" Dorothy asked, surprised.

"It'll go to the answering machine."

"You're not taking your calls? Em, what's wrong?"

"I wasn't in yesterday. The work's piled up. I don't want to talk to anyone for a while until I get caught up on things."

Her friend stared at her a moment before understanding stole over her face. "Something's happened between you and Brad."

Emily let out a long, tired exhale. She and Dorothy had known each other too long and too well for her to be able to hide matters of the heart. "Dot, please don't ask me to talk about it now. I'm not ready to."

Dorothy got up, circled the desk and put her arm around Emily's shoulders. For a long moment, all she did was hug her.

"When you are ready, you know where to find me," Dorothy said. Then she walked to the door and let herself out.

Emily stared at the empty chair across from her—the chair he had sat in that first afternoon he'd carried the heavy time capsule up all those stairs. She closed her eyes and saw his dirt-smudged face, the sudden grin that had imbued his handsome features with such irresistible fun.

When she opened her eyes a moment later, she looked down to discover that the desktop was wet. It was only then that she realized she was crying.

"I THINK KEN KERR TOOK the copy of the second page of the gardener's letter from Emily's desk," Brad said into the phone.

After work Brad had swung by his place to shower and change before calling Emily. When she didn't answer any of her lines, he tried the Mission house. No one answered there, either. He'd finally decided to give Ed a call.

"How do you know?" Ed asked.

"He gave himself away in the coming attractions section of the current newsletter when he announced that Emily is attempting to identify the plant that the gardener described in her letter. Look on page two, bottom right."

Brad could hear the sound of pages rustling in the background. Then Ed began to read the item aloud. "'Dr. Barrett will present her findings about the plant and its possible medicinal properties in a future article. The gardener, Agnes Hopper, died soon after she wrote her letter for the time capsule, when she went to the rescue of neighbors trapped in a house fire.'"

"He knew the letter was written by Agnes Hopper," Ed said, understanding what Brad had been getting at.

"You think that only someone who had seen the second page of that letter would have known. Have you talked to Emily about this? Verified she didn't say anything to Kerr?"

"Haven't been able to get ahold of her."

"She swung by the office here earlier on her way to work to pick up another copy of that second page of the gardener's letter. Told me she intended to catch up on her curator duties today, then concentrate on identifying the plant, so she might not be answering her phones."

Not answer her phones? That wasn't right. She knew he'd be calling.

Brad felt the beat of his heart as his hand gripped the receiver. "I'll catch her at work then. Are you going to talk to Kerr?"

"Next up on my agenda. Tell Emily to give me a call when you see her. Max Zirinsky has released the time capsule artifacts to the Historical Society."

Brad agreed, hung up the phone and immediately dialed her work number again. When it went to the answering machine, he disconnected the line.

He did not have a good feeling about this. Snatching up his keys, he headed for the door.

THE SKETCH AGNES HOPPER had made of the medicinal plant she had found to treat her headaches was quite amateurish and faded from time. If Emily wasn't mistaken, the various parts of the plant were not drawn to size. But the drawing still had a certain haunting familiarity.

Agnes had written that the white flowers appeared between July and October. She had found the ones she'd gathered growing between thickets. The plant was a prolific seed producer and had readily adapted to her garden. A small amount of the ground-up seed with her morning cereal had helped to relieve the deep headaches that had plagued her since adolescence.

Emily carefully studied the sketch, writing down her

observations. Stem—vinelike. Leaves—definitely cordate. The heart shape was unmistakable. Flowers—large and trumpet-shaped. She took a closer look at the faint ink smudges and for the first time saw the star-shaped outline in the center of the flower.

Well, no wonder the plant looked familiar. She had seen it before. Family *Convolvulaceae*. Genus *Ipomoea*. A morning glory!

A knock came at the door. Before Emily could call out for whoever it was to come in, the door swung open and Phoebe charged inside.

"Emily, I think you'd better come down to the meeting room. Now. He won't listen to me. He won't listen to anybody."

Phoebe's face was white—with concern or shock or both, Emily couldn't tell.

"Who won't listen? Oliver?"

Phoebe was already out the door.

Emily jumped up and skirted her desk to follow. They scurried down the stairs together and across the hall to where the managing board met. Even before they reached the room, Emily could hear the shouting.

She yanked open the door and rushed inside. Oliver stood at the head of the long table, holding a gavel in his hand and looking as if he was ready to pound someone with it at any moment.

"You're not a member of this managing board and you have no right to speak to me like that!" Oliver screamed. "Now get out of here!"

Ken stood at the other side of the long table, knuckles resting on the top, his skin white, his jaw tight.

Dorothy was on her feet, halfway down the length of the table, her hands stretched out to both Oliver and Ken in mute supplication. Wayne and Josh sat side-by-side in front of a computer monitor in what looked like a terrified stupor. The time capsule contents were spread out before them on the table.

"It's time you told me and everyone else what you did with the missing documents, Oliver," Ken said. "Now I've asked you very politely, considering the circumstances. If you don't answer the question, rest assured you will discover that I can be a great deal less polite."

Ken's voice had the deadly softness of a man on the edge. Even Oliver—angry and twice his size—sensed it and flinched.

Emily knew now why Phoebe had come to fetch her. Ken was the one who wasn't listening to her.

Quickly stepping to his side, she tried to get his attention. "Ken, tell us why you believe Oliver took the missing documents," she said in what she hoped was a calm and reasonable voice.

Ken kept his eyes on Oliver as he answered. "I was driving home from the grocery store early that Monday morning after the time capsule contents were stolen. I saw Lester shove a letter in my mailbox, then jump into his pickup and take off. I followed him, watched him go into an apartment that I later learned was his girlfriend's. I returned to my place to see what he'd put in my mailbox."

"He was blackmailing you about something he found in the time capsule?" Emily asked.

"He didn't want to blackmail me. He wanted to sell me the proof of who had killed my grandparents. His note said that he had a newspaper article giving the whole story. Told me I could have it for a hundred thousand dollars cash."

"The article that was in the *Bulletin* dated the same day as the time capsule," Emily said.

Ken nodded. "I was supposed to enclose the money in a white box and put it in a clothing-donation bin on the other side of town. I had until Wednesday at 5 p.m. The note said that if I complied, the newspaper would be in my mailbox Thursday morning. So I got the cash together and found a white box."

"But why pay him, Ken?" Dorothy asked. "You found the subsequent article—the one that labeled the deaths an accident. You knew that first story wasn't accurate."

"He was trying to get revenge on you for threatening to have him fired," Ken said. "He wanted that first story circulated to embarrass you and your family. If I hadn't bought the paper, he would have found another way to circulate the information. Don't you see?"

Emily was beginning to.

"The first story was accurate, wasn't it, Ken?" she asked. "It was the second story that a talented writer fabricated for Dot's benefit."

Emily watched the truth dawn on Dorothy's face. "Ken?"

"That *Bulletin* that was in the time capsule was also in the archives at the paper," he said. "I knew it was there. And I knew it matched the story my father told me of what had happened that night. When you came looking for old copies of the *Bulletin,* I destroyed it."

"You wrote the second story that said Agnes was trying to rescue her neighbors?" Dorothy asked.

"There was still a lot of the old typesetting equipment around. Didn't take much effort to insert the subsequent story over another in a later issue. By the time I converted it to microfilm, the image looked perfect."

Dorothy sank into the nearest chair and put her face in her hands. "Dear God, Agnes did kill them."

"No!" Ken shouted. "She didn't! The first page of her letter that was in the time capsule makes that clear!"

"You saw the first page of her letter?" Emily asked.

"I waited at that collection bin all Wednesday night. I was going to get Lester on film so I had proof for the police. When he didn't show, I drove to his girlfriend's place Thursday morning. There was no answer at his front door, so I went around the back. Through the window I saw him lying on the floor. The back door was unlocked. I went in. He'd obviously been dead a while. I thought he'd been in a fight with someone. The first page of Agnes's letter was on the table next to the empty tin of seeds. I pulled some trash bags out of the drawer, carefully collected everything from the time capsule, wiped my prints off what I'd touched and locked the back door behind me on my way out.''

"You were the one who put them on Dot's back porch," Emily said.

"After I read through them," he admitted. "Dorothy, please, look at me."

Dorothy's head came up, her face covered in sadness. "Ken, I'm so sorry. Your whole family."

"Agnes was a widow," Ken said, his voice an entreaty. "She didn't have any money. The first page of her letter talked about how her ex-father-in-law, Clarence Smithson, was paying her to be his guinea pig at his apothecary shop. He was making her take concoctions he'd mix to see if they would work. They were making her sick. She said they were even making her see things sometimes. Dorothy, do you understand? It was something that Clarence Smithson fed Agnes that made her go crazy that night. She wasn't responsible. He was."

"Oh, Ken," Dorothy said on a long sigh. She looked at him with gratitude and affection.

"When I put the stuff from the time capsule on your back porch," he continued, "the only reason I included that copy of the *Bulletin* was because I knew Emily had already read the article and might mention it to you. I clipped Agnes's letter to it and a typed note saying that the fire was Clarence Smithson's responsibility. I knew when you read her letter, you'd realize the truth. But that bastard over there got to the documents first and stole the letter and my note."

"Get out of here before I call the security guard," Oliver sputtered.

"All you care about is covering up your ancestor's duplicity in the deaths of my family and Dorothy's," Ken

said. "You don't give a damn about her feelings or anyone else's and never have. If you don't produce the first
page of Agnes's letter right now, I swear I'm going to rip
that gavel out of your hand and—"

"No, Ken, please," Dorothy interrupted.

"I'd like to see you try it!"

"Oliver, don't," Dorothy said.

Ken charged around the table, his eyes wild, hands
clenched, clearly headed for Oliver's throat.

Emily stepped into his path and grabbed his arm. "Ken,
it wasn't one of Clarence Smithson's concoctions that
caused Agnes to go insane."

"Emily, please get out of my way," he said, anger
seething in his words.

She gave his arm a shake until his eyes met hers. "Ken,
listen to me. The medicinal plant Agnes drew a sketch of
in her letter was a morning glory—a variety we call today
'Pearly Gates.' She was grinding up its seeds to help her
with her headaches. Morning glory seeds contain hallu-
cinogenic compounds. The night your father woke up and
heard her speaking of demons and setting fire to the
drapes, she was hallucinating, no doubt from an overdose
of the seeds."

Ken stared at her for a long moment. "Is this true?"

She dropped her hand from his arm. "Yes."

"But Oliver didn't know that, did he?" Ken said. "He
read the first page of Agnes's letter about her being Clarence Smithson's guinea pig. Mr. Historian here knew all
about the fire and what my father reported, believed it had
been his great-grandfather who was at fault. Isn't that
right, Oliver?"

The truth of Ken's accusation was written on Oliver's
face. He straightened to his considerable height, as though
being taller than his accuser could somehow put him in
the right.

"No matter what I or anyone may have thought," he
said, "Emily is telling us Clarence wasn't at fault."

"But you thought he was, which is why you took the letter and my note to Dorothy. You were going to let her suffer, cover up what you believed to be his crime. You damn bastard."

"You can't speak to me like that!" Oliver screamed as he stomped toward Ken waving the gavel. Ken shot around Emily and advanced to meet him.

"No! Please!" Dorothy yelled.

Her desperate plea was followed by an awful gasping sound that brought Ken and Oliver to an immediate halt and turned everyone toward her.

Emily watched in horror as Dorothy's face went ashen, her eyes rolled back in her head and she fell to the floor.

She raced around the table and dropped next to her friend. "Dot? Dot?"

Dorothy didn't answer. She lay unconscious.

"Ken, call 911," Brad's voice said from behind Emily.

She started, unaware he was in the room until that second. He came down on his knee next to her. One of his hands rested on the pulse point in Dorothy's neck while his other held out the keys to his car.

"Emily, go get my bag and what looks like a small silver suitcase out of the back seat."

His voice was perfectly calm and even, but commanding.

She grabbed the keys and was on her feet the next second, running out the door.

DOROTHY ARRIVED at the Courage Bay E.R. in full cardiac arrest. Nothing Brad had been able to do for her at the museum or in the ambulance on the way had changed her status.

She'd been in V-fib at the museum, multiple spots in her heart trying to beat, not able to pass blood up to the brain. He used the portable unit he carried to shock her heart, knowing he needed to stop all that uncoordinated electrical activity for a second to allow the primary pace-maker of the heart to take over and coordinate the beat.

But her heart hadn't taken over the beat. And she wasn't breathing. He had the ET tube in and Ambu bag attached and was performing CPR when the paramedics arrived.

By the time they rolled her into the E.R. trauma room, he'd spent forty minutes trying to resuscitate her and failing.

Quickly handing off the blood he'd drawn in the ambulance to a nurse for analysis, he concentrated on putting in a transvenous pacer. But even with that he was still unable to get capture.

His watch told him it had now been forty-two minutes. Time was running out. Desperately, he tried to think what else he could do.

"Stay with me, Dot," he commanded. "Damn it, come on. I know you can do it."

"YOU SHOULDN'T HAVE COME, Wayne," Phoebe said.

Emily took one look at his gray face and decided Phoebe was right. They had all followed the ambulance to the E.R. and were now in the hospital's waiting room.

"Would you like me to call your wife?" Emily offered.

"We're not waiting for his wife," Phoebe said as she took Wayne's arm and pulled him to his feet. "I'm driving you home," she announced. "Call me, Emily, when you have news."

Emily nodded to Phoebe as she escorted Wayne out the door, and fervently wished she had something constructive to do.

She'd called Ted on her ride in and told him what had happened. He was going to get Holly and come down. All she could do now was wait.

And keep reliving that awful moment when Dorothy collapsed.

Kneeling beside her friend, wanting so desperately to

help her and not knowing how, had been one of the worst moments of Emily's life.

That's how Brad felt when Julie fell.

The unbidden thought had filled her mind with certainty. She understood his commitment to medicine now on a far more personal level.

Seconds crawled by. Emily tried to focus on the things around her. Oliver and Josh sat on the bench across from her chair, clearly buried beneath heavy thoughts.

Ken sat on the couch to her right. When she saw his haggard look, Emily went to sit beside him and put her arm around his shoulders. If there was anyone who was feeling worse than she was at this minute, it had to be him.

"I was ready to kill him," Ken said after a moment, glancing at Oliver.

"Looked that way," Emily murmured, knowing the fight was out of him now.

"I've always loved Dorothy," he said.

"I figured as much. But I'm guessing you never told her."

He shook his head. "I was a decade older than her. Didn't even graduate high school. She was getting a doctorate."

Emily didn't know what to say. Maybe Ken had done the right thing. Maybe he'd been a fool to let such a deep love pass him by.

"Winslow's got to save her," he said.

"If anyone can," Emily said, knowing her voice was not quite steady, "he will."

Josh got up suddenly and marched over to stand in front of Ken. "I took Agnes's letter," he blurted out. "And your note."

Emily could feel Ken's twitch of surprise. She eased her arm from his shoulders.

"What are you talking about, Josh?" Oliver demanded as he sprang to his feet and came over.

"I heard you on the phone with Dad that afternoon after the ceremony," Josh said to his grandfather. "You told him that Agnes Hopper's letter could hurt the family and even the business if word got around that a Smithson had drugged her. I didn't know what you were talking about until I drove by Holly's and saw Ken putting the trash bags on the back porch. I opened them after he left."

Josh turned back to Ken.

"I read your note and the letter," Josh said. "That's when I understood. That's why I took them."

Ken stared at Josh.

Josh's eyes skipped to Emily. "I also took the second page of the letter off your desk, Dr. Barrett."

"Why?"

"Because it said her name was Smithson. I didn't want you to know about her connection to my family. I didn't realize it was only a copy. I took the map out of the trash bags because it showed that the Kerrs owned the land around the oak tree. I thought Clarence Smithson had stolen their land. I swear I didn't know Agnes Hopper was related to Dr. Mission. If I had, I would have destroyed the *Bulletin* with the fire story as well. I would never do anything to hurt Holly."

"Josh, I'm ashamed of you!" Oliver said.

Josh whirled on his grandfather. "Ashamed of me? I saw the ransom note you got demanding a hundred thousand dollars for that letter, directing you to put the cash in a blue box and drop it in the clothing-collection bin. I heard you on the phone trying to raise the money. You were going to pay Lester and destroy the letter."

Oliver looked away, not able to face his grandson's accusation.

"Well, I destroyed the letter for you," Josh said. "Lived up to my family name. You know what I'm ashamed of? I'm ashamed that I'm no better than you."

Josh blundered out of the room.

Looking both embarrassed and defeated, Oliver mumbled something incoherent and trailed after him.

Emily and Ken were alone in the waiting room.

A quiet moment passed.

"Doesn't look like I'm going to have to research much to fill up the next newsletter," Ken said.

"You won't print what we just heard," Emily said.

His eyes met hers. "You sound pretty sure."

"Dorothy is your hot button. When it comes to people protecting their family, you bend over backward to help them out. You proved it by rewriting the Himlot and Fitzwalter *Ranger* letters."

"What makes you think I did that?"

"You rewrote history so that Dorothy would feel good about hers, even though you knew that Agnes Hopper had been responsible for the death of your ancestors. Then you decided to do it again to bring together two feuding, basically good men who should be on the same side."

"I used to watch those two play together when they were kids," Ken said. "They were the best of friends."

"And your revised editions of their ancestors' letters have made them friends again."

"Someone else could have done it," he said.

"But no historian would have. As you told me, you're no historian. But you are a damn good writer. And after reading your column for so many years, I couldn't help but recognize your distinct style and, more importantly, the positive images in those letters."

"Are you going to tell them the truth, Emily?"

"I wouldn't dream of it."

He returned her smile.

"I am curious about how you're going to explain the originals of those letters never showing up, however," Emily said.

"I'm still working on that one. No way I can duplicate the primitive materials and ink, much less age them. The historians in the Society would see through any forgery I could produce. Maybe, as time passes, people will forget that the originals were never sent to the Society."

Emily hoped that Ken was right. "Did you type that note that was in Dorothy's mailbox?"

He nodded. "When the news reported that the first page of the gardener's letter and the *Bulletin* with the fire story were missing from the returned time capsule documents in addition to the *Ranger* letters, I assumed she'd pulled them out so as not to cause Oliver pain. That would be like her."

"Yes, it would," Emily agreed.

"When the *Bulletin* was returned, I admit that confused me. But it wasn't until we were in the board meeting today that I realized Dorothy had never seen the first page of the gardener's letter. Or my note. That's when I figured Oliver had gotten to them first and was trying to keep her from the truth."

"One more question, Ken. When Lester didn't show that night to collect the money, did you retrieve your white box out of the clothing-donation bin?"

Ken nodded. "I had to. It was all my savings. Although I would have given it if that meant I could keep the story from Dorothy. I would have given anything."

She believed him.

CHAPTER SIXTEEN

CPR. THAT'S ALL BRAD COULD DO at this point. Despite all the sophisticated advancements in medical technology, he was back to the basics of manually keeping a heart beating.

Dorothy had received all the medications appropriate for a heart attack; he'd used every intervention that his medical training and experience had taught him to apply. There had to be a reason she wasn't responding. He said a silent prayer that he'd find that reason before it was too late.

He'd told Emily he lived here. It hit him how true that was. Every nerve ending in his body came alive as he pushed himself to be smart enough and quick enough to help the sick and injured who ended up in these trauma rooms.

When he failed, death etched its mark on him. But when he saved a life, somehow he, too, felt saved.

A nurse came running in with the results of the blood work. "The serum potassium level is at 7.9."

"Way too high," Brad said, feeling a surge of hope. This was something explainable, something he could fight. "Give her ten units of insulin. And a glucose drip."

Brad watched the fast competent fingers inject the medications into the IV lines. He continued CPR as the second hand on the clock loudly ticked in the quiet room. It had been fifty minutes since her collapse.

Time slowed to a stop.

Suddenly, the nurse was yelling. "I've got a pulse! A good pulse!"

Brad's eyes flew to the instruments. "Her heart's beating on its own," he said, somehow remaining calm. "A good cardiac rhythm."

"Her pressure is one-twenty over seventy," another nurse on the team reported.

He studied Dorothy's face as he continued to monitor her vital signs. Gradually, the gray pallor receded to be replaced by a pale pink.

She made gasping motions.

He quickly removed the Ambu bag and gently pulled out the ET tube.

As soon as the tube was out, Dorothy took a big breath, the kind Brad recognized as consistent with life. He couldn't ever remember hearing a more beautiful sound.

Alec materialized from behind him and clapped him on the shoulder. "Well, damn. She's going to make it after all. Great save. I'm impressed."

Brad was simply grateful. That he'd been standing at the open door of the meeting room when Dorothy collapsed. That she'd hung in there long enough for him to find out how to help her. And that out there, somewhere, in a very busy universe, his prayer had been heard.

She opened her eyes and looked at him, blinking in confusion. He smoothed the matted hair off her forehead and smiled.

"You're in the E.R., Dot. Try not to talk. We've had a tube down your throat to help you breathe, so you're going to be sore there for a while. But we're taking very good care of you, and you're going to be fine. Just fine. Do you understand what I'm saying?"

She smiled at him. He could see her hand move. She was making a thumbs-up sign.

He clasped her hand within both of his, gave it a kiss and laughed.

THE MOMENT SHE SAW BRAD'S FACE, Emily understood Dorothy had made it. Relief made her giddy and reckless, forgetful of everything except the fact that he had saved her dear friend.

She threw her arms around him, heedless of the tears that flowed down her cheeks as she thanked him from the deepest part of her heart.

He held her close and told her not to worry, that everything was going to be all right.

The doors into the waiting room burst open and Ted and Holly rushed in.

"She's gotten through the worst of it," Brad reassured them.

Knowing they needed his attention, Emily pulled out of Brad's arms and stepped away.

"Her vital signs are stable," Brad told Ted and Holly. "She's awake and lucid. I've called upstairs to the ICU. They're getting a bed ready for her. As soon as she's settled, you'll be able to go up and see her."

As Emily listened to Brad address Ted and Holly's continuing questions, she turned around to see that Ken had left. He'd only stayed long enough to be sure Dorothy was okay.

Now that she, too, knew her friend was on the mend, Emily decided that the time had come for her to also quietly slip away.

BRAD COULD NOT FIND EMILY. It had been three days since he'd turned around after answering Ted and Holly's questions to discover she'd disappeared from the E.R. He'd gone up to see Dorothy in the ICU the next morning and had found her surrounded by the kind of beautiful flowers that could have only come from the Botanical Gardens.

But Emily was nowhere in sight. Dorothy had since been moved into a private room, and the moment his shift had ended today, he'd gone up to see her. She was doing very well and with the right medication, diet and exercise, should recover completely.

When he'd asked her where Emily was, Dorothy had simply said, "Around."

She wasn't around. Nor was she answering any of her numbers. He'd driven by the gardens and her home numerous times. Neither she nor her car had been there.

After leaving word at the nurses' station to call him immediately if Emily came to see Dorothy, he finally broke down and dialed Ed's number.

"Emily was here a few minutes ago," Ed said. "At her suggestion I had the guys check Lester's remains for evidence of ergine and isoergine alkaloids. Just got the results back. She was right. He was full of the stuff. Looks as though he ate the morning glory seeds that came out of the tin from the time capsule. He probably hoped they'd be a narcotic like the gardener's letter implied."

Brad had overheard Emily's explanation for Agnes's behavior while he stood at the door and watched what had unfolded in the Historical Society's board meeting. He was not surprised at Ed's findings.

"Lester must have been reacting to those powerful hallucinations when he went off the deep end in his girlfriend's kitchen," Brad said. "Have you learned who took the time capsule contents from him?"

"Ken Kerr came in yesterday and admitted to removing the artifacts from the kitchen after Lester's death. He says the *Ranger* letters weren't there, but he put the rest of the stuff in trash bags and left them on the Missions' back porch. Turns out it was Josh Smithson who took the letter off Emily's desk."

"Josh told you that?"

"Yeah. He also admits that he took the map and first page of the gardener's letter out of the trash bags on the Missions' back porch before Holly got to them. Josh destroyed everything he took. Refuses to say why. Just walked up to me, confessed what he'd done and asked me to lock him up.''

''What's going to happen to him?''

''Knowing the high-powered lawyers his father and grandfather will hire, it'll probably be pleaded out to a lesser charge, which might frost some historians but frankly won't bother me a bit. The kid did wrong and is ready to take his punishment like a man. You have no idea how refreshing that is to see in someone his age.''

''So, who took the *Ranger* letters?''

''We may never know. I'm surprised Emily hasn't told you all this.''

''We've been…missing each other recently. Know where she is now?''

''If she isn't at the hospital seeing Dorothy, probably packing.''

Packing?

''I assume you're going with her to that B and B this weekend?'' Ed asked.

''Right,'' Brad said. He thanked his friend and hung up before Ed could ask any more questions that he was going to answer with a lie.

After avoiding his calls for days, now she was going away and not even bothering to tell him. She couldn't make it any clearer that their relationship was over. He headed for his car with a heavy step.

Something had happened. But for the life of him, he couldn't think what. Their days and nights together had been perfect. Every minute he spent with her was perfect.

A mental and physical weariness gripped him as he drove home. He'd once worked fifty hours straight in the E.R. and hadn't felt half this bad.

He pulled into his parking space and collected his mail on the way to his apartment. When he saw the legal-size letter with the return address of a local law office sandwiched in between the bills, he felt a trickle of unease.

One of the hazards of being an E.R. doctor was the

likelihood of frequent lawsuits. When a trauma patient died, bereaved family members sometimes reacted with anger and disbelief, shortly followed by the conviction that the doctor had somehow failed their loved one.

Brad had been lucky to escape such legal proceedings so far. Looked as if his luck had run out. He slit open the envelope and pulled out the papers inside.

But the legal documents he read had nothing to do with a malpractice suit.

His cell phone rang. He pulled it from his pocket and answered.

"You wanted to know when Emily Barrett visited Dorothy Mission?" the nurse asked on the other end of the line.

"Yes."

"She's with her now."

"DOT, YOU LOOK GREAT," Emily said with enthusiasm as she walked into her friend's room holding a vase of fresh flowers.

Dorothy was sitting up, her hair pinned to the top of her head, wearing a new bed jacket and even a little lipstick.

"The makeup was Holly's idea," she explained. "Said she was tired of looking at her bedraggled mom. I can't thank you enough for staying with her and Ted these past few days, Em. Making sure they're eating properly and all. They were so beside themselves with worry. They would have been lost without you."

Emily set the flowers next to the assortment she'd already brought. "I was so beside myself with worry, I would have been lost without them."

"I'm sorry for scaring everyone so much."

Emily sat on the edge of her bed. "You're forgiven only if you promise never to do it again."

Dorothy sent her a smile. "I promise. So, tell me what's happening with the contents of the time capsule."

"You sure you're up to this?"

"I'm feeling as good as new. But I remember the argument in the board meeting, and I'm anxious to know what happened when I passed out on everyone."

Emily filled her in on the scene in the E.R. waiting room and the subsequent admissions that had been made to the police.

"Well, now I understand what this note from Oliver is all about," Dorothy said as she retrieved a card from her bedside table and held it out.

Emily took the card and read the message inside.

Dear Dorothy,

Please accept my sincerest apologies for my inconsiderate actions toward you and your family. Best wishes for your quick recovery.

Sincerely,
Oliver Smithson

"That's quite an admission for Oliver to put in writing," Emily said.

"I'm not surprised at Oliver's behavior," Dorothy said. "Nor Josh's. The Smithsons have been so tied up in honoring their family name that they forgot the real meaning of honor."

"Can you forgive them for trying to hide what they thought was the truth from you?"

"Oh, I already have," Dorothy said. "Even if I had seen the first page of Agnes's letter with Ken's note and thought that Clarence Smithson had given Agnes something that caused her to lose her faculties, I never would have taken it out on Oliver. I would have done everything I could to cushion the blow for him."

"And that, Dorothy Mission, is one of the reasons why I'm proud to call you my friend."

Dorothy squeezed Emily's hand.

"I should have realized before that Lester wouldn't try to blackmail Dean and Gerald," she said. "Lester knew very little about *Ranger* history. If he had attempted to read Himlot's letter, he wouldn't have realized why it made no sense. But I am surprised he didn't try to sell Dean his ancestor's letter, since Dean made such a big deal about its importance at the ceremony."

"Actually, Dot, we don't know that he didn't."

"What do you mean?"

"Remember Dean was pushing you to offer a reward and then suddenly he was calling you and telling you he was content to let the matter drop?"

"I see. You think that's because he got a ransom demand for his family's letter and decided to pay it. Do you think Gerald got one, too?"

"Gerald didn't make a big deal over his ancestor's letter at the ceremony. Since he kept pushing you to offer a reward, I doubt Lester sent him a ransom note. But we know Lester sent one to Ken. And Josh says he sent one to Oliver. And, according to the Courage Bay clothing drive for needy families, they received two hundred thousand in anonymous cash donations that week."

Dorothy nodded in understanding. "Since Ken took his money out of the clothing bin on Wednesday night when Lester didn't show, that leaves Dean and Oliver's payoffs. A hundred thousand each. They must have been very upset when the documents didn't arrive Thursday morning in their mailboxes."

"I don't feel particularly sympathetic, considering their motivations for the payoff. Besides, the money is going to a very good cause."

Dorothy shook her head. "It's all been about fear regarding their families, hasn't it? Oliver worrying that his grandfather had done something terrible. Dean and Gerald upset at the possibility that their ancestors hadn't been heroic."

"And in Dean and Gerald's case, that's really kind of

silly when you think about it. Their ancestors were good men. The fact that they didn't perform any specific heroic deeds on the day their ship sank shouldn't cast any aspersions on their family name."

"But because their descendants thought they were heroes, they had a special pride," Dorothy said. "Think of the Fitzwalters and how they lived up to that image of heroic self-sacrifice when they kept their bank open during the crash. And as officeholders, the Himlots have consistently supported programs to help the less fortunate."

"Yes, they were living up to the heroic image that had been passed down to them. Tradition can be a wonderful thing when its message is so uplifting."

"Which brings me right back to my earlier dilemma. What do I do with my copies of the real *Ranger* letters?"

"What do you want to do with them?"

Dorothy let out a deep breath. "I can't destroy a piece of history. My whole career has been dedicated to preserving it. But I can't destroy the good that's come from Ken's kind lies, either. I wish I could put these Himlot and Fitzwalter letters in another time capsule—one that wouldn't be opened for another hundred years."

"Then why don't you?"

"I was only joking, Em."

"Dot, think about it. A new time capsule would be a great project for the Historical Society. The energy that everyone would put into the task could help them to forget the negative aspects surrounding the uncovering of the last time capsule. And you'd be able to write out the whole story of the Himlot and Fitzwalter saga like the true historian you are, then seal it inside the new time capsule to be buried later this year."

A smile drew back Dorothy's lips. "I wouldn't be tampering with history, merely consigning its revelation to the hands of a future historian in the year 2104. I'm going to call the other board members and get started on the project tomorrow."

"You're being released tomorrow?"

"Providing all the tests they took this morning come back okay. My doctor promised she'd stop in first thing tomorrow to let me know for sure."

"Dot, that's wonderful."

"Speaking of wonderful things and doctors, Brad came to see me a few minutes before you arrived."

"I know he did, Dot. I waited until I saw him drive away before I chanced coming up to see you."

"Is it that important for you to avoid him?" Dorothy asked.

She nodded.

"Well, I'm sorry, Em, but I don't think you're going to be able to avoid him much longer."

"What do you mean?"

"He's at the door."

Emily spun around to see him standing there, watching her.

BRAD LED EMILY into the nearest empty hospital room and closed the door behind them. He reached for her only to have her immediately draw back.

Despite the fact that part of him had anticipated she would, he could not keep the stab of disappointment at bay.

"I've been trying to find you for days," he said.

She said nothing, just waited.

Holding up the legal documents he'd received in the mail, he asked, "Emily, what does this mean?"

She glanced at the papers. "What they say. If you want a father's legal right to your child, all you have to do is sign those papers and return them to my lawyer. It will become effective the day he files them in court."

"When did you realize I knew about the baby?"

"It doesn't matter."

"It does matter. Please, Emily, I need to know."

She was trying to sound tough, but the words simply

came out sad. "When I found out you'd read my *personal* journal."

Which had to have been four days ago when she returned to her place—the exact time she'd stopped answering her telephone.

"I know you'll be a very good father," she said. "But if you don't want the responsibility—"

"Of course I want the responsibility. I want to be a father to our child, Emily. More than I can say."

"Then all you have to do is sign the papers. When the baby is born, we'll work out visitation through my lawyer." Her eyes darted to her watch. "I have to be somewhere now, so if you don't mind—"

He took a step forward, blocking her path to the door. "Emily, I didn't find out about your selecting my sperm when I read your journal."

She looked straight at him for the first time since he'd found her in Dorothy's room. Confusion clouded her face. "What?"

"I've known from the first day I met you—the day you were brought into the E.R. and pulled that psychic routine on me."

"But it was only after you read my journal that you—"

"—learned how much you loved our baby already? How well you understood and liked the man I am even before you met me? How unbelievably, impossibly sweet you are inside?"

Tears welled in her eyes as she turned her face away. He stepped toward her and gathered her in his arms.

"I've never read anything more beautiful or touching than what you wrote to our baby. God, Emily, I will never, ever be sorry for having read your journal. I have only one regret in all this. I wish I'd gotten you pregnant that first night we made love. Because then you'd know that what I feel for you is not about the baby."

Gently, he kissed her forehead, the tip of her nose and her lips. When she gave a little sigh and her body relaxed into his, the tiredness that had weighed him down for days melted away, leaving him feeling buoyant and hopeful.

"I still have school debts. If I don't accept that job at the L.A. trauma center, it's going to take me longer to pay them off on the salary I'll be getting at Courage Bay Hospital. I don't have a lot to offer you right now. But I do have a good profession and an income that will soon be respectable."

"Brad, I don't need your money to support our baby."

"That's not what I'm offering. Emily, I love you. I'm asking you to marry me."

She pulled back to look him in the eyes. "Are you sure? This has been so fast."

"I'm dead sure. I have been for days. Emily, please, tell me you love me."

Her smile was lovely and deep and lit up her eyes. "I love you, Brad. I think I've loved you since the moment I read your sperm-donor questionnaire and told the Crispin Fertility Clinic that I was buying your entire donation."

"You did that?"

"I wanted you all to myself, even then."

He hugged her to him, incredibly touched and happy. "We're going to have a bunch of beautiful babies, Emily. But be assured, the rest are going to be conceived the good old-fashioned way. With lots and lots of practice."

And that promise he sealed with a kiss that came straight from his heart.

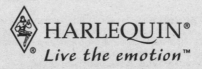

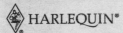

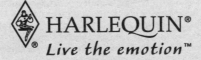

HARLEQUIN *Super*ROMANCE

What if you discovered that all you ever wanted were the things you left behind?

GOING BACK

John Riley's Girl
by Inglath Cooper
(Superromance #1198)
On-sale April 2004

Olivia Ashford thought she had put her hometown and John Riley behind her. But an invitation to her fifteen-year high school reunion made her realize that she needs to go back to Summerville and lay some old ghosts to rest. After leaving John without a word so many years ago, would Olivia have the courage to face him again, if only to say goodbye?

Return to Little Hills by Janice Macdonald
(Superromance #1201) On-sale May 2004

Edie Robinson's relationship with her mother is a precarious one. Maude is feisty and independent, and not inclined to make life easy for her daughter even though Edie's come home to help out. Edie can't wait to leave the town she'd fled years ago. But slowly a new understanding between mother and daughter begins to develop. Then Edie meets widower Peter Darling who's specifically moved to Little Hills to give his four young daughters the security of a small-town childhood. Suddenly, Edie's seeing her home through new eyes.

Available wherever Harlequin Books are sold.

Visit us at www.eHarlequin.com

HSRGBCM

Two on the Run
by Margaret Watson
Superromance #1205
On-sale May 2004

The last thing Ellie Perkins
expects as she reaches
her car after work is to
find herself facing down a
man with a gun. But Mike
Reilly gives her no choice.
He's injured and on the
run in an attempt to clear
his name. And he needs
more than Ellie's car—
he needs her help. So
Ellie gets caught up in a
desperate race to outwit
the villains and save lives.
Not exactly the way she'd
imagined meeting the
man of her dreams.

Available wherever Harlequin books are sold.

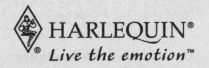

HARLEQUIN®
Live the emotion™

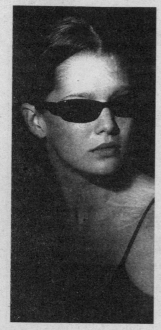
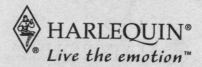